C000165900

ABOUT THE AUTHOR

Maggie Allder was born and brought up in Gamlingay in Cambridgeshire, the second daughter of a village police officer. She studied at King Alfred's College, Winchester (now the University of Winchester) and later at Reading university, and taught for 36 years in a comprehensive school. After exploring and appreciating more orthodox forms of Christianity, Maggie became a Quaker, and is happy and settled in the Quaker community in Winchester which inspired the unnamed community referred to in her first novel, Courting Rendition, and upon which her second novel Living with the Leopard is loosely based. Maggie volunteers for a not-for-profit organisation, Human Writes, which aims to provide friendship to prisoners on death row in the USA.

A Vision Softly Creeping is the third book of a planned trilogy.

A VISION
SOFTLY
CREEPING

MAGGIE ALLDER

Copyright © 2018 Maggie Allder

The moral right of the author has been asserted.

Apart from any fair dealing for the purposes of research or private study,
or criticism or review, as permitted under the Copyright, Designs and Patents
Act 1988, this publication may only be reproduced, stored or transmitted, in
any form or by any means, with the prior permission in writing of the
publishers, or in the case of reprographic reproduction in accordance with
the terms of licences issued by the Copyright Licensing Agency. Enquiries
concerning reproduction outside those terms should be sent to the publishers.

This is a work of fiction. Names, characters, businesses, places, events
and incidents are either the products of the author's imagination
or used in a fictitious manner. Any resemblance to actual persons,
living or dead, or actual events is purely coincidental.

Matador
9 Priory Business Park,
Wistow Road, Kibworth Beauchamp,
Leicestershire. LE8 0RX
Tel: 0116 279 2299
Email: books@troubador.co.uk
Web: www.troubador.co.uk/matador
Twitter: @matadorbooks

ISBN 978 1788039 635

British Library Cataloguing in Publication Data.
A catalogue record for this book is available from the British Library.

Printed and bound in Great Britain by 4edge Limited
Typeset in 11pt Aldine401 BT by Troubador Publishing Ltd, Leicester, UK

Matador is an imprint of Troubador Publishing Ltd

To my four sisters and my three brothers-in-law.
What would I do without you?

PROLOGUE

It must have been in the early 1960s. I suppose I was about four years old. We had family in Switzerland, on my father's side, and at that time it seemed to me as if we visited a lot. Later I realised that it was only once or twice a year but time did not mean much to me then, and I remember our visits as being far more frequent. We were sitting in a bar in the little village in the Bernese Oberland which we always visited, because that was from where the family originated and in some cases still lived. There was a long pine table and the adults were drinking white wine, but my two brothers and I had glasses of sweet lemon tea, served cold. Everyone was talking in Swiss German. My mother spoke, I realised years later, with a distinct accent that came from first learning High German and only later, to please her husband, the local language, but she was fluent and charming and Papa's family loved her. My older brothers Rolph and Walter spoke a little of the language and their attempts to join in the conversation were applauded by the assembled crowd. I didn't like to try, although I understood something of what was going on, so I sat in silence, swinging my legs on the wooden bench and looking around me as the light outside faded.

The place interested me. The overhead lights were without shades, so that you could see the coils of the elements, two quite different shapes of coil. None of the tables matched. Some, like the one at which we sat, were long, rough pine. Next to us was a circular table made of some sort of reddish wood, like the sort of table we might find at Granny's house. Granny was Mummy's mother, and lived in a place called Surrey.

I was a little bored with the conversation, which I suppose was over my head. I think I recall that the people we were with were interested in Rolph's progress at school, but I'm not at all sure I can rely on that memory. I remember seeing a couple who seemed to me to be ancient, coming to sit at the round table. They looked like all the older people I saw in those days in Switzerland: their faces were creased, their hair dark, their clothes what I would now call 'casual', but which I then just thought were outdoor clothes. Since the conversation at our table bored me, I watched the old couple, and saw three people closer to Mummy and Papa's age, who came in shaking snow from their coats, and shook hands with the older couple, and sat down. It all looked quite ordinary, except that there was something my four-year-old mind found odd. It was to do with the expression of the two men, the older man and the man who was Papa's age. I found them somehow not quite right, although for the life of me now I can't imagine how I knew that, at such a young age. Anyhow, I went on watching while the waiter brought them wine or beer, and still it didn't look quite right to me.

When the waiter brought the brown paper parcel over and gave it to the younger man, both men seemed relieved. The younger man passed the parcel to the younger woman, who smiled and put it in her bag. Even from where I was sitting I knew that the atmosphere at their table had relaxed.

I remember tugging at Papa's arm, trying to catch his attention. "Papa, Papa," I demanded, "what is the secret?"

At first Papa didn't notice my nudging, but one of the people I didn't know nodded to me and said, "Hans, dein Sohn braucht deine Aufmerksamkeit."

Papa turned to me, and smiled. "Karl, what is it?" he asked. "Can you ask me in German?"

"No, Papa," I said. "Papa, I want to know their secret." And I pointed to the people at the next table.

"What do you mean, Karl?" Papa looked at me with a question in his eyes. "What secret?"

I repeated myself. "Papa, I want to know the secret. Their *secret!*" And I stood on the wooden bench and pointed again. "*Their* secret!"

The people at the next table looked across at our group. I could see alarm in their faces.

"Karl," said Mummy, putting a kind hand on my arm, "sit down and be good. Those people don't have any secrets!" Then she smiled at the adults who were sitting with us. "Well, not secrets we ought to know!"

The grown-ups around me laughed, and someone said in accented English, "We all have secrets which other people shouldn't know!" And for some reason I did not understand everyone laughed again.

I must have made my demands to know the secret quite loudly. I remember seeing beyond the bulk of Mummy, who was making me sit back on the bench, that the people at the round table were frowning at me, and almost at once they stood and left, leaving half empty glasses on their table.

Later I heard one of the women I did not know in our group talking to Papa. "He doesn't miss much, your little one, does he?"

And Papa answered, "It seems so. Although it's hard to know what is imagination sometimes. Our little spy!" he added, beaming round the table and reaching across to tussle my hair.

CHAPTER 1

I really just existed during the flight across the Atlantic and the drive down to Hampshire. I was very aware, as I went through security in Houston, that I was carrying a deeply subversive document, or at least a document *they* would consider subversive. I had never been so grateful for the electronic tag on my passport. I was one of the good guys, or so they believed, and the check was cursory. We flew overnight and I barely slept, but the plane was quiet and the service in business class unobtrusive, and I lay back with my eyes closed, reliving the last few months, and the pretty American stewardess left me alone.

Driving down from Heathrow to Amy's village was harder. Since my training, when I was in my late twenties, I have rarely been aware of any prolonged stress symptoms, but my heart was pounding and my mouth was dry. I have driven a lot, in all sorts of vehicles, but I twice found myself making silly mistakes. Once I realised I was driving on the right, the result of being in the States, I suppose, and I took a wrong turn on a road I know well, leaving the motorway to head for Amy's village. I told myself it was exhaustion. I had barely slept since I saw Alice in that awful place, but I think I knew, really, that it was grief.

I arrived at Amy's at about ten in the morning. There was a gradual thaw in progress. They had not had as much snow in Hampshire as in more westerly parts of the country, although even in Amy's village there were dirty piles and heaps beside the roads, where conscientious local citizens had cleared paths and lanes. Amy's drive was white but it had obviously been cleared, probably several times. She had family living nearby and of course they would see to it that she was all right. In fact, knowing Amy, half the village would come to her aid if needed: retired colonels, the postman, the son of the vicar and no doubt the few American residents, brought up to believe in good neighbourliness, as long as their neighbours were fellow whites, and not too radical in their politics.

Amy must have heard the tyres of my car crunching on the snowy gravel. She came to the door wearing a beautiful Norwegian-style knitted jumper in shades of grey and red, but looking haggard despite her immaculate turnout. I left my bag in the car and almost ran to her. We embraced there on the doorstep and I could feel her shaking in my arms as I held her. When we parted she had tears in her eyes.

"Oh, Karl!" she said, and then gulped. "Come on in."

We went into the kitchen and without asking she poured me coffee and put a plate of homemade biscuits in front of me.

I had intended to be strong. I thought I might bring comfort to Amy, who had just lost her much loved sister-in-law, but when I looked up at her red eyes and strained face, it was suddenly all too much.

"Amy," I started, intending to say some words of comfort, although I can't imagine what. A comment about executions being quick and painless? But we both knew that was not necessarily true. Some inane remark about dying for what one believes in? But nobody should die for their beliefs in a free country, only for their actions. Perhaps some cliché about being in a better place? But I did not believe that stuff then, and I had no idea whether Amy did, although of course she was a pillar of the local Anglican church.

"Amy," I started again, and then suddenly it was all too much. I could see Alice's face, not as I had seen her behind

2

bullet proof glass in her prison in Texas, but the way she had looked in the soft light of the cottage in Wales, where only a few weeks ago, we had talked together about politics. I, fool that I was, had been supporting the status quo, and Alice had been disagreeing, and even as we talked I had wanted to reach out and touch her. She was so strong and so vulnerable. By common consent, though, we rarely had any physical contact. That part of our relationship was long since over, although to be honest I often longed for her. I will never know, now, whether she felt like that about me.

Then it all washed over me. Alice was dead, and although I had tried, I was not entirely innocent of her fate. She was gone. And then I was crying. I did not have a few controlled tears in my eyes, I was not weeping gently, I was howling, my grief suddenly overflowing, overwhelming. I managed to put my coffee mug down on the table, and then I just let go. My body was racked with misery, I was choking on it, consumed by it, it was too much, I could not even express it. In my mind, I saw Alice's serious face, and I saw her as she had been when I had last seen her in that awful place, and I wailed and shook from head to toe.

Amy stood up and came to me. She stood beside me and held me tightly, the way I suppose she would hold one of her daughters or a grandchild if they were distressed, and she said nothing. And I just cried. When the worst was over my grief turned to sobs. I could not stop. I could feel the tremors in Amy's body as she stayed close to me, and I knew she was crying too.

After a time – who knows how long – we both established a little more control. Amy poured my cold coffee away and poured fresh for us both, and we went through to her sitting room. The log fire was burning, the Afghan rug in front of it glowed with the reds and ambers of the weave, and the globe light made one dark alcove beside the chimney look secretive.

3

We sat beside each other on the deep settee, and drank our coffee, still both with tears in our eyes.

"It will be over now, won't it?" checked Amy.

"Yes, at about six last night. US time."

"There was nothing on the news," said Amy.

I thought about that. "They'll say what they want to say when they're ready." I said. "When it's politically expedient." I thought about it. "They won't make much of it over here," I added. "There are a lot of English people who are against the death penalty, and they don't want awkward questions about the lack of due process. She was never tried, you know, not in open court."

Then we talked about practical issues. The grandchildren had not been told, and nor would they be. They were being brought up to support the current regime. It was safer and healthier, and after all, we had got here through proper democratic processes. It helped that the military did not disclose names. Alice would forever be prisoner 999101T, the 'T' standing for 'terrorist', to distinguish her from the majority of death row prisoners in the USA, largely Blacks and Latinos, or Muslims of any colour, there for murder, or at least being charged as party to murders. Her body would be cremated and the remains sent to her closest family member, who was Amy, as long as she paid the required charges. Otherwise they would be buried in Chasserton, in the bleak cemetery there. I told Amy how to claim the ashes and where to pay the fee, and we finished our coffee and held hands, providing some comfort on that bleak, cold morning.

★ ★ ★

When the Anti-Terrorist Task Force, the ATTF, was formally constituted by an Act of Parliament and they gave us uniforms for formal occasions, I was allocated to the Central South region of England. This was around the time of the New Alliance. There had been a lot of big changes in the country quite quickly. We had left the European Union, the United Kingdom had split up when Scotland and Northern Ireland chose to go with Europe, and we were hand-in-glove with the USA, which we in the Organisation had known had been the intention for several decades, since the 1990s certainly. The majority of English voters supported these changes, but there were still campaigning groups who operated mostly through the internet, suspicious of the changes and anxious about the loss of human rights. As well as that, we had to contend with several groups of religious extremists. The ordinary fundamentalist Christians were no problem. They instinctively embraced the right. The survivalists and conspiracy theorists were unpredictable and we had to keep an eye on them all the time, and there were Islamic extremists and radical Greens to contend with too.

That was when I bought my flat in Hampshire. In line with departmental policy I chose a large, anonymous town with quick rail links to London and various points south. It had been a London overspill town following the Second World War, and there were streets and streets of dull, red-brick houses and a huge ring road with periodic roundabouts, keeping the traffic out of the centre. My flat was in a mixed development of houses and flats, with a few bungalows for old people, close to a park and to the ring road. It was very modest, but I loved it because the living room and bedroom windows looked out over a wild, green patch of trees and unruly undergrowth. I had just one bedroom, but the living room was spacious and I bought a very expensive bed-settee, although I do not know who I thought might come to visit. It was hardly likely that my brother Rolph would do a concert in such a provincial town! I could have afforded a much larger and more glamorous apartment but I liked the compact nature of what I had. It felt

5

as if I were asserting who I was, rather than fitting into the expectations of my ATTF colleagues and bosses.

I tried to ease my way in gradually to the work in Hampshire and Dorset. The relationship with the regular police was not entirely comfortable and there were lower rank ATTF operatives who had been working in the area for a while before I became the regional commander. I made it my business to know each ATTF recruit personally and I enjoyed the feeling that I was building a team. I kept records of the families of Other Ranks and made sure I remembered birthdays and asked after relatives. I was careful never to tread on the toes of the men and women who had been in the field in the Central South while I was based in London, involved more in the international aspects of our mission and with technology.

I liked my new role immediately. It was more hands-on than my London activities although I was using all my London surveillance skills. It was just that I had the added ingredient of personal contact: contact with informers but also contact with suspects. It made me feel more human.

That was how I came to meet Alice. Alice had been on our radar for a long time, since before the ATTF was formally constituted. She was a teacher in an academy in southern Hampshire, and a member of one of those left-leaning religious groups which are so attractive to a certain sort of middle-class person.

To all intents and purposes Alice seemed like a perfectly respectable woman, not too far from retirement after a full career in teaching, involved in her religious group but in an innocuous sort of way, a bit of a do-gooder, perhaps. Our records told us that she had been in several quite significant relationships but that none of them had led to marriage. None of her family posed any sort of threat to civil society. She had first come to our attention through the American authorities, which did not like Alice's regular trips to Texas to visit on death row through some amateurish organisation with which she was connected. Our surveillance was therefore cursory. We did not really see Alice as a danger. She was an irritant at the worst.

A couple of lads from Alice's year group had managed to attract our attention. I cannot remember the details now, but they had probably circumvented restrictions on the internet and accessed websites we considered suspicious. As often as not when we needed to check out teenagers it amounted to nothing, so we always started out with the police or lower ranks doing the interviews. If we managed things well, we were able to avoid giving minors records that would stay with them into adult life. I visited the school when the boys and their parents had already left, hoping just to meet Alice, to see what I made of her. If I had been busier that week I dare say I would not have bothered. Such small matters can change a life.

She was sitting at a desk in her office when I arrived, rows of photographs of students arranged in classes on the wall in front of her, and book shelves above housing more files than books, but with a Bible and a copy of the handbook of her religious organisation there as well. There was a blue settee against one wall, a coffee table in the corner and a matching blue armchair under the window. Above the settee was a huge cork notice board with various typed lists pinned up and, to my surprise, some really lovely enlarged photocopies of photographs.

If Alice was surprised at my arrival, she did not show it. The office door was open and I just walked in, holding out my hand to shake hers so that courtesy forced her to stand and extend her hand too.

"Commander Wyss," I said. "ATTF. You must be Alice Owen."

"Good afternoon." She was polite but reserved. "How can I help you? Your colleagues and the boys left a few minutes ago. They've gone to Lee Dawson's home. I can give you the address, if that would help?"

"No, no. That's fine," I said. "Sergeant Moss will report back. If it's all right with you, I'd just like to check your records." Then, before she could answer I asked, "Are these photos of Brazil?"

Alice's face lit up. "They are!" She exclaimed, surprised. "How did you know?"

I stepped across to the notice board to look more closely. "I was there a couple of years ago," I said. "There's something about the light... Did you take these?"

"I did. I spent Christmas there to celebrate my 50th. It was summer, of course."

I looked again at the photograph which had first caught my attention. "These Catholic churches are amazing, aren't they? Although protestant Christianity is on the rise now. The influence of America, I suppose."

Another photograph further along had been taken somewhere in Europe. France, I guessed. The picture was taken looking from one room in a café through a door into a conservatory area. "Is there a theme here?" I was intrigued.

"I'm interested in spaces," explained Alice. "The way doors and windows separate areas, but at the same time make them accessible."

I was impressed. "Do you travel a lot?" I suppose the answer might have provided some useful background, although I am sure we must have had records of all Alice's trips abroad. Already Alice interested me.

"As much as I can." Alice was not a beautiful woman. Quite plain, in fact, but when she smiled her whole face lit up. I thought, *I would have loved to have had a teacher like you.* Then she added, "It's not so easy now, of course." She was referring to the travel restrictions imposed on English nationals as a result of our rigid immigration controls.

"There's always the USA," I said, a leading comment designed to illicit remarks from Alice which might have

8

indicated whether or not I needed to consider her a risk.

"Yes," she agreed. "There's always the States." I could not tell what, if anything, she meant by that and just then I found I did not want to pursue it.

"Can I see the records of Lee Dawson and Frankie Sahel?" I asked. It was, after all, the official reason for my visit.

"I'll print them off for you, if that'll help." Alice turned to her DeV, the large device so often found in offices, clicked on a few buttons on the screen and watched as the printer regurgitated sheets of neatly ordered A4. She took a stapler, clipped them together, and handed them over.

I thought about Alice Owen as I drove north up the M3. I thought about that smile and about her photography. I thought about the ordered office in which she worked, the speed with which she located the records of the boys. It was easy, while I was working in London, to forget that subjects were actually people with lives and personalities quite apart from the activities which caused us concern. Alice Owen, I thought, was so much more than just a person of interest. But then I realised, she was not. She was exactly that: a person of interest – and I was very interested.

★ ★ ★

I remember my next meeting with Alice being just a few days later, but that is unlikely. It was probably at least a week before I went back to the school. As I had expected, the two boys we had needed to interview had done nothing much to worry about, they had been led to the websites they had visited by a short video on the internet, not by anything that had been said at school. We let them off with a warning.

Yet I wanted to see Alice again, and I did not fool myself into thinking it was for work reasons. I accessed her DeVs, the big networked desk DeV at the school and her rather smart new

9

device at home, and chose a day when she had no after school appointments or meetings. I wore my uniform again, because nobody questions an ATTF officer on duty, and arrived at the school about half an hour after classes had finished.

The receptionist was still at her desk, wearing headphones and carrying on a conversation which seemed to be about child care. "Well, if you've paid her to work from two thirty on she should be able to meet the children from school," she was insisting as I walked through the door. Then she saw me, finished her conversation with, "I've got to go now, love," and smiled at me. "Problems with my daughter's babysitter," she explained. "She's supposed to meet my grandchildren from school, but... Anyhow, how can I help?"

"I've got an appointment with Ms Owen," I said. "For four o'clock. I'm sorry I'm early."

"Right you are." The receptionist did not know whether to look impressed or worried. That is the effect of the uniform. She dialled a number and when it was picked up at the other end she said, "Your four o'clock appointment is here, Alice." Then, to me, "She'll come up to meet you in just a minute, if you'd like to take a seat."

When Alice arrived, she looked very slightly flustered. I guessed she was a person who kept on top of her diary, and that an unexpected appointment would throw her. When she saw me a series of expressions flickered across her face: surprise, concern, and – was I mistaken? – pleasure. I do not remember what I said but I saw that the receptionist was listening in despite the head phones over her ears, so I winked at Alice and she blushed ever so slightly.

Even early on I did not want to play around with Alice. It was not that she was a serious person, more that there was something about her to be taken seriously. At one time, perhaps when I was a child, ordinary members of the public would have thought it far-fetched to believe that spies made relationships in order to keep a watch on people, but the disclosures of the second decade of the twentieth century, of under-cover police officers living for years with green activists and animal rights supporters in order to infiltrate their organisations, put paid to that scepticism. Of course, we did the same in the ATTF, but that was never my intention with Alice, although I do admit with some regret that at first I sold the relationship to my commanding officer with that excuse.

I remember the first time I took her out to dinner. I did not so much ask her, as tell her. I took advantage of the fact that she was in her office and that a couple of kids, miscreants no doubt, were pretending to study on their DeVs right outside her office. Given the flimsy fabric of the internal partitions of the school, they could quite possibly hear some of what went on between us. Alice could not really argue, and I did not want to give her time to reflect. I just told her I would pick her up at seven, and left.

★ ★ ★

I was absurdly pleased, when I pulled up in front of Alice's little terraced cottage that evening, to see that she had made some effort to dress up. It was the first real encouragement she had given me, unless you could count the blush in the school reception area, when I winked at her. She was wearing a light, flowing cotton skirt and a white peasant blouse, and she looked cool on that hot evening, and happy. I took her to the place in the High Street with the courtyard garden behind it. It had once been a pub but in the last few years it had moved up-market and even on a weekday you needed to book a table, especially on a day with such glorious sunshine. We had a corner table and ate good French food, and we talked and laughed together all evening. I had wondered if conversation might be a bit stilted. I knew, of course, of Alice's religious affiliations and her political leanings, and I half expected that she might try to convert me, or at least demonstrate that sort of judgementalism so typical of the left when they talk to or about the rest of us. Instead we talked about food, about travel, about books and films and music. She confessed to having no love of celebrity culture and amazed me by telling me she had never once watched the new fly-on-the-wall series about the House of Lords, now officially but not popularly renamed *the Senate* to conform to the norms of our new best friends. Then we walked back to her cottage through the summer dusk, and I desperately wanted to hold her hand, but I waited. On her doorstep I only kissed her on the cheek, and left at once.

I remember, though, the first time I really kissed Alice. It seems almost ridiculous that a man like me, an officer in the ATTF, a man with rather too much history with the opposite sex, should remember in such detail that first, wonderful evening.

I had not yet invited Alice to my flat. I had several times picked her up from school, wearing my ATTF uniform, well aware of the fact that our friendship could do Alice no harm in the increasingly right wing establishment of the English education system. Usually we went out for meals. Once we drove down to the coast and drank cocktails at a little place I knew overlooking Poole Harbour, and we went to a concert of chamber music in a little church over one of the city gates. The tickets cost me a huge amount, it was some charity function organised by parents of a local music school.

At first Alice did not ask me in. I would walk her back to her cottage, or drive her home, kiss her on the cheek and leave at once. I did not want to take advantage of her. In the back of my mind I was aware that while my presence in her life might do Alice good at work, it must surely set up conflicts for her in her religious group. As we came to know each other better I realised that her faith was both less dogmatic and more demanding than I would have expected, and I found that I did not want to disturb it. It is one thing I feel glad about, when I look back at it now.

After a couple of months, she started inviting me in, and when winter arrived she surprised me one day by suggesting that she cook dinner for us at her place. We ate roast pork then profiteroles which Alice had made herself, and drank the whole of an excellent bottle of wine I had brought back from one of my ATTF trips to France. We were talking about a book Alice had recently read, and I remember that she ran upstairs to find her copy, which she had volunteered to lend me. I stood when she stood, and was waiting at the bottom of the stairs when she came back down. It was not calculated. I just looked at her, and she looked at me. Then she dropped the book on the floor and walked into my arms. It was, perhaps, the best moment of my life to date.

After that I invited her to my flat. I used to pick her up from school on Fridays and take her to her place to shower and change. If I had been working all day I would buy food while Alice got ready, then we would drive over to my place and I would cook. Those were wonderful evenings. I had never entertained guests in the flat, despite the sofa bed, and the place felt like a refuge. When we were there together I did not feel like an officer in the ATTF and I did not think of Alice as member of a suspect religious organisation. Perhaps we were fooling ourselves. We made love frequently and with passion, but when I look back now the moments I remember most fondly are of holding her as she slept, both turning over together so that we were in each other's arms all night long. Alice slept with her mouth slightly open and made little noises, not quite snoring, in her sleep. If I woke in the night I would savour the feel and smell of her hair against my face and the gentle sounds of her sleep, and feel that life could hold nothing more. I used to take her breakfast in bed. The thought of her was in my mind day and night, so that I was always happy and always looking forward to the next time I would see her. Even now, after all that has happened, I am glad we had that time. It was, beyond doubt, the happiest year of my life.

★ ★ ★

It was late summer the following year that things came to a head. Not with Alice. With Alice, everything seemed fine. She was happier at work, I thought. I had managed to help her to sort out a couple of issues with her pupils, using my surveillance and IT skills, not seriously affecting anything, just correcting injustices. Of course, Alice did not know what I had done but she was no fool, and I am sure she guessed I had not stood idly by. We had settled into a pattern where there were only two subjects we never discussed: my work and her religious group. I did not say as much to Alice, but of course I loved her.

I had a lot of freedom as a regional commander. My area included two large ports and a lot of coastline, which of course was officially the business of the port and border authorities, but which brought some interesting material to my desk too. The ATTF had become increasingly important and quite a lot more visible. We automatically outranked the police, which they hated, and the uniform instilled a degree of fear generally because our powers were significant and largely unstated. People variously likened us to the KGB, to US federal agents and to guardian angels.

I wrote monthly reports and spoke regularly to staff in London over the internet. Our Skype calls were safely encrypted and we had some of the best computer buffs in the world in our employ. Even so, I travelled regularly up to London for meetings and to conduct interviews, and we did a lot of group training in some wonderful locations. I think

14

it was during that lovely, straightforward year with Alice that they took us out of the country to a Scottish castle, to learn the latest advances in computer surveillance. These were team building exercises too. Since regional commanders had so much autonomy there was always the danger of loneliness, of being sidetracked or of losing one's way ideologically. I suppose they were keeping us sweet and keeping us loyal, as well as keeping us all on top of our game.

The Secretary of State for Internal Security was a new post, introduced into the Cabinet at the time of the New Alliance. Officially this office took some of the responsibilities from the Foreign and Commonwealth Office and from Communities and Local Government. Internal Security had so far always been awarded to a peer of the realm. It was too great a risk to allow such a post to go to an elected representative who could, of course, lose his or her job in the next general election. It was a prestigious and powerful post, and much hated by the Left. The Secretary of State for Internal Security at that time was Lady MacDonnel-Watts, *Gracey* to what was left of the tabloid press and *Lady Grace* to us in the ATTF. She was fearsomely insightful and ruthless, divorced from her American husband, so rumour had it, because she could no longer tolerate the way he pronounced his vowels. Lady Grace was our boss, and as a regional commander it was my privilege to be summonsed to see her at any time.

I had lived for quite a while in the capital, and had a great affection for it, although nowadays if I needed to stay overnight I was always booked into a very smart hotel close to the London Eye, overlooking Westminster, where the ATTF had some sort of contract. I usually travelled on the Underground to Russell Square when I visited Lady Grace. It was not the closest station to her Bloomsbury apartment in a 'period' mansion house, but Russell Square was my old stamping ground and I enjoyed the short walk.

A maid in a black uniform and a white apron let me in, and took me through at once to the drawing room where Lady Grace usually entertained her officers. It was an elegant room, with traditional English country house furniture of the sort made trendy at that time by Phillips, Forbes and Watson, and with the alcoves on each side of the fireplace lined with books. It was the end of the summer and still quite warm, although I had noticed golden leaves on trees by the tracks on my rail journey up to London, and Lady Grace had a small fire burning in the hearth.

"We'll have coffee, please Sherine," she smiled at the maid. Then, to me, "I have remembered correctly, haven't I?"

When I smiled and nodded she added, "The Brazilian, I think. And shortbread."

I walked across to Lady Grace's huge armchair and she stood. I held out my hand to shake hers, but instead she pulled me closer and air-kissed my cheeks, as if I were a society guest. "Karl, it's lovely to see you," she said, smiling and sounding genuine. "Sit down, sit down!"

I sat, looking around me. The magazines on the coffee table changed each time I visited, of course, and there was a new and rather beautiful picture above the fireplace, but otherwise the room was exactly as I remembered it from my last visit. It spoke of tradition, of Englishness, of safety and predictability – all the things the ATTF was trying to protect.

We made small talk until the coffee and biscuits arrived, discussing the tree planting programme in the nearby Regents Park and the improvement in air quality right across London. Then, when we had our coffee cups on side tables next to us, she got down to business.

"I'm hearing good things about you, Karl," Lady Grace said, smiling. "Your region has seen greater personnel loyalty than any other region, and the intel your agents have passed to us has been excellent."

"Thank you." I ate a delicious shortcake slice and waited for the 'but' which I was sure was on the way.

"Yours is an interesting region, of course," she added meditatively. "You have two large ports, both hosting nuclear submarines, and well-established families of immigrant origin, and then those wonderful middle-class enclaves near the Forest and around the Cathedral. In some ways, your region is like the South East, but perhaps less wedded to London."

"That's right," I agreed. "I did some work down in Kent when I was stationed up here, and there are some things which are similar, but some really significant differences too."

"Such as?" Lady Grace brushed crumbs off her tartan skirt onto the Persian rug at her feet.

"Well…" I started. "The biggest difference, as I see it, and the most significant, is our relationship with the police."

"Tell me," she instructed.

I sat back in the corner of my settee. "In Kent," I explained, "when I worked with Commander Pickett, I found the police really cooperative. Their police and crime commissioner was very supportive of our work. He had been elected, if I remember rightly, on a pro-ATTF ticket and he did everything he could to help us. Whereas in my region I have to deal with three of them, and only the Wiltshire man is genuinely cooperative."

"Ah yes," smiled Lady Grace. "Francis Fox. We were at pre-school together!"

"Right!" I smiled. The ruling classes were as close as ever with each other, despite Alliance propaganda about democracy and fair chances for all. In those days it did not bother me at all.

"So, who is Hampshire?" she asked. "Dorset is that neo-socialist, isn't it? What's his name? McGreggor? McNaught?"

"MacCormack," I corrected. "And Hampshire is Meadows. Sally Meadows."

"Mm." Lady Grace looked thoughtful. "I've never had any dealings with Meadows and I only came across MacCormack once, when we were drafting the new human rights bill in the Lords – the Senate. To be honest, he seemed like a decent chap, despite his wayward politics."

"I think he is," I agreed. "But that doesn't make him cooperative. Still, the biggest problem is definitely Meadows."

"Explain!"

I thought for a moment. "It's hard to put my figure on." I told her. "MacCormack will flatly refuse to help if he feels that we are out of line, but Meadows usually sounds cooperative. Yet somehow, any time we try to work with the Hampshire police, things go wrong." I decided to put my cards on the table. "Last week I fed her some misinformation. I told her we were planning a raid on one of the Southampton halls of residence, and her police arrived an hour before the time I had given her. If we had genuinely been planning a raid she would have put the kibosh on it." I laughed. "As it was, the block was empty, due for refurbishment."

Lady Grace smiled. "So how did Meadows explain that?"

"A misunderstanding. It seems she thought I had asked her to do the raid."

"Tricky," agreed Lady Grace. "Do you think her actions are seriously harming our mission?"

I thought for a moment. "No," I said. "No, I don't. If I had thought that I would have written you a report sooner, or come up to see you. It's just not very helpful, and it's something I have to keep my eye on."

"Yes." We were both silent. I could hear a hoover somewhere in the background, several heavy oak doors away.

"You do seem to have your hands full," ruminated her Ladyship, looking into the coals of the fire. "And you haven't mentioned your religious left yet."

She was referring to Alice's group, and others like it, scattered right through my region, small in number but sometimes quite vocal. I had justified my relationship with Alice by writing a report on them almost a year ago.

A small frown appeared on Lady Grace's forehead. "Karl, my friend," she said. "I think we need to talk. Alice Owen... What is the state of play there?"

I suddenly felt I was on uncertain ground. Of course, I had to be honest. It was part of our code of honour in the ATTF, and anyhow the chances were that Lady Grace knew it all, already.

"I'm in a relationship with her," I said. It sounded silly to my own ears – adolescent.

"Of course," her Ladyship smiled kindly. "How could you not be? She's very much your type, except that..."

"Yes." I sighed. "Except for her religious and political leanings. I know. I do know it."

"I wonder how she justifies your relationship to herself?" she mused. "And to her community."

"I don't know," I had to admit. "We don't talk about it."

"No." She paused. "You wouldn't, of course. It's the elephant in the room."

"Yes."

She looked meditatively into the embers, that small frown appearing again.

"I think, Karl," she said, "that we've reached a crunch point. If Alice were a different person – say an Anglican – my suggestion at this point would be that you go ahead and marry her. You've given good years of your life to our organisation, we have utilised your single status over and over again, but there are not many years until your retirement and I would like to think of you living comfortably with a wife who loves you. I don't suppose she would change her religious affiliation, would she?"

I was surprised, but I knew that that was not a way forward.

Suddenly my mouth felt dry and at the same time I needed to swallow. "We've never discussed it," I said, "but I know she wouldn't. She's really deeply committed."

"And yet she loves you?" Lady Grace was probing gently.

"Yes, I think so," I agreed. "I hope so. We've never discussed that either."

It was Her Ladyship's turn to sigh. "You know where this is going, don't you?" she asked.

"Yes." I could feel a sort of heaviness creeping over me, that sense you get in a nightmare where you know you are going to fall over the cliff but you cannot stop yourself.

"I don't think it can go on like this," she continued. "Sooner or later this situation is going to give you divided loyalties. You're going to get hurt, or she's going to get hurt, and really we can't have that." She looked at me very directly. "You've got two choices, Karl. Either she changes her religious affiliation and you marry, which is what I would prefer, or this relationship has to end."

I should have foreseen this ultimatum when she invited me to Bloomsbury, but I had not. Now it seemed so obvious, and so grim. Of course, I had to do one or the other, and I knew which it would have to be. I was sure Alice loved me but she would not – could not – stop believing the things she believed in. I felt a deep despondency fall on me. How could I end it? What would I say? How could I bear it?

Lady Grace must have understood how I was feeling. She walked across the room and sat beside me, placing her beautifully manicured hand on one of mine.

"I do know," she said. "It's very hard. You sell your soul to the organisation in our line of work." She paused, then said, "Of course, you don't know the real reason for me divorcing Henry…"

"Oh!" I had never thought much about it nor, at that moment, did I much care.

"Like your Alice, we all have to have something we believe in more than anything else," she went on. "And like your Alice, it is vital that we remain true to ourselves, whatever the cost."

"Yes." I knew she was right, but the cost was so great.

Lady Grace patted my hand and went back to her armchair. "You're a strong man," she encouraged me. "You'll manage this. And you don't have to abandon her. Stay friends. Use your influence to protect her if you need to, although I will deny it point blank if you ever say that I gave you that advice. We're not unreasonable. We haven't asked you to use her so far, and we probably won't. Discuss things with her. Work slowly. See if you can wean her away from her extremist friends. I've read her file. I think she's a good woman, just misguided."

"Thank you," I said. Why? Because Lady Grace thought my Alice was a good woman? Because she had just given me the hardest piece of advice I would ever have to follow?

As I left, Lady Grace said, "Come and tell me when it's done, will you?"

"Yes," I agreed, numbly.

She held on to my hand when we shook. "No," she said. "I don't mean *keep me informed*. I mean come here, in person." She gave me one of those penetrating looks, but added kindly, "You're going to need a friend, and I'm not sure there is anyone else in your world you can confide in."

As I walked away she called out uncharacteristically, "See you soon!" and then went back inside.

★ ★ ★

It could have been worse. Alice could have made it worse, and I loved her all the more because she did not. I did not feel I could put it off. It seemed unfair to Alice to leave her thinking all was well between us, when I knew it was not. I

21

arrived home that evening and texted her at once, 'Dinner tomorrow – we need to talk.' My brief message was, I think, enough to warn her. I did not dare take her back to my flat. I did not trust myself to go through with it, knowing that my bed was in the next room, knowing what it would be like to hold her in my arms, to feel her holding me. We went instead to a very expensive restaurant outside her city, and ate snails in garlic, and laughed together, but warily, both knowing what was to come. Over brandy and coffee by the lounge fire in the bar afterwards I told her we could no longer go on.

I thought she turned pale, but I could not be sure in that dim, atmospheric light. She sat very still for a moment, then sipped her brandy deliberately.

"I know," she said. "I always knew it couldn't last."

"Alice, I'm sorry." I wonder if she realised how sorry I was.

"Yes," she agreed. "Yes, I'm sorry too." She paused, then put her hand on my sleeve. "It's been a good year, Karl," she said. "I wouldn't have missed a minute of it, but we're very different, you and I. Our lives are heading in different directions."

"They needn't, Alice…" I was preparing to make a last-ditch attempt.

"Yes, they do need to," she interrupted. "We could try for a while, telling ourselves it doesn't matter, but sooner or later one of us would wake up in the middle of the night and know we couldn't go on. And then where would we be? One or other of us would have burnt our boats. It would be desperate."

I knew she was right. We were both believers, believing in opposing faiths. "Can we stay friends?" I asked, almost plaintively.

She smiled. In fact, I would say she grinned. "How could

we not be friends, Karl?" she asked, and lent over to kiss my cheek. "Friends for life," she said, and in that she was right. It was just that life was not all that long.

'Life' turned out to be nine years.

CHAPTER 2

I went back up to Bloomsbury within the month. I would have gone sooner but there was a crisis involving a US soldier stationed in the Fort Lee compound at Primrose Barracks and it took some sensitive management to sort it out. In theory, under the New Alliance treaty, we are equal partners with the US, but of course might is right, and they have far more military and economic power than us. Then I had to de-brief one of our operatives and deal with quite a lot of paperwork. In the ATTF we have strict priority lists and I could not go back to talk to Lady Grace on a personal matter while there were issues of national security to deal with.

It was October when I finally made it back to London. I had seen Alice once since that horrible evening. I picked her up after school, wearing my uniform of course, and took her for a drink at a local pub which I knew was frequented by a number of the parents of her students. I wanted them all to know that she still had my protection. She seemed quite calm, a little quiet perhaps, but she laughed when it was appropriate and looked me in the eye. She was a brave woman. I accessed her DeVs too, to make sure that she was not in any danger. Until around the time of her retirement Alice wrote a sort of intermittent journal on a little tablet DeV. It was mostly spiritual. It included quite a lot of self-analysis and some issues she intended to pray about, but she also wrote about her ordinary everyday life. From reading her journal I was able to tell when she had cleaned her house, what she had eaten for dinner and what she was worried about at work. There were gaps, though. She was working hard and struggling with the direction in which education was moving. I enjoyed reading what she had written, but if I was accessing it the chances were somebody else might be too. I had tried to persuade her to stop, which would have been something of a small sacrifice for me, but I think she thought that I was being unnecessarily cautious. She still drafted her letters to her Texan pen friend on her DeV too, and then printed them off to send. Both the journal and the filed letters provided a similar insight into Alice's life and if I found myself missing Alice particularly I would read those documents and feel closer to her.

Lady Grace seemed pleased to see me. She already knew that Alice and I were now only friends. I was pretty certain that surveillance on us officers was limited, but I dare say there were operatives watching Alice and it was not impossible that my excellent deputy, Pearson, could have talked to headquarters. On this occasion, Her Ladyship had asked me to call round after dinner, and once again we sat in that large, warm drawing room, this time drinking a rich burgundy and nibbling cheese straws and olives.

"So how has it been?" She asked me, looking concerned. "Tough, I imagine?"

"Yes," I agreed. "Very tough. Although…"

"Although?" she asked.

This was something I had hardly put into words before, even to myself. "Well," I hesitated, and started again. "Well, Lady Grace, it is odd but I feel as if I have done right by Alice."

"Go on," she prompted.

"I suppose – I suppose that in the back of my mind somewhere I had a fear, a sort of lurking suspicion, that I was somehow making Alice betray her conscience." Then I thought how that sounded. "I mean, I didn't seduce her. She came into the relationship of her own free will." In my mind's eye, I pictured her coming down the stairs with that book she

25

had intended to lend me, then dropping the book and walking into my arms. "I didn't need to seduce her," I added sadly.

"No, I'm sure," Lady Grace was either encouraging me or comforting me. I was not sure which.

"I'm still keeping an eye on her," I added, wanting to be totally open. "And I've seen her a couple of times."

She was quiet for a few minutes. She was burning solid fuel in the fire. Was that really environmentally acceptable? One of the coals broke and flared up, hissing as trapped gas met the flames. Then she sighed.

"Well," she said, "you've proved your loyalty in one of the hardest ways imaginable. It won't go unrewarded, you know. And now I have a slight change of job description for you, if you are interested. It involves some more foreign travel, and it requires someone with tact and – how can I put it? – humility. We were impressed by the way you handled the Primrose Barracks escapade. Do you think you might be interested?"

There followed a conversation which, I believe, will not be on record anywhere, and which I see no need to repeat here. Services like ours operate in this way the world over, and I suppose always have done. It is sufficient to say that when I left Lady Grace's drawing room my status within the ATTF had changed and I was, incidentally, a wealthier man.

Technically, from that evening onwards I was still Commander of the Central Southern Region, but much of the routine work was shouldered by Pearson. My role became far more varied, and even more sensitive. I did not think then, and I still do not, that it was a consolation prize because I had put the ATTF before Alice. I believe that only a single man could do the work they were giving me, but it needed to be a single man who was not in danger of becoming emotionally involved. I loved Alice, and Lady Grace knew it. My love for Alice would stop me from becoming entangled in the lives I infiltrated. My love for her anchored me to my region, despite the problems with Meadows and the dull routine of anti-terrorism work in schools. My love for her stopped me from minding that I had not been officially promoted despite my increased responsibilities. My love for her helped me to relate to married operatives when they struggled with domestic issues, and that made me popular with Other Ranks. But in the end, my love for Alice could not help me to save her life.

★ ★ ★

For the next few years life seemed, in some ways, quite settled. My new, more secretive role took me all over England and Wales, and also to a surprising range of places in Europe. The European Union officially disapproved of the policies of our government. They were concerned because our new Bill of Rights, which we had created to replace the European Convention of Human Rights to which we were no longer signatories, gave citizens fewer freedoms and certainties than European governments still guaranteed, and it did not like us polluting the western region of Europe while they maintained such strict environmental regulations and we did not. Nevertheless, there were politicians in most countries who were less opposed to developments in England and Wales than they allowed to be known publicly. The global conglomerates were powerful lobbyists and money is as important in political circles as it is anywhere else. I consulted with high ranking police officials in France, Germany and Italy especially, and we had a number of meetings in Greece with an organisation similar to our own, but still secret.

Back in the Central Southern Region, Pearson carried a lot of responsibility, but rarely took any major decisions without checking with me. As far as my official status went, I was still the regional commander and attended public functions in that capacity whenever I was in the area. I saw Alice when

I could and I thought about her even more, although with less joy than in the past. She was more or less working her way towards retirement. I saw how tired she was when each term ended and how taxing she found the political constraints which were imposed on her work. Occasionally I accessed her work DeV or that of her line manager, to cleanse her record of any politically dubious comments and to help her in her work with her students, and when I found I was missing her more than usual I read her journal, which she tended at that stage only to write at weekends. I still had not succeeded in convincing her of the danger of writing it online. Anyhow, it was innocent enough.

I think at first, and despite everything I had said to Lady Grace, I did hold out the hope that Alice would change. Her Ladyship's recommendation that Alice should become an Anglican and that we should marry had created a dream in my mind in which exactly that happened. On long flights to the States, or if I could not sleep following a meal in an officer's mess in some warm European country, I would make up stories in which she became disillusioned with her left-wing idealism. After all, is not that the usual direction of political travel? Do they not say that people tend to be idealistically left in their youth and move to the right with old age? I even tried to suggest as much to Alice when I took her out to dinner, the year before she retired.

I had been in Greece, I think, advising on border controls, and had taken a few days off afterwards to sail with a fellow officer. It was late May. Junior Baccalaureate exams were about to start at Alice's academy and she looked tired and jaded. Over pâté and green salad, I asked her if everything was all right.

She hesitated. "More or less," she said. Then, "No, not really. I'm worried about a couple of my kids."

"Go on," I encouraged.

She sighed. "Oh, it's just the usual," she said. "Kids who're

28

unhappy at home, anxious to get away, applying to military colleges to do their advanced baccalaureates. They'll end up as officers, I suppose, with a lifetime of killing ahead of them."

I ate some more pâté and thought about it. "Alice," I suggested, "are you sure that a military academy would be such a bad thing? You know, they have excellent academic results and their students have good work prospects, whether they sign up afterwards or not."

Alice had that worried frown, a frown I had rarely seen when I first knew her. "You wouldn't understand, Karl," she said.

"Then tell me," I suggested, knowing we were embarking on a subject we had tacitly agreed never to discuss.

Alice toyed with her wine glass, then smiled a rather woebegone smile. "When kids are little," she said, "they have an innate sense of right and wrong. You know that, don't you? Didn't you ever hear your nieces complain *it isn't fair*?"

"Well, yes, of course," I agreed. "I used to say it myself!"

"The thing is," Alice was not going to be distracted, "I believe – in fact, I *know*, that we all, if we want to, if we are ready to listen, have consciences that will guide us."

"Okay..." I was not sure where this was going.

"If these kids go to the military academy," she said, glancing around to make sure the people at the next table were not listening, "then they will learn not to listen to their consciences."

"Brainwashing, you mean?" I thought Alice was being melodramatic. "They'll just -"

"No, not brain*washing*," Alice interrupted. "Brain *polluting*. There is a Light inside each one of us, Karl, and it really doesn't suit the military. They'll want to extinguish it." She looked very sad. "Karl, I don't want my kids to go through life out of touch with their own spirits."

Afterwards I wondered if that was what Alice thought I was

doing – going through life out of touch with my own spirit. I think that was the first evening when I really, consciously, doubted whether the life I was living was good.

Perhaps, though, I might have given it no further thought if, a year later, Lady Grace had not asked me to visit the East Anglian region.

★ ★ ★

I drove to Cambridge, avoiding London. It was a pleasant enough drive, although I felt sorry for ordinary motorists who were stopped regularly at checkpoints. Of course, my car had ATTF number plates and a chip, and since I was meeting Reginald Palmer at a rather prestigious hotel in Cambridge for lunch, I was in uniform. Both police and ATTF personnel waved me past, the ATTF even saluting.

Before the New Alliance ours was not an organisation ordinary people knew about. We wore no uniforms and were considered by politicians to be a rather dubious wing of the police, or maybe MI5, involved in undercover work. It must have been hard for those organisations, I reflected, when the ATTF was established by a very early act of the new parliament, the uniforms introduced, and the first post of Secretary of State for Internal Security established as a high-ranking cabinet position, and the only person to whom we were answerable. Now we outranked the police and were both feared and respected everywhere. Of course, we had been working towards this for decades, but outside a very restricted circle and one or two conspiracy theorists who nobody listened to, the public had not seen this coming.

Cambridge had a park and ride system and some very strict regulations about cars entering the city, part of the new Clean Air Initiative, but my ATTF status saved me from having to bother with that. I arrived at the hotel half an hour or so before

I was expecting to meet Palmer, so I walked in the famous walled rose garden at the rear of the beautiful building, and wondered what Alice was doing. She was counting down the months to retirement by then, and I was trying to encourage her to take up a new hobby. She was quite a creative person. I thought she might try painting.

To my surprise, she was thinking about moving. That spring she had told me that one of her more extreme friends, a woman called Sky, had encouraged her to look at the new all-green flats built in the park where the old leisure centre used to be, and Alice had decided at once to buy one. I was taken aback. I thought that her cottage was homely and it really reflected her personality, but when I asked her, Alice said that Victorian properties always needed something doing to them, and that her house needed to be empty to be refurbished properly, to make it carbon-neutral. Of course, Alice would mind about things like that. So, she was selling her house to one of those developers who claim to make properties totally environmentally friendly, and was buying her flat.

I had to agree, when she showed me round, that it was an attractive property in its way, although I thought it lacked the character of older houses. Alice was happy, though. Without telling her I arranged to have the flat swept for surveillance bugs one evening and was not totally surprised to discover that there had been several well-hidden gadgets, mostly in the light fittings. I had no idea whether they were installed in all the flats, or only some. They were not the work of the ATTF, and I planned, if I could, to discover whether the local police labelled Alice a *person of interest*. I had realised, with some sadness, that Alice's commitment to her group was unwavering and there was that problem of her pen friend on death row in Texas. That was about the time that Alice had stopped writing her journal online at my insistence, rather reluctantly, but she still wrote to Simon on her DeV and then printed the letters off, including colourful photographs of the places she had visited. I thought I really needed to persuade Alice to stop doing anything personal on her DeV. It might not be easy.

Reginald Palmer was not at all what I was expecting. I suppose his name had conjured up visions of a gruff, broad-browed Norfolk man reflecting his Anglo-Saxon origins. In fact, the man was olive skinned and dark haired, with fine features and small hands and feet, despite his medium height. He walked across the hotel lobby and flashed me a cheerful, relaxed smile. "You must be Commander Wyss?" he said, his hand outstretched to shake mine. "Commander Palmer. Interesting surname. Swiss? Austrian?"

"Swiss," I replied, smiling. "Whereas *Palmer* is as English as it comes!"

Palmer smiled as he led me towards the restaurant. "You're right," he agreed. "The wife tells me it dates back to the Crusades." He chuckled and added, "It seems my ancestors carried palm crosses in the Holy Land. Although," he added as an afterthought, "I can't think why!"

He was a well-read and amusing man. Generally, of course, regional commanders are. They are mostly recruited from Oxbridge or, like me, from Durham, with a smattering of graduates loyal to England, whose degrees were nevertheless awarded by Scottish universities before the vote to leave the European Union. Over lunch we agreed that we would use first names, and Reggie insisted that the following evening I would go to dinner at his home. "Rosie loves entertaining," he claimed. "You do eat meat, don't you?"

★ ★ ★

Lady Grace had talked about seconding me to the Anglian region, but she had also referred to my month's placement as a break. The organisation had booked a room for me in the hotel where Reggie and I had eaten lunch, a quiet, airy room overlooking the gardens. It seemed that nothing was expected of me until the following day, so I walked into the centre of the city and explored the green space behind the colleges. I ate dinner in a pub frequented by students, and listened with amusement to their self-consciously intelligent conversations. In the corner three girls, perhaps in their mid-teens, unwittingly represented the town element of *town and gown,* and I enjoyed overhearing their unsophisticated remarks about fashion and manicures. Then I walked back to the hotel, briefly considered messaging Alice but decided I should not, and went to bed.

Lady Grace was right; it was a break. Reggie was one of those very able leaders who makes being in command look easy. He smiled and chatted to everyone he met, and drove lazily with one hand on the steering wheel and, it seemed, only one eye on the road. Nevertheless, it was clear that he did not miss much. One day, perhaps three or four days after I had arrived, he surprised me with a question over a pub lunch. "So, our Gracey is worried about you?" he queried. "Have things been tough in the south? Do you want to talk?"

I took a deep breath. Operatives at any level were discouraged from sharing personal details and while I assumed Lady Grace trusted Reggie, it was always possible that her agenda was very different. What if she had certain concerns about his region and wanted me to form my own opinion without being influenced by her?

I decided to be cautious. "I suppose a job like ours is never totally straightforward," I said. "We're lucky to have someone like Grace MacDonnel-Watts looking out for us."

Reggie gulped down some more beer. "I think so," he agreed. "Rosie and I owe her a lot."

The bait was too tempting to ignore. "You do?" I asked.

Reggie looked across the lounge bar to where the barmaid was pulling pints and laughing with locals. "Mm," said Reggie.

"Well, it's not much of a secret." He glanced sideways at me. "Rosie is Dutch," he explained. "She didn't want us to leave the European Union and she totally opposed us making the New Alliance. She signed petitions online and demonstrated in Trafalgar Square – the works. When she discovered I'd been ATTF and not regular police all those years she was all set to leave me." He looked deeply into his half empty tankard. "It would have broken my heart."

"So what did Lady Grace do?" I had met Rosie on my second day in Cambridge when I had gone to dinner. She had seemed cheerful and friendly, and the home seemed relaxed, if a bit chaotic.

"She invited us to dinner," Reggie said. "Rosie was dead set against going but Lady Grace phoned her while I was in the office and talked her round. And over dinner she explained the philosophy of the ATTF in a way that I couldn't, so that Rosie saw how we are motivated only by the need to protect and defend the country. She seemed to understand – I mean, Lady Grace did – how Rosie was feeling. To be honest, she converted Rosie. Like a religious conversation, almost. And now it's fine."

"Goodness!" I was really surprised. I must admit, I even wondered at the wisdom of having a man in the role of commander whose wife was so shaky on our basic philosophy. But then I thought, *if Lady Grace had been able to convert Alice, and I had married her, wouldn't I be better at my job, not worse?* I thought I would be: better, happier and stronger. *Lucky thing!* I thought, looking at Reggie, but I only said, slightly sarcastically, "I love happy endings!"

★ ★ ★

The revelation about Reggie's marriage was the first of three big surprises that month. The second occurred when we met the local police and crime commissioner. Xavier Booth had an office

34

in the centre of the city, above an internet café and computer supply shop. His name and title were on a large plaque next to the door, and underneath was a noticeboard, behind glass, advertising the times when his office was open and reminding people that they could make appointments, or drop in on spec. There were also posters of the sort you always see outside police stations: notices about having pets chipped, about phoning a certain number if you are suspicious of someone or something, a couple of missing person posters and a large sheet announcing a marathon, to take place in a couple of months, in aid of *our brave men and women on the front*. We had two fronts at the time but everyone was talking about the Caribbean, so I assumed that that was what was meant there.

Xavier Booth was waiting for us. He seemed to have no staff present, not even a receptionist sitting in the lobby and waiting room area. He was standing at his window looking out on to the market square, a big, bald man in rather ill-fitting clothes, with a small cross on his tie pin.

"Ah, gentlemen!" he said as he turned. "Reggie, good to see you. Commander Wyss, isn't it? Welcome to Cambridge! Or are you already familiar with our lovely city? Not a graduate, are you? Sit down, sit down!"

We sat. "No, Durham," I said. "One of a small minority."

"Ah yes, minorities!" exclaimed the Commissioner and smiled benignly. "Very much a matter of concern for us, minorities!"

We were obviously diving straight in. The commissioner turned to a low table and produced a cafetière, then three assorted mugs. Without asking us he poured the dark, murky contents and pushed a plastic milk container and some sweeteners towards us.

"Which are your largest minority groups, Sir?" I asked. Of course, Reggie and I outranked the commissioner but there was no point in rubbing it in.

"The largest group? Eastern Europeans perhaps, but they really aren't much of a problem." He gulped some coffee, and scratched his bald head. "Wouldn't you agree, Reggie?"

"Oh, I think you're right," agreed Reggie. "They came here to work before we left the EU and, to be honest, they've been working ever since. I don't know what the economy of the region would have done without them."

"And of course," the commissioner chipped in, "they're white. Now, I know that isn't something we're supposed to mention but the truth is, their children speak the lingo like the native born – well, they *are* the native born – so there is nothing to make them stand out. Difficult surnames to spell when it comes to keeping records, but that's about it."

I waited, and when he looked as if he was going to add nothing further I asked, "So any troublesome minorities?"

"Well... I would say we have two groups in our sights. One you might expect. We have a couple of towns on the edge of our area where a previous regime chose to settle large numbers of asylum seekers. And then there's the Gypsies."

"Gypsies!" I was really surprised. We had a lot of homeless people travelling around our area, living in vans and even caravans, putting up tents and squatting in empty properties, but as far as I knew none of them were Gypsies.

Reggie took over. "Oh, we've always had Gypsies in this region," he explained. "Some real, authentic folk with strong links to Eastern Europe and Ireland, and some ne'er-do-wells. It's the real Gypsies who are the problem."

I was amazed, and it must have shown on my face. "Why?" I asked. "How many of them are there? Why are they a problem?"

"Well, they might not be a problem," mused the commissioner. "Our difficulty is that we don't know."

I looked at Reggie. "They're a very closed community," he

started to explain. "Well, maybe not *closed*, so much as *close*. We never really know what they're up to."

I thought back to my initial training. We had done some very in-depth study of a number of cultures and religions, but I did not recall learning anything about Gypsies. "*Are* they up to something, do you think?" I asked.

"Could be," said the commissioner. "Could be."

"People trafficking," explained Reggie. "Perhaps."

There had been a time, until a couple of years after we had left the European Union, when people smuggling had been a big problem. Back then it had seemed as if everyone wanted to come here to make new lives for themselves. That had all stopped, though, and as far as I knew we really did not have to deal with that issue any more.

"Not bringing people in," clarified Reggie. "Taking people out. Helping them to escape."

"Oh, I see." That was, I knew, a growing problem. Since the establishment of the New Alliance, our regime had been heavily criticised for our human rights abuses, especially for our treatment of the poor and of those who were disloyal, who did not have the best interests of the country at heart. We had strict border controls. We especially did not like professionals to leave the country, or people whose revelations might further harm our standing in the world. We had to be fairly vigilant along the coast in my region, especially at the ports and the small airports, but there had been nothing to indicate to me that criminal people smugglers might be involved yet.

"You don't have that problem?" queried the commissioner.

"Not as far as I am aware..." I said, but my mind was in overdrive. It was something I would need to talk to Pearson about when I got back. "Not established gangs, although I suppose it is only a matter of time..."

"I'm not sure we have established gangs either," said

Reggie. "In a way, it might be easier if we had. What we *do* have is a sort of passive resistance to the regime."

"Not exactly passive," the commissioner interrupted. "Possibly quite active, but definitely not gangs. Not in it for the money."

"So, what are they in it for?"

"Idealism," muttered Reggie, and sighed.

"Or not even that," the commissioner pondered. "You know; the Gypsies have lived here for hundreds of years. They've never integrated, just lived their own lives. Used to drive social workers mad in the old days, when we were keen on getting everyone educated! And they're not integrated now. It's as if they are immune to the politics of the day. They just keep on doing what they choose to do."

"And they choose to help people escape?" I asked.

"Well, that's just it. We think so. But so far, we've had no proof. Just rumours."

"And a few ends that don't tie up," added Reggie.

The more I thought about our conversation with Xavier Booth, the more uncomfortable I felt. It had not taken me two minutes to realise that if people were helping undesirables to escape, it was just the sort of thing Alice's group might get involved in. They would think nothing of taking criminal action if they thought they should. Despite being, normally, very law-abiding, they would never allow themselves to put man-made rules above what they thought was the right thing to do. Of course, that was the problem with Alice and that Texan murderer too. Most sane people would run a mile from establishing such a warm and open friendship with someone who was known to be a killer. I thought of all those letters I had intercepted. She wrote to him as a friend, as an equal. Alice's group seemed to think everyone was potentially a friend, and definitely an equal. I sighed. It was such an attractive characteristic, but so dangerous.

★ ★ ★

A week or so after that, Reggie picked me up from my hotel as usual and announced as I settled into the passenger seat, "We've got an interesting day today."

The intervening days since our meeting with the commissioner had been fairly routine. Reggie's region seemed less diverse than mine. Although his area, too, included quite a lot of coastline, he had only one really large port and a single airport of any significance. I had sat in on a few meetings with Other Ranks and helped in the debrief of a very bright, young, undercover operative, but there had also been the usual paperwork and a liaison meeting with Border Controls in Luton.

"We're heading out into the country," Reggie explained. "There are a couple of people I want you to meet."

It was a pleasant morning. The countryside was flat, the fields ploughed, surrounded as often as not by ditches rather than hedges, the trees golden, the sky blue with white cumulus clouds floating lazily overhead. We were both quiet for a while, then Reggie started talking, almost as if he were thinking aloud, reviewing his region.

"Compared to most areas," he said, "we've really had very little trouble in East Anglia. I think it goes back a long way, our good fortune." He indicated right and we turned off the A road onto a narrower lane. "I knew old Xavier before the New Alliance," he went on. "He's a good man. A law-and-order man, of course, but compassionate."

I remained quiet. *Compassion* was not a word used often in ATTF circles, and I was intrigued to know where this was going.

"Way back," Reggie continued, slowing down as we passed through a small, sleepy village with no sign of human life, but with a black cat asleep in the sun at the side of the road. "Way

39

back, before we left the EU, Xavier was a bit of a pioneer in the treatment of extremists."

He turned to look at me, only one hand on the steering wheel, as was his way. "Do you remember when we had that rush of terrorist attacks across Europe and here in England, and half the time the young men responsible turned out to have psychiatric problems?"

I did remember. I had been undercover in France during part of that time, liaising with the French Right. It was the year we finally left the EU.

"Well, our estimable commissioner set up a sort of alternative to the government's failed *Prevent* programme. Do you remember *Prevent*?"

"Oh, yes!" *Prevent* had been a misconceived attempt to get immigrant communities to give information to the police about their own, radicalised, people. Of course, it had led to a lot of bad feeling and achieved very little. "Well, old Xavier decided to do something different. He talked to social workers, schoolteachers, religious leaders – any community leaders he could work with – and got them to tell his people if they thought a person was in need of psychiatric help. Not if they were being radicalised, you see? Just if they were vulnerable. And then he tried to get them help. It didn't always work, but he achieved a lot. People trusted old Xavier after that."

"Do you?" I asked. I would not trust our commissioner, Meadows, under any circumstance.

"Oh yes, I do." Reggie spoke with absolute certainty.

★ ★ ★

We entered the village past an old railway station, some retail outlets and then an early twenty-first century housing estate with lots of green space, past a school and a cemetery, before turning right and pulling up outside a vicarage.

Without explaining, Reggie said, "We're here!" and switched off the engine.

A middle-aged woman came out of the house. "Reggie," she exclaimed. "Right on time!" They hugged each other and then she held out her hand. "You must be Reggie's colleague. I'm Mia, Will's wife."

"Karl," I said, shaking hands.

"Well, come on in," invited Mia. "Will's just with a parishioner." She smiled at us. "He'll be glad you are here. We haven't yet discovered how to end a meeting with Vicky! She always has just one more thing to get off her chest!"

★ ★ ★

Over ginger tea and home-made chocolate muffins I realised why Reggie had spoken as he had in the car. Will was, of course, the vicar in that rather isolated village, and he and Mia had been long-time supporters of Xavier's alternative to *Prevent*. They had achieved one notable success several years ago, and it was this that Reggie wanted me to hear about.

"The whole family was a bit odd," explained Mia. "Not a church family, but with some sort of Christian beliefs gleaned from the internet."

"Almost survivalists," Will added. "You know, like those Americans who believe that civilization as we know it is about to end, and that after that it will be each family for itself?"

"They saw conspiracies everywhere." Mia smiled, "They told me about you lot a long time before the ATTF were public knowledge, so some of their sources of information must have been reliable!"

Will, who perhaps should have been watching his waistline, took a second muffin and continued the story. "They had two sons." Then, looking at Mia, "Or was it three?"

"Three," corrected Mia, "but Jeremy was living away from home. He wasn't involved."

"Right. Well," continued Will, "the older of the two remaining sons was a youngster called Enoch."

Mia giggled. "They all had these Old Testament names. Poor kids!"

Will grinned. "It probably didn't help," he suggested. "I dare say the boys were teased at school, and felt different from other kids, and the parents didn't like them mixing with the families in the village. They ended up homeschooling them. The first we knew of a problem brewing was when they started distributing homemade leaflets around the village. It was odd stuff, I think they just copied and pasted it from various internet sites."

"It was certainly stuff from the States," agreed Mia. Looking at Will she said, "Don't you remember the leaflet that talked about the right to bear arms?"

They both chuckled. "I do," said Will, continuing. "It was a bit of a nuisance, actually," he said. "The Guides and Scouts were having some sort of campaign to make the village litter-free and no sooner had they cleaned everything up than another batch of leaflets would be delivered and dropped all over the place by people who weren't interested." He chuckled again at the memory.

Mia turned serious. "Still," she said, "we would never have seen the problem coming if Mrs Broomfield hadn't spoken to Will."

"Mrs Broomfield was the mother," Will explained, addressing me. "Two farthings short of a penny, if you ask me, but devoted to her husband."

"Yes," agreed Mia, "but frightened of Enoch."

"Yes." Will looked very serious as well. "Very frightened." Again, he was looking at me. "Enoch had got hold of a gun," he explained. "Mrs Broomfield came to warn me. He

42

was planning to come to church on Sunday and shoot the congregation."

"Because we don't practice Believers' Baptism," explained Mia, as if it made perfect sense. "And because we pray for the Royal Family."

"What did you do?" I asked. Who would have thought that the life of a country vicar would be so exciting? Or so dangerous!

"I phoned the police and crime Commissioner." Will said. "He had been elected a couple of years earlier. I thought he was a bit right wing for my liking…"

"We're woolly liberals," interrupted Mia, cheerfully.

"Yes, but all of us church leaders had been told about Xavier's anti-terrorist strategy and I thought he was the man we needed."

"So, what happened?" I was ignoring the comment about being woolly liberals, thinking it was a bit of a risky comment for Mia to have made.

"Exactly what should happen," said Will. "The police came out with a psychiatric social worker and took Enoch to some institution or other. They took away the gun and warned the rest of the family, who all claimed to know nothing about Enoch's plans."

"Obviously not true," interrupted Ma, "since Mrs Broomfield had spoken to Will!"

"And that was the end of it," concluded Will, with obvious satisfaction.

"Much better than the *Prevent* programme," gloated Mia.

On the way back into Cambridge, Reggie and I discussed Enoch's story.

"Where is he now, the son with the shotgun?" I asked.

"I'm not sure. In some residential community, over near Cromer, I think." He was quiet, then added, "Mia told me that Mrs Broomfield came to church once or twice after that, but she didn't really like it. She told Will it was too tame!"

★ ★ ★

Will and Mia were my third surprise in East Anglia. The morning we spent with them and the light lunch we ate together challenged my way of seeing the world. It had started when Mia had made that comment about being woolly liberals. She had said it so cheerfully and unselfconsciously, and there had been no glance from Will signalling *be careful!* I thought about my region, and wondered whether people in the south would dare to be so relaxed about their views. Obviously, liberals or not, Will and Mia were no threat to the status quo. Quite the opposite, they were working with the authorities to achieve peace and to avoid complications. I found myself contrasting, as I drove south past a series of roadblocks and checkpoints where I was waved through and saluted, the reaction the villagers might have had to Enoch being taken off to some sort of residential community near Cromer, with popular feeling if the ATTF had gone in, tasers blazing, and arrested the young man and removed him to who-knew-where. I started to wonder whether there might not be a place in our society for woolly leftists, and then I started to think about Alice's group. Should we mistrust them as much as we did? I briefly wondered about talking to Pearson about it, but I thought the poor man would only worry, and would probably feel the need to report my wavering commitment to higher authorities. Then I thought of discussing my thoughts with Lady Grace. After all, it had been her idea that I should visit East Anglia. No, I needed to think carefully, I decided. Would Lady Grace suspect that I was being influenced by Alice? As I drove along I realised that I was. Her comment about people being out of touch with their spirits had stayed with me, and was a little perplexing because I was not quite sure what it meant.

★ ★ ★

I thought a lot about my route into the ATTF during that easy drive south. When I looked back on my years at Durham it seemed as if I were a different person then. Perhaps one's youth always looks like that from the perspective of middle age. I was happy and, compared with the rest of my life, carefree. Well, maybe that is not quite true. I did have lots of cares, but they were the concerns of youth and when I observed them through the filter of time, and of course with the knowledge of how they turned out, they seemed like minor worries and incidental anxieties.

There are a few memories which still stood out in a landscape that was blurred and vague. I remembered a group of us sitting in a pub talking about politics until the pub closed, then moving on to a small park, sitting on benches and on the ground, arguing about capitalism and the nature of the Good Society. I thought that that must have been before I went to Professor Narin's lectures.

Of course, I remembered when my girlfriend, Phoebe, phoned me from Manchester and told me she was pregnant. I still had a memory that was crystal clear, of arriving at Manchester station feeling desperately cold, and hugging Phoebe, and us both crying. I remembered, too, but rather less clearly, arriving back in Durham, relieved that it was all a false alarm but at the same time in some way disappointed, as if it were an anti-climax. Was that when our relationship ended? I thought perhaps it was, although at the time I did not realise it, and we went on seeing each other with less and less enthusiasm until the end of our second year at university. I knew I dated a lot of girls in my third year, but I could not even remember the names of most of them, forty or more years on. Perhaps I thought I was in love with one or two of them but it was a long time – decades, even – before I felt that easy connection I had shared with Phoebe when we were teenagers, and then, of course, it was with Alice.

After university my life had taken some very unexpected turns. It had started with a seminar, perhaps really it was more of an informal discussion, with Professor Narin, who was a visiting lecturer. I expect the subject was global capitalism. It usually was. Some students were looking again at a new form of left-wing politics. They were deeply opposed to the developments which, in nascent form, were going on in front of our very noses: the trade agreements which would eventually give international companies the power to sue national governments, the enormous wealth of CEOs who seemed to be answerable to nobody, and the ever-increasing gap between the rich and the poor. Others of us followed the revolutionary thoughts of Narin who believed in a sort of social Darwinism, claiming that as the old ruling classes faded out it was both natural and good that a new ruling class, the oligarchs he claimed would emerge in the twenty-first century, should take over. He provoked us all by saying that democracy had to be tempered by men and women with vested interests and a well-grounded knowledge of how the world really worked, because if we depended a hundred per cent on the vote of the ordinary citizen we would end up being ruled by soundbites and prejudice. Narin predicted that the House of Lords would never be completely reformed because democracy was better served by having meritocrats working within it, rather than elected representatives. Back then we were experiencing our first ever female prime minister. I remembered that I was not impressed. I had known that my brother Walter and his new wife Nancy thought she was wonderful but I had thought that they demonstrated the truth of what Professor Narin was suggesting. It seemed to me that they had no idea what her government was really doing to the fabric of our society.

I was an idealist, of course. I would like to think I still am, although my ideals are very different now. Anyhow, it made me an easy target for recruitment. By the time I was twenty-four and had a master's degree behind me, I had also been initiated into the organisation dedicated to the maintenance of law and order, to a sensible modification of democracy in order to achieve a stable society that would benefit everyone, and to an ever-closer union with the USA.

The years which followed were, I suppose, strange. I became rather distant from my family because it was impossible to talk about my work. I was trained, groomed even, by the organisation, and became something of an expert in electronic surveillance. The *RIPA Act* (Regulation of Investigatory Powers) which came into force at the beginning of this century, gave us far more power than the public and most members of parliament realised, and increased the influence of our organisation hugely. I was one of the group which trained several FBI field workers on the use of chips in smart meters, the meters which replaced standard gas and electricity meters in England and Wales in the second decade of the century.

There was a lot going on. Outside my areas of expertise, I could see all sorts of other strategies designed to move the nation in the direction in which we wanted them to go. I remember, before I knew Alice, watching TV in the London flat of some girlfriend whose name I have forgotten, and realising that a new ploy was being used in advertising. Several times in one evening I heard phrases like *'America's favourite chilli'* or *'the number one best-selling cleaning agent in the whole United States'*. Suddenly I realised what the unspoken message was, beyond *'Buy this product!'* It was, *'If it comes from America it must be good!'* Documentaries on TV strengthened the message. We were shown how a policy of zero tolerance had reduced crime rates in New York City and how the police in the State of Mississippi were being trained to avoid racial profiling (rather belatedly, in my opinion, and without any observable outcomes), but we were rarely shown how Sweden or Japan managed these things, although their crime rates were so much lower and their systems, no doubt, far more effective. There were those who fed stories about the EU, about undemocratic processes, ridiculous regulations and expensive bureaucracy into the British media, until there was an almost general acceptance of the idea that we were somehow being cheated of some sort of national sovereignty by our links with Europe. In our organisation, we knew that there was a long-term plan to drive us into the arms of the Americans, to whom the EU had become a serious threat. As a young man, I believed the propaganda.

My membership of the organisation, in fact the very existence of the group, was not publicly acknowledged until well into the twenty-first century when we left the European Union and made the New Alliance. Then I wore my uniform, if not with pride, then certainly with the confidence that I had spent my life on the right side, serving the good of my country. That is what I thought then, and that was what I was wondering about when I drove back from Cambridge.

I had seen less of the homelessness problem in the east than was obvious in my own region, although Reggie assured me it was there. Their food banks seemed to be well supported by more affluent citizens so the loss of benefits was not biting as strongly as in the south. More than these things, though, I was impressed by the way the ATTF worked with other organisations. Police and crime commissioners are elected and Xavier Booth made no secret of his warm relationship with our organisation, yet he had been re-elected twice. Then there were Will and Mia, self-declared woolly liberals, who nevertheless welcomed Reggie into their home with open arms and worked with the police and the ATTF when the need arose. I saw in the east an image of the England I had signed up to protect, the England I wanted to see re-established in my more complicated Central Southern Region. I was beginning to question whether, in fact, we were too hard line, and my questioning left me feeling insecure. At about the same time that I drove back into my region, the first time I recognised the men at a checkpoint, I realised that what I really wanted to do was to visit Will and Mia without Reggie being present. I wanted to know how they could be liberals and still support the regime.

CHAPTER 3

During my month in the east I had of course received numerous updates from Pearson about my own region. There had been some trouble with the churches, starting in the coastal towns but spreading right across the region. The Alliance supported and even encouraged charitable activity, of course. It was an important part of good citizenship, and it also helped the consciences of the middle class to rest easy at night when they contemplated the loss of benefits for the poor and the sick. On the other hand, we did not want over-zealous do-gooders to establish a sort of piece-meal welfare state to replace the one we had almost succeeded in dismantling. Our vision was of independent, hard-working people who took responsibility for their lives and the lives of their families. Too much charity encouraged dependency. That a few people would go to the wall was inevitable, but it was the price we had to pay to establish a strong, resilient society.

Pearson and I discussed the problem at length a couple of days after my return when, wearing casual clothes, we visited one of the churches on the outskirts of Alice's city. Like a lot of the evangelical churches, this church was thriving. They had established strong contacts with a US west coast Christian community a while before we left the EU, and were in many respects ideal citizens of the New Alliance. I browsed their bookcase and found several paperbacks imported from the US, complete with American spelling and references to American culture. That seemed good. However, the church had a strong adherence to Biblical teaching and they took seriously the teaching to love their neighbours. This they were trying to obey by starting a feeding programme which operated every evening. When Pearson and I visited, there must have been well over a hundred people there, of all ages, and the food ran out before everyone was fed.

The next day I asked for an appointment with the pastor of the church. She was an elegant woman in her forties with gleaming white teeth, dressed in quite a trendy fashion with an embroidered waistcoat which sparkled in the office lights. I congratulated her on the commitment of her congregation and we discussed faith schools in an upbeat manner, until I was reasonably sure she was on my side. Then I explained why I had reservations about the feeding programme. "There is such a thing as tough love," I said, using the jargon I had read in a book on their bookstall about raising children. "Sometimes we have to allow a little pain for people to learn how to live good lives."

I saw that she was feeling uncomfortable, but I wanted to win this move of the game.

"To put my cards on the table, Pastor Wells," I added, "I have another concern. When we visited your feeding programme we counted eight people working flat out to prepare and serve those people. Am I right?"

She nodded, uncertain about where I was going, a little frown on her well made-up face.

"Eight people," I said, "who could have been telling others the Good News. Eight people who could have been talking to their neighbours, organising events, praying for the lost, who instead were feeding people who would be just as hungry again the next day."

Pastor Wells looked stricken.

"What we need," I said, ignoring my feelings of hypocrisy and clinching the deal, "is churches which don't just feed people, but churches which change people's lives. If you can do that, there will be no need to feed them, because they'll be feeding themselves!"

In the end, we achieved a compromise with the Council of Churches. Out of love they would operate feeding programmes once a week, normally on Sundays. The greater part of their energy would be spent on evangelism. My field workers reported that even the group Alice belonged to was abiding by the new guidelines, at least as far as the weekly food distribution went. I reported the development proudly to Lady Grace, and received an approving email in return.

★ ★ ★

In fact, despite my rather confused thoughts and reflections as I drove home, for several weeks after I got back from East Anglia I felt really positive. Reggie's set up, with the agencies cooperating as they did, seemed quite inspiring. I doubted if I would achieve much with Meadows, she had a deep-seated grudge against the ATTF, but Fox in the small part of Wiltshire for which I was responsible, was already working well with us, and I thought I might be able to get somewhere with MacCormack in Dorset if I played my cards right. I shared my hopes with Pearson, and we were beginning to plan a way forward which would involve isolating Meadows, when Meadows herself took the initiative.

Her office phoned me first thing one Monday morning. Meadows liked her staff to do all the routine work associated with her post, although she loved attending commissioners' meetings, which were usually hosted in the House of Lords (or should I say *the Senate*), and appearing alongside mayors or MPs at important functions. Her minion asked me if I could meet Meadows at eleven that morning. I swallowed my impatience. The invitation was more of a summons, and Meadows knew that I outranked her, and that I oversaw a much larger region than she did, and was likely to be busy. I was tempted to say it was not convenient, but with the vision of the friendly working relations I had glimpsed in the east, I curbed my pride and agreed to be there.

I suppose I knew as soon as I walked into her office that Meadows was up to something. She was seated behind her large, oak desk, wearing one of those fashionable trouser suits which women wore at the time, with two rows of brass buttons down the front and epaulettes on the shoulders, so that she looked vaguely military, or perhaps like the Little Drummer Boy of Christmas legend. Her smile did not reach her eyes, but then I am sure my returning smile was more of a grimace too.

"Karl," she said, again ignoring my rank by using my first name, "thank you for coming."

I remained formal. "How can I help you, Commissioner?" I asked, sitting down before I was invited to do so, and crossing my ankles in a relaxed pose, to show that I was unimpressed.

She sat down too, looking perhaps a little disconcerted. "Well, really it's a question of what I can do for you," she said.

I doubted if there was anything very important that Meadows could do to assist the ATTF, but it would have been hopelessly undiplomatic to say so. "That's good," I said, in a tone of voice which spoke of doubt.

"Some information has come to my ears," she said, and paused, waiting for me to ask. I tried to appear bored. When it became evident that I was not going to ask, she said, "It's about a woman in this city. She's a rather anti-social element. I'm surprised you haven't realised already because I'm told you know her."

I felt trouble coming, but I refused to let my concern show, and just raised my eyebrows in an enquiring fashion.

"Alice Owen," she said, almost gleefully. "She's a member of that strange group that meets in that place behind the

Guildhall. We've known about her for a while, as I believe, have you. And now the Americans are showing an interest."

"Ah," I said, trying to keep my expression and my voice neutral. How could I be ignorant of it, if the Americans really were truly concerned about Alice?

"Yes," insisted Meadows, pressing home the advantage she must have known she had. "Major Wallace came to see me while you were away. Ms Owen is involved with someone in Texas who is no friend to their country, or ours."

"Pearson hasn't mentioned this," I said.

Meadows sat back, her expression gleeful. "Well, no, he wouldn't," she said. "Major Wallace understood that you might be – how shall I put it – romantically involved with Ms Owen. Under the circumstances, he thought it best to circumnavigate your office." As if lecturing a junior officer, she added, "Our relationship with the Americans depends on trust, you know. Major Wallace does not trust you."

"Right," I said. I knew Meadows had seriously wrong-footed me. If I found out that a US officer was involved with one of my suspects, I would not trust him, either. I realised that in my attempts to protect Alice in the less-than-friendly environment of her work, I had advertised our relationship widely, at least among those whose surveillance skills were good enough to have detected what I had been doing. I thought quickly.

"But your information is rather seriously out of date," I improvised.

Now it was Meadows' turn to look surprised.

"Yes," I continued. "Alice Owen and I are no longer together. We found that she had no more useful information to give us." *Alice, I'm sorry,* I thought, knowing I was misrepresenting our relationship to save my own skin.

Meadows looked perplexed, but then her frown vanished. She picked up a piece of paper from her desk and looked at it closely. "That's strange," she said. "According to my records Ms Owen received a call from you the day after you got back from Cambridgeshire, and you went out to – let's see – *The Inn by the Willows*, two nights ago."

I tried to stay calm. It was unnerving how much they knew about Alice, even after I had swept her new flat for bugs.

"True," I said. "I congratulate you on the accuracy of your surveillance. Although," I added, "if there had been anything untoward about me meeting Ms Owen, I doubt if I would have taken her to quite such a public place!"

Meadows was looking a little uncomfortable now. "Perhaps you should explain this to Major Wallace," she said. "In fact, perhaps you should have explained this to Major Wallace some months ago!"

If there was any truth in that remark – and there was – I was not going to let Meadows see that I saw her point. I rose from my chair and replaced the cap I had removed when I entered. "Perhaps, Commissioner," I said, "Major Wallace should have used proper channels, and have come to me with his concerns. Good morning. It was a pleasure, as always, to talk to you." I turned sharply, emphasising my paramilitary training, and left.

Once out in the street I took a deep breath. Now I really did have a problem. Far from creating a good working relationship with Meadows, mirroring Reggie's relationship with Xavier Booth, or simply isolating the commissioner, I realised that I had on my doorstep someone who was working directly against me. Meadows and I were, in effect, enemies. It would be hard for me, and I understood with a rush of cold fear, very dangerous for Alice.

★ ★ ★

Until then, there had been little about our surveillance operations that I had not shared with Pearson. If he were to run the region during my not infrequent absences, he needed to be up to scratch on everything we had in hand. Yet I was not comfortable telling Pearson about my conversation with Meadows. Of course, he knew I had been seeing Alice, and I am sure he realised that the relationship had been replaced by a friendship years earlier. Even so, I was a little ashamed at how vulnerable my actions had left me, and I began to wonder whether he had disapproved all along. Not for the first time I wondered whether Pearson had been the one to talk to Lady Grace about it in the first place? Was he writing regular reports about me? And perhaps, more dangerously, was he writing regular reports about Alice? I really doubted it, Pearson seemed like a loyal man, and a sensible one, but there was really no way I could find out. One thing I was sure about, though, was that if Meadows knew of my weaknesses I needed to be very careful.

★ ★ ★

Alice invited me to her leaving celebrations. I was, at first, surprised, but then flattered. She had never asked me to anything that was happening in her religious community, but perhaps that was not so extraordinary. On the other hand students and staff were used to seeing me at the school, and I could believe that it was more comfortable for her to have someone alongside her during the festivities. I checked with Alice and on her recommendation, I wore uniform, both to the departmental meal at a local restaurant, and to the events of the last day of term, after the students had left.

Actually, Alice made me chuckle on that last day. She also made me worry. There were several people leaving and each was invited to give a brief talk to the assembled staff. Most thanked their colleagues for all the support they had received, spoke of missing the students, and of the things they hoped to do next. The assembled teaching staff looked weary. The retirement age had risen steadily over the years and there were a lot of grey heads in the audience, no doubt belonging to people who wished they could retire too. Alice was retiring relatively young. She was good with money and had inherited quite a lot from her parents, divided exactly equally with her brother DD. When it came to Alice's turn to speak she started with the usual routine, thanking the senior management of the school, the governors, the staff counsellor who advised staff on ideology, and also the cleaning staff, which I thought was a nice touch. Then, at the point where most staff spoke about spending more time with their grandchildren, or moving to Cornwall, or seeing everyone again when it was time to invigilate for baccalaureate exams, Alice branched out on her own.

"I came into teaching, as I'm sure we all did," she said, "full of idealism. I am still idealistic now." She smiled across at me, where I was sitting with one of the deputy principles. "I am not sure what I will do with my retirement. For a start, I think I might sleep for a month!" Everyone laughed. They did all look so very weary, like people who had just flown back overnight from somewhere a long way away. "I don't know what I will do," repeated Alice, "but I know I will relish the time to be involved, at last, with the things I really want to do. I hope that in whatever I end up doing, I will help to change our world, at least a little, for the better." Cheekily, Alice grinned at me, and sat down.

There was a slightly nervous round of applause. Alice had not actually said anything ideologically incorrect – not quite. After all, who could fault anyone for wanting to change the world for the better? Yet everyone knew, I suppose, that Alice was rather out on a limb in her political and religious life, and there did seem to be an implied criticism of society as it then was. Should people be suggesting that our world needed changing? Was not our country, now that we were in the New Alliance, stronger and healthier than it had been since Victorian times?

I saw a few people glance at the staff counsellor. His concerns were really with the academic content of the curriculum, with putting the right slant on historical and geographical material and checking the way literature was taught. The personal views of the staff were the business of the senior management of the school, the ATTF and sometimes the police. I saw eyes follow Alice as she came and sat beside me, smiling almost conspiratorially at me. I smiled back, I did not want anyone to think I was disturbed. I did not want anyone to think Alice was in trouble. At the same time, I knew I had to warn her. Meadows was on her case. Her new apartment had been bugged. The Americans were not happy about her friendship with that Texan prisoner. She needed to be rather more circumspect.

★ ★ ★

We went over to my flat for dinner, a practice we had resumed, although now Alice slept on the sofa bed, to my great regret. It was a warm July day and I made Greek food, which seemed appropriate, and we drank retsina. Afterwards, sitting by the wide-open windows looking out over the wild jungle of brambles and trees behind the flat, which I so loved, I broached the subject.

"I don't think your colleagues knew what to make of your leaving shot, today," I started.

Alice chuckled. "Oh, they knew what to make of it, all right! It's just that they didn't know what to do about it! Could you see the principal's face from where you were? He will be glad to have me out of his hair!" Then she turned more serious. "Thank you for being there, Karl. You made the whole leaving business much easier."

"Good – I'm glad I helped," I said. "But Alice, you were taking a risk, you know."

Alice chuckled. "Oh, I don't think so," she said. "Not with you sitting there!"

She did not understand. "Alice," I tried to explain, "there are people watching and listening everywhere. You don't realise…" I did not want to tell her what I knew, indeed I could not legally do so, but she needed to be less cavalier, for her own good. I started again, "You know, Alice, in my line of work I see things that you don't see. There are powerful people watching society, protecting us from all sorts of extremism. You really don't want them suspecting they need to watch you!"

"Why would they think they should watch me?" asked Alice. "A retired schoolteacher with no political influence, just looking forward to a peaceful retirement!"

"Alice…" I paused. "Alice, that's one way of looking at it. Here's another. You're a member of a suspect religious community. You're friends with a known criminal in the USA. Who knows what else you might be into? Why would the authorities *not* want to keep an eye on you?"

"But Karl," she looked a little perplexed, "so what if they keep an eye on me? I haven't done anything wrong!"

"No." That much was true. "But Alice, it's not just what you have done, it's what you might do, too. It's what you *are*. Alice, you really need to take my word for it. You truly are running risks."

Alice was quiet for a few minutes, then she refilled her glass with the last of the retsina (leaving none for me) and said, "Honestly Karl, I think your job has made you paranoid! But I don't want you to worry about me. I've finished at the academy now, so there's no more danger there. I stopped writing my journal online when you asked me to. What do you want me to do? What other precautions do you want me to take?"

Of course, what I wanted was for Alice to leave her religious group and start to worship in some safe Anglican church somewhere, stop writing to her Texas pen friend and take up some innocent and totally non-political hobby. Then I wanted her to marry me. Well, there was not much chance of any of that, so I went for the one change I might achieve. "I really wish you'd stop storing your letters to Simon on line," I said. "Just hand write them. It's so much harder to intercept handwritten letters!"

"Honestly?" She seemed genuinely surprised. "You don't really think anyone reads them, do you?"

We looked at each other and Alice blushed slightly. I guessed that it was dawning on her that I must have read her letters, and once or twice, very discretely, she had mentioned me. I dare say she was trying to remember what she had said. She looked thoughtful. "Well, okay Karl, if it'll set your mind at rest, I won't draft my letters online anymore."

She was as good as her word. When I had finally persuaded Alice to stop writing her journal online I had bought her a beautiful leather-bound notebook from Spain, and she had started using that. I still read it, of course, whenever I had the chance, but nobody else could. Now her letters to Simon would be equally as inaccessible to Meadows and her American crony, Major Wallace. I had done what I could.

CHAPTER 4

I did not help Alice when it came time for her to move, just a
week after her retirement. Her friend Sky had volunteered
to help, along with several people from her community,
and I knew I would be out of place and that they would be as
uncomfortable as I would be. Into the bargain, it was just at
that time that Lady Grace summonsed me to see her, not in
her Bloomsbury flat this time, but at a hotel on the south coast
where she was on holiday with some family members: a niece,
maybe, and a couple of very small children. We sat outside on
a warm late July evening and watched the sun set, and drank
gin and tonic like a couple of old friends.

I was seeing her Ladyship at her most informal. She had
been down on the beach playing with the little ones, and her
hands looked slightly less manicured and her hair a tiny bit
less well coiffured than usual, and she was wearing elegant,
wide-legged linen trousers and silver-heeled sandals. I was
in uniform, having spent the greater part of the day with the
Dorset police commissioner, MacCormick, so what with the
hotel staff knowing they had a titled guest, and me representing
such a fearsome organisation as the ATTF, the service we
received was excellent!

Lady Grace had invited me down, not to give a routine
report, but because she wanted to discuss a specific and rather
tricky piece of surveillance.

After the usual courtesies, Lady Grace introduced the
topic in hand.

"Karl, do you know a Major Wallace? A rather gruff American stationed at Primrose Barracks?"

I was surprised. "I know *of* him," I said. "He's had more to do with Commissioner Meadows than with me."

"Pretty much what I'd expect," commented Her Ladyship. "They're two of a kind."

"So, is he in our sights?" I prompted. I rather hoped he was.

Lady Grace thought for a moment. "Well, yes and no," she said. "There's a strange sort of link between Wallace and your Alice. Did you know that?"

"I'm not surprised," I said, keeping my conversation with Meadows to myself. "Alice writes to a prisoner in Texas."

Lady Grace re-crossed her legs and took her last sip of gin and tonic. She raised a finger to a waiter, hovering a discreet distance away, and a second round of drinks was brought to the table. Just at that moment small, twinkling lights came on among the plants around the swimming pool and soft lamps began to glow where we were sitting. It was getting dark.

"It's just bad luck, as far as I can tell," said her Ladyship. "I got my PA to look into it, and that organisation which Alice belongs to, the one which allocated that particular prisoner to Alice, works pretty much at random. They try to match the interests of pen friends but definitely not the politics. I don't suppose they even knew the background."

"Do *we* know the background?" I asked, beginning to feel uncomfortable.

"We do now," said Lady Grace, "now that we know that our American major is interested. I've made it our business to know. And you need to know too."

I sipped my drink, and waited. After a minute or so, Lady Grace went on. "Do you remember the outcry, the year of the Rio Olympics, when Americans finally became aware as a nation of what we had known for decades, that there was a widespread but rather disorganised policy of killing black and Latino citizens in the US? Do you remember the *'Black Lives Matter'* campaign?"

"Of course," I said. "Well, it's never really ended, that campaign, has it? Just gone undercover, I think."

"You're absolutely right." Her Ladyship had the ability to make me feel good about knowing things that every ATTF officer should know.

"Well, you probably realise that there's a big cover-up going on now. The official story is that the police are anti-racist, and that all citizens are equal before the law. As they are here."

Did I detect a note of cynicism? It seemed unlikely, but...

"Well," her Ladyship continued, "Simon, Alice's pen friend, is Latino. He was arrested, charged and sentenced for something he did not do. The murder he is supposed to have committed was the work of a police officer. And now some evidence has emerged which would prove the point. It *would* prove the point if it got out, but of course, it will not be allowed to get out. That is, unless…"

"Unless?" I prompted.

"You said *'Black Lives Matter'* has gone underground, and you are right. But that doesn't mean the activists have gone away. What we don't know – what Major Wallace doesn't know – is whether Simon and his family have been contacted about this new evidence. Or whether Alice has been contacted…"

"Ah!" Now I could see how it all linked together. The Texan authorities would have every reason to want to suppress information like that. I thought for a minute. "Alice hasn't said anything, and I think she would have." I sipped my gin and tonic. "Or written anything in her journal, as far as I know." I had the grace to blush at this acknowledgement that I read Alice's private writings, although Lady Grace would have expected nothing less. The second gin and tonic was stronger than the first. A double? I was supposed to be driving back. It

63

crossed my mind to stay at the ATTF place in Bournemouth, the flats where our undercover operatives stayed while checking out foreign language students. "She's sure he's innocent. That much I do know. But as far as I can tell, it's just because she thinks he's a nice guy. She can't believe he'd commit a murder."

"Well," smiled Lady Grace, "in this case her instincts are sound. What a pity she's not on our side!"

It was almost dark now, and a light sea breeze had sprung up. I shivered. Was Alice really not on our side? In all the time I had known her I had just thought of her as naïve, a typical, rather innocent, member of the public. I could not think of her as the enemy.

"So, Karl," Lady Grace continued, "this is what I want you to do. I want you to go to Texas and find out for yourself what is going on. Do whatever you need to do. Check the police. Check the family. And then report back to me. Report *only* to me. There are lines," she added obliquely, "even in these days of necessity, which we will not cross in this country."

★ ★ ★

It took Pearson and me several days to organise my trip to the States. We were concerned because this time I would be travelling as a civilian, since we did not want to alert the Texan lot to the fact that we were getting involved. They are happy enough to make use of our excellent surveillance, but very reluctant to admit to any possible difficulties they might be having, and under the last two presidents they have pretty much denied point blank to having any problems at home. I decided to try to see Alice again before I left. Following my discussion with Lady Grace I felt I needed to check, just to be sure, that she had not been contacted by the undercover *Black Lives Matter* group.

I wanted to make the evening special. I had subscribed to a couple of films, both featuring ethnic minority groups and both with excellent reviews. Alice loved documentaries so one of the films was a dramatised biography of the life of the first non-white American president. We called him 'mixed race' but of course in the States everyone who is not pure white is *black* or *Latino,* and typically, the rest of the world had accepted without querying it, that the US had its first black president. I hoped that a film featuring race issues might provide a vehicle for a discussion of *Black Lives Matter.* To my surprise, though, Alice chose the lighter-hearted offering. It was a Bollywood re-make of *As You Like It.* She chose well. It was a lively, amusing and beautifully choreographed production. I avoided doing anything else while it was showing. Sometimes I catch up on messages on my pocket DeV while I'm watching a programme, but I wanted to be ready in case Alice gave me a lead-in.

Alice was an easy person to be with. It was almost as if a lot of the normal complications of the human ego had been ironed out of her life. She was relishing retirement, happy about her move, and more relaxed than I had seen her in years. When we had watched the movie, and while we were drinking a small tot of Kahlua before bed, I introduced the question of race relations in America, although it came less naturally than if we had watched *The Enigma of Black Leadership.*

"That was really fun," I said, referring to the film. "The Americans are missing a lot, in their rejection of black culture."

Alice looked surprised. "Well, they haven't *all* rejected it, have they? When I last went to Texas to visit Simon the taxi driver to the prison had black gospel music on his car DeV, and he was white."

"Yes, that's true," I agreed. "But I don't think they value black culture, any more than they value black lives."

Alice wrinkled up her forehead. "Karl," she said patiently,

"you know my views. There's something good in every person, and so it's dangerous to generalise. Well, that's what *I* think. Do you think it would be excessive to have half a glass more of Kahlua?"

It seemed to me that Alice would not have been able to be quite so cool if an undercover organisation had contacted her, and I let it pass, feeling reassured.

★ ★ ★

I came home from the States feeling deeply uncomfortable. Over the years I had done all sorts of things in the service of my country, and justified them to myself with the conviction that I was working for the overall good. My ATTF training had been built on Professor Narin's teachings, and the regular upgrades in our training and the ATTF team spirit all contributed to a sense that the ends justified the means, although I don't remember us ever using those words.

Ingratiating myself into the family of Alice's penfriend had been all too easy. They lived in Corpus Christi, in a lower middle-class Latino district in the Bay area, in a little two-bedroom frame house with a small front porch and white plastic chairs arranged on the scrappy grass at the bottom of the steps. It had proved almost impossible to meet Simon's wife, which is what I had hoped to do, because she worked at a Catholic home for seniors and travelled to and from work by bus. His daughter Maria was still in high school, but she worked some evenings and most weekends in a local fast food outlet, clearing and wiping tables, and being paid less than the recommended minimum wage now that any regulations governing pay had been scrapped by Congress. All I had to do was visit the rather unattractive premises early on a Saturday morning, dressed casually and pretending to be a lost tourist, and in no time at all I was asking Maria to show me the sights of her city when she got off work that afternoon. I felt guilty, although of course I was planning to do her no harm, but I was old enough to be her grandfather and she was much too trusting. It was because I said I was in law enforcement, and because Americans find my type of English accent both attractive and safe. They really should not.

I had no intention of encouraging Maria to become fond of me. It would have been better if she had already been involved with a boyfriend, then I could have asked them both to show me around, and I could have treated them a little, so that the whole experience would have been positive without doing any harm. However, Maria had no boyfriend. She confided in me easily – much too easily – that with her father in prison and her family struggling financially she had no time, between work and school, for boyfriends.

We took a tour of historic Corpus Christi. It was at the Surf Museum, of all places, that she explained how her steady boyfriend, whom she had dated since her freshman year, had ditched her when he had discovered that her father was on death row. She wept, too, when she confided that her mother, whom she called *Ma,* no longer visited her husband. Apparently, she claimed it was down to the expense and the difficulty of getting there. Stanleyville is out in the countryside a couple of hours north of Houston, and Maria's family car was not up to the trip. Maria visited alone, using Greyhound buses.

When I left, having discovered that as far as I could tell the family had nothing to do with the underground *Black Lives Matter* movement, I intended to end the friendship I had established so easily with Maria. Then, on the last day, when I had packed my hire car ready to drive back to Houston and fly home, she told me that she had fallen out with her father. It seemed she had spoken to him on the phone and told him about me. She had claimed I was her boyfriend. He had been unhappy. Well, if I had a seventeen-year-old daughter seeing a man my age I would have been pretty unhappy too! But Maria was stressed and lonely. There had been a huge row and in a teenage strop Maria had said she would not visit her father anymore. In a moment of weakness, not wanting to cause her more distress, I promised we would stay in touch. On the flight home, I felt deeply uncomfortable. I had not joined the ATTF to meddle with the vulnerable feelings of teenagers. I felt dirty.

★ ★ ★

"Morning boss!" said the ever-cheerful Pearson. "I hope you had a good trip."

Had I? I had very mixed feelings on that score, but of course I could not tell Pearson. "Not bad," I said, "as these things go."

"Well, I hope I'm not going to ruin your day," Pearson commented, "but there's trouble at mill!"

"Tell me," I sighed.

"Meadows," Pearson summed up in one word.

My heart sank. I felt I had left my last encounter with the Police Commissioner having established my seniority, but of course I had known it was unlikely to end there. "What's up now?" I asked.

"She says we're not doing our job," Pearson said.

"In what way?"

I could hear Pearson sighing at the other end. "It's the problem of vagrants," he said. "She says that the police are inundated with complaints. They're trying to do their best, but Meadows feels we're not backing her up. It seems that a village police officer was trying to move a rather belligerent homeless family on from a village green in one of the villages – Mistlethrush, perhaps – and she asked a uniformed ATTF operative for help. The officer declined."

"Oh dear!" I thought for a moment. "Do we know who our operative was?"

"Saunders," said Pearson. "She's very reliable. She was obviously doing something else. I haven't spoken to her yet, I thought you might want to do that. And to be honest, I think Meadows is just looking for a fight."

I thought about it. "Can you get someone on the case?" I asked. "I want to know homeless numbers in the whole region. I want to know where they are and why they're homeless. I want to know who has registered complaints, and when, and why. And I want to know what line the police are taking. Then we'll tackle Meadows – when we're on top of the situation."

"Right, boss!" It was really a pleasure working with Pearson. "I know just the chap to do the research!"

★ ★ ★

Sitting in my flat the day after my return, I was aware of the heavy cloud still hanging over me. I had started seeing my first serious girlfriend, Phoebe, when I was about the same age as Maria so I knew how deeply a teenager could fall in love. I wanted to talk to someone about what I had done, but I could not think who. Instinctively I knew that Lady Grace would see my concerns as a weakness. She was a strong and compassionate woman, but experience informed me that she would have no patience with the reservations I was feeling. Through meeting and talking to Maria and, I will admit, a little light romance, I had elicited the information our organisation wanted. Her Ladyship had already expressed her pleasure, both with the work I had done and with the outcome. As far as she was concerned, I believed, that door would now be closed.

Of course, it was completely impossible that I could talk to Alice. Apart from the fact that I could not let her know the nature of my work, I also knew how very shocked she would be about what I had done. Using other people was utterly anathema to Alice's community and I feared she would despise me. The truth was, I realised, I despised myself. I vaguely thought about talking to Alice's sister-in-law, the indomitable Amy, but I knew that that was also not a possibility, even if I spoke in general terms. Yet the burden of that short time in Corpus Christi was heavy to carry. For the first time in years – well, probably decades – I wished there were a God to whom I might go for help. If Alice found herself in a fix, I was sure that that was what she would do. From reading her journal when she left it lying around, I even knew the terminology. She would hold the problem in the Light. Not that I could do that, when I did not really believe in The Light!

That was when I thought again of Will and Mia, in Cambridgeshire. The idea of them came suddenly into my mind and I knew at once that I would go to see them. I felt a sense of relief, having decided on a course of action. I checked with Pearson that all was well in our region. He was still looking into the question of the rising visibility of our homeless, and we agreed we would deal with that problem in a week or so. Then I took a few days' leave, found Will and Mia's phone number on my DeV, and arranged to see them the following evening. I suggested I might stay at the pub in the main street, called *Church Street* for obvious reasons, but Mia insisted I should stay with them. "It might be a bit chaotic," she said, "as the twins are just back from summer camp in the States, but it would be lovely to see you. Any friend of Reggie's, you know…"

I was grateful for the warmth of my reception. I was not quite sure what I was going to say, but whatever it was, I felt that Will and Mia could help.

★ ★ ★

70

I drove down there on a bright, golden September morning, passing through the middle of London just for the experience and because I could. It was years since I had driven in London. I was out of uniform, and feeling out of role too. My visit to the vicarage was hardly typical behaviour for a regional commander, although I reminded myself that it was Reggie who had introduced me to Will and Mia.

Having set off so early, I arrived at the nearest small town by coffee time. We had agreed that I would be there for lunch, so I stopped off, parked the car in a residential neighbourhood and used the satellite navigation on my DeV to take me to a low-lying area, a water meadow with a children's play area. I found a bench, took off my jacket and enjoyed the feel of the gentle, early September breeze. School had started, so the only children playing on the equipment were little, and I listened to their mothers talking to them using that patient, interested tone of young mothers all across the world, nurturing and kind, switching easily and apparently without thought between various Eastern European languages and English. I remembered what Reggie and Xavier Booth had said about the hard-working immigrants who had arrived before we left the EU. These little ones, I supposed, would be their grandchildren, as English as me, with my mixed Swiss and English heritage. For a few minutes I felt good, thinking of the peaceful, stable country we were creating for them. Then I remembered Maria, the warmth in her eyes and her embrace when I left, and a wave of guilt washed over me. I found myself wondering who, exactly, was paying the price for all this stability. In her letters to Simon, Alice had several times mentioned the quality of integrity. Did I have integrity, I wondered? In the real world, not the innocent world in which Alice lived but the world of global companies and vested interests, of secret alliances and propaganda, was integrity even a possibility? I looked at the little ones, holding up their arms to be lifted, giggling as their mothers eased them down the slides, calling out as their mothers pushed them on the swings, and I hoped that integrity was possible. I hoped it, but with a sinking heart I doubted it.

★ ★ ★

Will and Mia greeted me warmly, as if they had known me for years. I saw what Mia had meant about a degree of chaos reigning, the result of her offsprings' recent return. The twins themselves were not there. They had flown in the day before school started, but Mia had mounds of clothes lying in colour-coded piles on the floor of the kitchen and the washing machine was churning away in the utility room.

"You'll have to take us as you find us," Mia said with a smile. "We have six weeks of peace and quiet while they're away, but this is the price we have to pay!" She looked happily out of the kitchen window to the washing line where summer clothes were lazily flapping in the breeze. She turned to me and smiled. "It's lovely to have them back," she said.

"Did they have a good time?" I asked.

"Oh yes – they always do!" It was Will who answered.

"Only I've never understood," commented Mia as she picked up a pile of navy blue clothes, mostly jeans and shorts by the look of it, "why, when there are excellent facilities on the site, they always come home without a single item of clean clothing!"

She dumped the pile of unwashed laundry on the floor in the utility room and grinned at Will. She obviously did not mind at all.

"It's a good thing they have such a strict uniform at the Long Road Academy," said Will, "or they wouldn't have a stitch to wear!"

Over lunch we talked about Episcopalian Youth Action,

the organisation which ran the twins' camp. Mia explained that she and Will had met in the original English organisation, which had merged with the American programme at the time of the Alliance. They talked easily about the ethos of service and spirituality, and about the importance of letting teenagers do things independently of their parents and their home churches. Neither of them showed any sign of wanting to know why I had come. After coffee, and after my small case had been deposited in the big double bedroom at the front which was obviously a guest bedroom, Will said, "Fancy a stroll, Karl? I have to pick up some papers from the vestry, and I'd like to show you the church."

We turned right out of the vicarage and passed some very old cottages on our left before we arrived in Church Street again. Several times people stopped Will to ask him something or to tell him something. An old gentleman with a baseball cap and rings in his ears said, "Afternoon, Vicar!" and a young woman pushing a buggy waved to him from across the street.

"One of the blessings," said Will, as we entered the churchyard and crunched along the gravel path, "of living in a village, is that you know everyone, and everyone knows you!"

"I think I might like that," I said, meaning that I might like Will's job. Of course, in my line of work the fewer people who really knew me, the better.

"Would you, indeed?" commented Will. "I wonder…"

★ ★ ★

The interior of the church was exactly what the interior of an English church should be. There were wooden pews (I imagined they must be rather uncomfortable if the sermon were long) and a wooden screen to separate the congregation from the choir and the altar. The floor had old, Victorian tiles and a strip of carpet up the middle. There were noticeboards

73

and a small bookstall at the back, and a children's play area, with a laminated notice showing a big, smiley face and reminding everyone: *'Children's QUIET play area!'*

Will crossed himself unobtrusively as we walked beyond the screen, and turned right into the vestry where a pile of papers was lying on a shabby table. "Ideas for harvest festival," explained Will. "I couldn't take them back on Sunday because of the rain, and me not having a jacket." Then, "Would you like to talk, Karl? I imagine you have something on your mind, to have come all this way, and this is a safe place for conversation. I'm sorry to say that almost nobody comes into the church during the week, even though we leave it unlocked!"

We sat in a pew half way down the main aisle. I was not sure where to start, but Will seemed entirely comfortable just sitting there. He had a sort of stillness to him.

After a minute or so, I spoke. "My job," I said, "throws up some complicated issues. I... I sometimes struggle to know what is right and what is wrong in any particular situation."

"I can believe that!" encouraged Will, and waited.

I sighed. "I have recently had to do something I don't feel too good about."

Will said, "Karl, are you asking me if I'll hear your confession? Because I will if that is what you'd like. It wouldn't be the first time."

I was surprised. "Goodness, no!" I said. "I don't even believe in God!"

We were both quiet, but when after several minutes I had said nothing further, Will prompted, "So?"

"So," I said. "So, I'm wondering... I'm a bit perplexed... I don't know how to balance the good I achieve in my job with the harm my actions sometimes do. I can't... I can't be more precise," I explained.

"No, of course not," agreed Will. "No need to be. So, you have a moral dilemma?"

74

"Yes." I thought for a while. Outside I could hear pigeons cooing and a tractor rumbling past. "Well, actually," I realised, talking aloud, "it's more than a moral dilemma. I'm a pragmatist. I've been a pragmatist all my life. I look at the practical effects of my behaviour. We mostly do, in my line of work, but somehow... various things that have happened... people I've met... The thing is, Will, I'm not sure pragmatism is enough."

It was Will's turn to reflect quietly. After a couple of minutes, he asked, "But surely even a pragmatist must have things he believes in? Or else, how would he decide on any course of action? What do you believe in Karl? I usually find that that's a good place to start."

That was easy. "I believe in serving my country," I said. "I believe that we need to create a society where people are independent and resourceful, and safe. I believe in people being responsible with their lives, and in learning to make good choices. I believe that governments sometimes have to make tough decisions, and that a good government does just that. And even if they sometimes make mistakes, I believe that a strong government is better than a weak one, just like a parent who is firm with his children is a better parent than one who lets them get away with anything."

"Ah!" Will was thoughtful. "Spoken like a good ATTF officer!" He was quiet for a moment or two, and then he added, "All those beliefs are political beliefs, Karl. Did you realise that? None of them is really personal."

"I really believe all that!" I insisted. "I've based my life on it."

"Yes, I'm sure you have." Will smiled at me, then looked up at the cross on top of the screen. "But what about your personal values?"

I was stumped. Looking back on it now, my failure to understand what Will was getting at was a reflection of my years of training and my immersion in the culture of the ATTF.

"So, let's look at it this way," suggested Will. "You are single, I believe, but I'm assuming you grew up in a family. Was it a happy family?"

I smiled. "Yes, it was. I'm one of those lucky ones who had two parents who loved each other and who stayed together."

"Brothers and sisters?"

"Brothers," I told him. "No sisters. I'm the youngest."

"Are your parents alive?"

"No." Papa had died a decade or so earlier and my mother, moved by my brothers to a delightful care home near to Walter's home, had given up the will to live, and died within the year.

"Right then," said Will. "A hypothetical situation. If one parent, let's say your mother, was still alive, and she was running out of money, would you help to pay her care home costs? Given that really, in your philosophy, she and your father should have made proper provision while they could?"

"Yes, of course!" I felt the need to explain more. "The family is the main building block of society. I do believe that."

"Mm," considered Will. "So you would help your mother because of your ideology, not because you loved her?"

"I – no! I didn't say that!"

"Didn't you?" Will was still looking ahead and up a bit, his eyes focused on the cross.

Had I said that? I thought back over my words. "I loved both my parents dearly," I insisted.

"No doubt," agreed Will, as if that was not the point. Then, "Right, another hypothetical situation. Do you have aunts and uncles?"

"Two aunts, very elderly, in Switzerland," I answered.

"Good," said Will. "Now, if one of them ran out of money for care, would you help her?"

"I'd expect her kids to," I answered, feeling a little uncomfortable. "They both have families."

"Right," Will was not going to be distracted. "But let's suppose the family of one of your aunts – the immediate family – couldn't help for one reason or another. Would you contribute towards her care costs?"

I thought about it. "Perhaps," I said. Then, "Probably."

"Right. Now the toughest hypothetical situation of all. Imagine you know a neighbour, an elderly woman with no family. Of course, she should have made provision for her old age but she has not. You have known her vaguely, the way one sometimes knows neighbours, for years. You see that she is no longer able to look after herself without some help, but she cannot afford help. She is distressed. She starts to call on you, asking you to perform simple, neighbourly tasks for her, like putting out her bins or changing a lightbulb. Do you help her?"

"Yes, of course!"

"Why?" asked Will.

"Because that's how society ought to function! Because it's all about good citizenship! Because people *ought* to help each other out!"

Will smiled. "But not because you care about the woman?" he asked. "Not because you feel sorry for her? Not because you can put yourself in her position and imagine how vulnerable she must be feeling?"

"Well, yes – that too," I said. "I suppose."

Will was quiet. I was feeling uncomfortable, as if I had failed a test. After another pause, Will started speaking again.

"We're in very different lines of business, you and I," he said, "but we both want to change the world. We even share some of the same values. I don't want people to be dependent, or irresponsible either, and it might surprise you to know that I also believe in strong government." Then he clarified his last point, "Strong, democratic government," he said. "Not totalitarianism, however benign."

I almost interrupted. The word *totalitarianism* was a loaded word, a word used by the Left and by those European nations which opposed the Alliance. Then I thought better and did not comment. This was not a political discussion. I wanted to hear what Will had to say.

"The big difference, if you ask me," he continued, "lies in our ideology. Or perhaps I should say, our motivation. You have explained where you are coming from very clearly and succinctly. I admire you. Now let me explain my beliefs. My ideology is no more and no less than love. Every action, big or small, must be motivated by love." He smiled at me. "Sometimes the outcome will be the same. If I could, I would also help my parents, my aunts and uncles and the lonely old neighbour, but I hope I would do it out of love."

To be honest, I felt indignant. It seemed as if somehow Will had told me that he was a better man than me. I was not going to let it pass.

"Love can be very dangerous," I suggested. "People have done crazy things out of love."

"They have done crazy things through being wedded to an ideology, too!" Will pointed out. Then he added, "But you are right. Let us say, love tempered with truth. Love accompanied by a sound assessment of the situation. Love that is not gullible."

I had nothing more to say. I realised that I needed to think through Will's comments. I could already see that while sometimes our very different ideologies would lead to similar actions, at other times they would not. Ideology had allowed me to cheat Maria, to leave her believing she had an English boyfriend. Ideology had created the situation where she had argued with her father. I knew for certain that love would not have done that. Especially not love tempered by truth.

But in that case...The implications were huge. If my ideology was faulty, then what was I doing with my life?

★ ★ ★

The rest of the day was fun, apart from the fact that my conversation with Will had left me with a lurking feeling somewhere in the back of my mind that all was not well in my life. It was time for afternoon tea by the time we got back to the vicarage. Mia had made great strides with the laundry, there were no more piles of washing lying around, and she was standing at the ironing board humming as she pressed clothes. "The twins get home around five," she said, "but we don't eat until seven. Will that suit you?"

The twins were charming. Charlie, the girl, had Will's mid-brown hair which she was wearing in a French braid, very fashionable. Harry was taller, fairer and a bit gangly, but with a lovely smile and dimples, which were going to break hearts in a few years. They were both confident, well-mannered kids who chatted easily with me. I had travelled quite widely in the States but I did not know Virginia well, and they did not know the Deep South as I did. We compared notes. Harry asked me what my job was, and when I said I was an ATTF officer he said, "Cool!" Will and Mia might consider themselves woolly liberals, but they were certainly not subversive! After dinner, the twins went off to study, grumbling because it was their first day back and the teachers had already started piling on the homework, and we watched the mid-evening news and discussed the effects of climate change on East Anglian farming methods.

I drove home after breakfast the next day, still thinking about Will's words. How much of a change would it make if I started acting out of love instead of taking my more pragmatic approach? Was it even possible to combine the dominant ideology of our time with Will's emphasis on love and truth? It was the first time in years that I had not felt sure about the work I was doing.

Bother Maria, I thought, as I drove up to my own flat. *Look where your affection for me has taken me!* Then, as I let myself in and opened some windows I wondered, *And how do I deal with the situation now?*

CHAPTER 5

Pearson's young investigator, fresh out of training school and as keen as mustard, had done a lot of work in a short time, researching the homelessness problem in our region. It was worse than I had realised, although I had, of course, noticed that there were young people sleeping in doorways at night, and various councillors had complained about *'feckless elements'* bringing their towns or cities into disrepute. Usually it was the police who dealt with vagrants. Generally, I thought, they just moved them on, shunted them out of residential neighbourhoods and town centres, but sometimes, I thought, persistent offenders were arrested. We had, of course, done everything we could to discourage the churches from feeding the poor, and that must have impacted on the homeless along with those no longer eligible for benefits, but the feeding station in the middle of Alice's city was still operating. I wondered if we should look into that.

I must admit that I was a little shocked by the statistics young Francis Moody had gathered. He was at pains to point out that they were not accurate. They could not be accurate, because our own actions regarding the disenfranchised (everyone without a permanent address) and those who had forfeited state help, meant it was harder to keep track of them. In fact, Moody had gone to the very organisations we most mistrusted: feeding stations, the left-wing *Alliance for Social Justice* and a couple of well-respected international human rights organisations. A good operative will do that. We may not like these organisations but we will certainly use them! From these sources, he had concluded that almost one in six of the population of our region was living in severe poverty, and he estimated that something like half of all of those were technically homeless. Almost fifty per cent of all homeless people in Hampshire and our section of Wiltshire were children, although Dorset fared slightly better, with forty-two per cent.

After Moody had briefed Pearson and me, and left with our promise of an official commendation, we sat in Pearson's office, which was in the pedestrianised High Street above a building society, and looked at each other. Then Pearson surprised me. With a smile, he said, "Congratulations, boss!"

I had planned to say nothing. Lady Grace had phoned just after I had been in contact with Will and Mia, arranging to go to Cambridgeshire. As I had anticipated she was pleased with the intelligence I had brought back from the States. In fact, she had been pleased with my performance for a long time, and I had been awarded a promotion – an official one, this time. My job description would not change but my salary would go up again. As would my pension. I might have been more pleased if I had been less concerned about the effect I might have had on Maria.

"Thank you." I assumed Pearson would have been notified in the normal way, although I had not scrutinised the staff list returns that week so I had not realised it had yet been made official.

We were both quiet for a moment. I wanted to say "I don't really deserve it," which is how I was feeling, but I knew that would be unwise.

Pearson broke the silence. "Appalling statistics," he commented, going back to the information Moody had given us. "You would think, given that the consequences are so awful if they don't, that people would sort themselves out and get work."

I agreed. "That's the idea." I thought some more, and suggested, "Do you think it's just taking longer than we expected to wean society off the old benefit system? Dependency must have been pretty deeply ingrained." I thought some more. "Actually, Pearson, I think it's a problem right across the country."

"Perhaps." Pearson looked worried. "Anyhow, it does suggest that we might need to take Meadows' concern seriously, doesn't it?"

I hesitated. "I'm just not sure how..." I was thinking that our concern was really extremist groups and subversive elements. The people who fell out of the system, for whatever reason, were not really our responsibility. Of course, they were probably nobody's responsibility. I felt a small nudge of sympathy for the police.

Pearson looked thoughtful, and toyed with a DeV pen on his desk. "I think, boss, that we need to be sure we keep the upper hand here. We need to be the ones to take the initiative. Don't you think?"

"Absolutely." I thought through the issue. "Let's talk to Saunders first, to see what really happened in Mistlethrush Village, and I'll talk to a few other regional commanders about what we are doing to support the police in their areas, and we'll take it from there."

"Right, boss." Pearson was clearly pleased with the plan, vague though it was. "And I'll write up that commendation for Moody. It'll be on your DeV by the end of the day."

★ ★ ★

I realised a couple of days later that the precautions I had insisted that Alice should take, writing her journal on paper and not drafting her letters to Simon on her DeV could have seriously backfired, at least as far as me watching out for her went. I was, in fact, alerted to the possibility of a problem by Pearson, and perhaps I would not have known then, if we had not decided to write a commendation for Moody, so that he felt a great degree of loyalty towards those in command.

Pearson phoned me a couple of mornings after our meeting.

"Boss," he said, "lovely morning. Something I think you ought to know."

"Fire away." I was sitting in my flat thinking about the birds I could see in the untamed jungle behind the building. I had heard that species previously unknown this far north were now making a regular appearance in the south of England, and was wondering whether to learn a little more about birds so that I would recognise them when I saw them. I expected Pearson's call to be routine.

"Moody popped into my office just now," said Pearson. What time did he start work, I wondered? It was only just after eight in the morning. "He's got real promise, that young man."

"Yes. What did he want this morning?"

"Well, it's a bit delicate," said Pearson hesitantly.

"Okay." I waited for the details.

"Did you know there are homeless people camping in the park in this city?" asked Pearson.

"I didn't," I said. "Which park?"

"The one where the old leisure centre used to be." Meadows paused. "Where Alice Owens lives."

"Ah!" I said no more. Pearson would tell me in his own good time. He was being tactful.

"I've put Moody onto that business of trying to find out what the police are doing about homelessness. It's not a pretty picture I'm afraid. To please the electorate, the police commissioner's staff are harassing homeless people in every way they can. There are even reports of violence. And of removing children from their parents and putting them into care."

I thought about this. "I'm not surprised," I responded. "Isn't that the point of elected police commissioners? So that they will respond to the concerns of those who voted for them?"

"Yes," agreed Pearson. "And their prejudices." Then he added, "And they're watching any groups of homeless people, to see if they're getting help from subversive elements in the community."

I realised where this was going.

"And?" I prompted.

"And Alice Owen has been to visit the camp in the park. Several times. And Meadows knows it."

I felt sick. It was typical of Alice. Why did she do these things? I would need to talk to her again.

"Okay, Pearson," I said. "Thanks for the warning."

"You're welcome, boss."

The next day there was an indignant article in the local paper about the encampment, rather exaggeratedly called a *'tent city'*, and I began to realise there was, potentially, a really big problem.

* * *

I had quite a lot on that week, because I had been to the States and to Cambridgeshire so recently, and because Pearson and I were meeting up more than usual, to discuss the homelessness problem. Or rather, we were discussing what to do about Meadows and her involvement in the homelessness problem.

I checked Alice's text messages, which were easy to access, and discovered that she was working in her charity shop one afternoon and was planning to meet her friend Jo for tea afterwards. I rather liked Alice working in the charity shop. Unlike feeding stations, the charity shops gave nothing away for free. It is true that it was run by an organisation which had been forced to move its headquarters to Ireland when we started taxing charitable income, and that its policies were undoubtedly left of centre, but these shops provided a good way for people to recycle goods, and even more importantly, they provided an outlet for the more affluent who had a conscience. It meant that by donating goods, or even volunteering to work in the shops, people felt that they were doing something, and thus it circumvented the asking of too many questions or the onset of too much guilt.

I phoned Alice when I calculated she was about to leave her flat, claimed to have been given the day off unexpectedly, and asked her to come over for a meal. She agreed almost at once, despite her previous arrangement with Jo, and that gave me a little surge of pleasure, because it showed me that Alice still cared for me. I knew she had not been out with anyone else since we had broken up.

I said that I would pick Alice up from the shop at four thirty, but I was ten or fifteen minutes early. I would like to say that this was a calculated move, designed perhaps to have a quick check on the shop, but that was not what happened. In all honesty, I think I just wanted to see Alice.

I parked outside in the street, a privilege of the ATTF to whom parking restrictions do not apply, and while Alice started tidying up for the end of the day and closing time, I looked around the shop.

Despite the homeless underclass in Hampshire, Alice's city is a wealthy little place. There are, of course, areas of poverty, but the cathedral, a large public school, a small university and an internationally renowned art school all conspire to make it one of those genial middle-class enclaves Lady Grace had commented on, during one of my many meetings with her. The goods in the shop reflected the general affluence of the area. Some of the items of clothing had high fashion labels, and there was some very attractive hand-thrown pottery on display. I checked to see whether any of it had been made by Amy, Alice's sister-in-law, but it had not. The books were mostly guide books, with quite a selection on Stonehenge. I knew the same charity ran a bookshop in the city too, so the sparsity of other books was not surprising. There was a good selection of CDs, though, and some vinyl.

Alice was ready to leave before half-past-four, because her colleagues volunteered to finish the clearing up, and we were soon on our way. I had been thinking about how to broach the question of the homeless encampment and wondering whether I should tell her in so many words that she had been seen over there. However, try as I might, I could not think of a way of warning her without telling her at least something about my work, and that I could not do.

An opportunity arose as we left the city. The road we were on took us past some relatively new houses, built when the city expanded during the second decade of the century. As we drove along I noticed that several had 'To Let' signs outside them. I commented on them to Alice and we talked a little about market forces and about the impact of the increasing American population on the city. I hoped Alice would say something, perhaps remark that English families also needed homes, but she did not give anything away and I let the subject drop. After a dull and rainy morning, the sun had come out, and I felt ridiculously happy to have Alice sitting beside me in my car.

I loved cooking for Alice. She was a perfectly reasonable cook herself, but she really appreciated having meals made for her, and often wanted to know about the ingredients. Afterwards we watched a football match, if I remember rightly, and then a quiz show. That was when the opportunity to warn Alice fell into my lap.

There was a whole series of satirical quiz shows broadcasted at the time. In fact, they had been fashionable for years and although they were a little subversive, I thought they were left uncensored for the same reason that the charity shops were tolerated: they gave the educated middle class an outlet for their anxiety about poverty and disenfranchisement without stimulating protest. That night there was a question, the answer to which was *'eviction'*, made to sound like an amusing topic by the droll quiz master speaking in his Northumbrian accent. I raised the topic of the encampment in the park. Alice said she knew about it, but she did not say anything about going over to visit. I wished she would trust me. Anyhow, I did my best to warn her off. Even then I was not at all sure I had succeeded, and soon afterwards I knew that for sure. Not content to do her bit by working in the charity shop and helping when her community gave breakfast to all comers on a Sunday, Alice and her naïve friends planned to start a school over there. I did not know it that evening, though. In fact, I was struggling to keep my distance. I really wanted Alice to come back to my bed. I might even have tried to convince her, except that Pearson phoned. He needed to talk to me, as soon as possible. We arranged to meet up the following morning, and by the time the call had finished the moment had passed. I tried to tell myself it was just as well.

★ ★ ★

"I spoke to Saunders," Pearson told me over a mug of coffee in his office. The window behind his desk was open and street sounds were filtering in, the sleepy conversations of people going to work, some delivery people unloading trendy fashion to the shop almost opposite, and then the tinny sound of the shopping mall clock striking nine.

"What did she have to say," I asked, "about that incident in Mistlethrush Village?"

"Not much." Pearson laughed. "She didn't even remember it at first!"

"So, what happened?"

"It's more or less what we expected," Pearson said. "Saunders was due to visit the primary school in the village to take an assembly. She was held up in traffic and was only just in time. A couple of police officers were in some sort of argument with a small group of men who looked as if they had been camping on the village green. The men were refusing to move on. The police officers called Saunders over and asked for her help. Saunders explained that she needed to be in the school, and gave them our local back-up number, which they must have known anyhow. Then she went and took the assembly. When she came out the green was clear. No campers. No police. She didn't give it another thought."

"No reason she should," I agreed.

"Meadows is looking for trouble," Pearson said.

"Yes, I know."

We were both quiet, thinking over the situation. Then Pearson suggested, "You know what, boss, I think it's time we did something quite radical."

"You do?" I was amused. Like many a mid-ranking and very established ATTF officer Pearson was really quite conservative. "What do you have in mind?"

Pearson looked almost gleeful. "Let's put someone in, undercover, into Meadows' office. What do you think?"

I left his premises a few minutes later chuckling. I had really had enough of investigating people I liked (or loved), people who were innocent, and people who might be misguided but who really only wanted to do some good. Investigating Meadows would be a very pleasant break. I neither liked her nor trusted her, and I very much doubted that she aspired to do good!

★ ★ ★

We thought of Francis Moody for the job, because he was such a promising young operative, but cursory enquiries brought to our attention that he had mixed socially with a couple of police officers, so he could be too easily recognised. We could have asked Lady Grace for help. She had access to a pool of personnel which could be put at our disposal, but both Pearson and I were uncomfortable about making our investigations official before protocol required me formally to report them. It was Pearson who saw the solution.

"We need someone from outside the region," he suggested. "Someone with IT credentials."

"That would be ideal," I agreed.

"So why not ask your contact in East Anglia? What's his name – the regional commander."

"Ah! You genius!" I exclaimed. "Of course, Reggie – Reginald Palmer. Then we just need to get the person in to Meadows' office."

Pearson sat forward. "Right," he said. "I'll find out if they are looking for anyone and you can tell the commander what we need."

"And if Meadows isn't looking for new staff just now?" I prompted.

Pearson grinned. He was enjoying the subterfuge. "Oh, I'll see to it that she is!" he announced. "One way or another."

And so it was that the lovely Josephine started work, a couple of weeks later, working as IT support, with access to the police computers right across the region.

★ ★ ★

Josephine turned out to be worth her weight in gold. I was a little surprised that Meadows had appointed her so quickly and with so little fuss. I had noticed that she tended to surround herself with young men or rather sycophantic

90

women of her own sort of age, whereas Josephine was smart, blonde, and hardly out of her twenties. Nevertheless, I was told by Pearson, who spoke with a decided glint in his eyes, that the IT section of Meadows' office had hit a crisis, with one key worker becoming ill and another resigning at short notice, when he was offered a better job in another part of the country. Although British-born, Josephine was a graduate of a mid-western American university and she had that sort of hometown healthy sheen about her, and a slight mid-Atlantic accent. She was working in the IT suite which was located in the mayor's official residence by the gardens close to the Guildhall, and Pearson began to meet with her regularly in a coffee shop in the High Street where a lot of police office personnel and other office workers tended to eat their lunches.

It took a couple of weeks, of course, for Josephine to transfer down from Cambridge, where she had worked in Xavier Booth's IT division, to move into one of the flats reserved for key workers, out towards the medieval foundation for old people featured recently in *A Fox Roaming the South* documentary, and to find her way around Meadows' IT system. The first information she brought us came at the beginning of October, and it was something of a shock.

I dropped into Pearson's office just after nine one morning. I needed to debrief a worker at the local library who monitored the reading habits of certain suspects. It is, of course, quite simple to see what information people are accessing online, but if they choose to take out old-fashioned books it is actually more difficult to monitor their interests. Our little, elderly, volunteer librarian kept a motherly eye on those who used the Resource Centre, which had once been the public library but which had become a charity manned by well-meaning citizens since austerity brought about so many library closures. I was really just checking in with Pearson, but when I entered his office he was sitting forward, frowning at a natty little pocket DeV which he had placed on his desk, the case still open.

"Hi," I greeted him, sitting down opposite.

"Hi," he responded, still frowning. "I've got our first intel from Josephine," he said, looking up. "I think you should see it." He pushed the DeV over to me.

The screen was small so I could not read the whole correspondence. It seemed to be some sort of report, presumably written for the eyes of Meadows. The key words which caught my eyes immediately were, '*Suspect has been informed by letter of impending execution of S999XXX*'. I knew that the numbers *999* always indicated that a Texan prisoner was on death row, and I guessed at once that *S* could stand for Simon. "The suspect is Alice?" I asked Pearson.

He took the DeV and scrolled back, re-reading the earlier part of the document. "It seems as if Meadows has Ms Owen in her sights," he said. "She's been monitoring her for a while."

"Well, I knew that much," I admitted. "Can we check that *S999XXX* is actually Alice's pen friend?"

"Easily done," said Pearson. "Upcoming executions used to be published on Department of Corrections websites until public opinion became rather queasy on the subject of lethal injections and firing squads. Now they keep the whole thing very quiet. But the military are always informed and somehow or other Amnesty International usually seems to know – although its information is not quite as reliable."

"And we have access to US military information?" I asked, fairly sure of the answer.

"Of course," confirmed Pearson, with that wicked gleam in his eyes again.

I sat and thought for a moment. "Alice will be upset." I stated the obvious. "Do we know how she will have been informed? Do they give some sort of official notification?"

"Not any more." Pearson turned to his larger, ATTF

issued, desk DeV and tapped a few keys. "Here we are. The prisoner is informed by the warden or his assistant, and it is then up to the prisoner to tell his next of kin. If he chooses to."

"So, Alice will have received a letter," I said. I felt a pang, thinking of her sitting happily in her flat opening her mail, and being confronted with that news. "Poor thing."

Pearson sat back in his chair, swivelled round and looked out of the window at people wandering up and down the pedestrianised area below. Then he turned back. "Boss," he said, "why is Meadows so interested in Ms Owen?"

"Well…" I could have given the reasons Meadows had given me: her membership of that faith group, her general lack of conformity to the outlook of the day. Pearson was a friend, though, as well as a colleague, and we were working together to infiltrate Meadows' office. "To get at me, I think."

"That's what I thought," agreed Pearson. "Is it the old police versus ATTF controversy, do you think?"

"In a way," I agreed. "She wants power, but we have more. She can't stomach it."

Pearson sighed. "You would hope we would all want the same things," he said. "That we might work together."

"They do in some places," I said, thinking about Reggie Palmer and Xavier Booth in Cambridge.

Pearson was quiet, then asked, "Will she do something unwise? Ms Owen, I mean."

"I hope not," I said, with feeling. Then I added, having thought more about it, "Well, what could she do?"

Pearson gave me a very direct look. "She could go to the press," he suggested. "She could chain herself to the railings of the American embassy. She could get her religious group to demonstrate in the High Street, or hold a prayer vigil, or distribute some leaflets."

"Yes," I agreed. "She could do any of those things."

"Boss," recommended Pearson, leaning forward and

looking me directly in the eye, "you need to keep an eye on Ms Owen. Don't let her get into something she can't get out of. Protect her."

"Thank you, Pearson," I said, and stood up. He meant well but I felt we had crossed a line. I was his senior officer. I did not think he should have spoken to me like that, however well-meaning his comments had been.

* * *

I phoned her as soon as I could, and told her how sorry I was. Alice seemed a little surprised that I would even know that Simon had been given an execution date, but I improvised and said I had read it on the Amnesty website. I hoped she would confide in me, but she did not. I felt a longing for her, to hold her and to keep her safe. Simon's death was going to cause Alice a lot of pain and I wanted to shield her from it. It flashed through my mind that I was acting towards Alice out of love, not out of the sort of ideals by which I had always tried to live, and very briefly I thought that Will would be proud of me. Then I suggested dinner on Friday, and Alice agreed, and I felt a bit better. At least she was going to let me in, a little, into this aspect of her life.

* * *

The second and third pieces of information via Josephine were rather more routine. One memo told us that Meadows was paying rather over-generous expenses to two women in her department with whom she was particularly friendly. I cannot say I was surprised. The next intel concerned vagrants again, and made it clear that, unofficially at least, homeless families were being directed to the encampment in the park. Pearson and I discussed this at length. Pearson had heard the same thing from several of our sources on the street, and did not think it was particularly significant although, obviously, it was not in line with government policy. Homeless people had to go somewhere and there were no resources for the local authorities to help them. He felt it was almost an act of kindness to tell such people where they might find others to help and support them. The fourth leak we received from Meadows' office was, however, really significant. Meadows had begun to use undercover officers.

Of course, there was a time when almost all undercover work was performed by the police. Even now they still work in secret when trying to break open serious crime rings and criminal gangs, but all the anti-terrorism and subversive activity issues were passed to us soon after the New Alliance was signed. According to Josephine, there were documents which lacked detail but which indicated that Meadows was putting undercover officers into charitable organisations and faith communities. From the documents which Josephine was able to send us it was not clear which charities Meadows was focusing on, although one remark suggested that the feeding station at the bottom of town by the river might be particularly vulnerable.

"She's exceeding her powers," noted Pearson.

"She's trying to catch us out," I answered. "She wants to prove we are not doing our job."

"She's a bitch," said Pearson, uncharacteristically, and then grinned. "But we *are* doing our job, so she's on to a loser there!"

CHAPTER 6

Unlike the police – or, at least, the police in their official capacity, more than fifty per cent of our work involves undercover operatives of one kind or another. Many are just observers who report back because they think they are supporting law and order, like our volunteer librarian, and some work for small monetary rewards or in order to have certain sanctions lifted. The latter can be less reliable. They are driven to work for the ATTF because of financial need, but their hearts are often with those on whom they are reporting, and we have to treat their information with a degree of caution. A very small number of skilled and vetted agents go in undercover the way the charming Josephine had done, and they are closely scrutinised for ideological orthodoxy and for certain emotional and psychological traits which stop them from being too vulnerable. I would have liked to have put a volunteer or a trained agent into the tent encampment in the park, but we could not find a volunteer or justify financially a trained man or woman. In the end, we found a young man whose situation was sufficiently desperate that he was prepared to report back to us, on condition that the label of *fecklessness* be removed from his girlfriend's record so that she could again receive proper health care. Daniel and Ariel moved to the tent encampment on the 16th of October, I think, and gave us their first report on the 17th. Putting an agent in the camp had been Pearson's idea, and I was glad. It meant that I had information about what Alice was up to over there, without having to take the initiative of spying on her myself. It did occur to me that this had been Pearson's intention, but if so it was done with such tact that I felt no need to acknowledge his kindness.

When we found out the extent of the involvement of Alice and her friends in the affairs of the people in the tent encampment, I must admit I was impressed.

"They've set up a *school*?" I exclaimed, as we sat in Pearson's office drinking whisky one early evening.

Pearson chuckled. "They have!" he said. "Several classes and a rota of teachers. From what Daniel says it's really quite impressive."

I felt conflicting emotions. To be honest, my first feelings were of pride. Alice was doing something really good, offering to children benefits which were being denied them because of the poor choices of their parents. I was never quite happy about the way we penalised youngsters when adults failed to run their lives intelligently, although I understood why it had to be done. Then, close on the heels of my sense of pride, came a feeling of alarm. By any standards – or, at least, by the standards of the day, the action Alice and her friends were taking was subversive. They were seeking directly to undermine the sanctions an elected government had put in place for good reason. It would not be allowed to go on.

Pearson was watching me, sipping his whisky in an appreciative manner.

"You've got to admit," he said, "Ms. Owen and her friends are enterprising!"

"They are," I agreed. "And generous."

"Why do they do it, boss?" Pearson asked. "I mean, what's in it for them?"

I thought about that, and offered some possibilities. "A mistaken idea of good citizenship? Religious ideology? Discomfort with their own comfortable lives during this period of transition to the new order?" Then I thought about

Alice, about the concern she had shown for her students while she was still working, and the ways I had occasionally helped her out. "Or maybe just out of kindness?" I added.

Pearson coughed and looked a little embarrassed. "I went to a Catholic school," he said, then paused and swivelled his chair to look out on to the dark and empty pedestrian precinct below.

"And?" I prompted.

He turned back. "There was a nun there. She didn't teach me. I think she might have been in charge of the department that dealt with children with special needs. But she used to do assemblies when the priest was called away." He smiled, remembering something from those long-gone days. "Anyhow," he continued, "we had a sort of joke, me and my mates, that all her little pep talks came down to the same message. In the end, all she ever said was that God is love and that we ought to love our neighbours as ourselves. *'The two great commandments'* she called her philosophy." He picked up his whisky glass, realised it was empty, opened the second drawer in the filing cabinet to retrieve the bottle, and topped up both our tumblers. Then he continued. "Ms. Owen and her friends are religious, aren't they? Do you suppose they're just doing this out of love?"

★ ★ ★

I had to catch the train back to my flat that evening. I had drunk too much to drive, and Pearson had drunk too much to give me a lift. Walking across the park to reach my flat I mulled over Pearson's words. I had never really understood Alice's motivation. I did not know, really, why she wrote to Simon. I suppose I had always just assumed it was something about her personality, and to be honest, until that evening I suppose I had seen it as a sort of weakness, a vulnerability from which I needed to protect her. But Pearson's comments had resonated with me. What was it Will had said when we had sat in his empty church? That I was motivated by ideology and he was motivated by love? Love is a complicated thing. I had loved my parents and I hoped I loved my brothers and my nieces. I had definitely loved my girlfriend Phoebe, in my youth, and I certainly loved Alice now. All these, though, were different from a love which might lead a person to help someone they did not know. I found it confusing. I had always thought that love was a feeling, an emotion, but now I wondered. Was is something other than that? More than that? Or were people fooling themselves, taking the moral high ground, when they claimed to act out of love?

As I approached my flat through the dark little, tree-lined footpath that led from the park, other thoughts crept into my head. I realised I might need to step in and do something dramatic to prevent Alice from getting into real trouble. I knew, although the general public did not, that it was not totally impossible that a person considered to be a seriously subversive element, could be made to vanish completely. Back in the first decade of the century they had called it *extraordinary rendition*. In Latin American countries and, since the third decade of this century in North America, they just called the missing people *the disappeared*. Alice would have no idea that such a thing could happen to her, but I knew it could. You have to have strong government to bring about the sort of radical changes we were aiming for.

★ ★ ★

I was beginning to wonder whether Pearson had a special soft spot for Josephine. It was either that, or he was excited about our activities within Meadows' office. Anyway, it was less than a week later that he phoned me at home, just as I was clearing up from a late and leisurely breakfast.

"Boss!" he said. "I'm glad I caught you."

"Morning, Pearson," I responded. "What's up?"

He sounded a little breathless. "A report from Josephine," he said. "You'll want to know. The police are planning to raid Ms. Owen's flat."

For a moment, for a fraction of a second perhaps, I felt panic. Then a familiar sort of quiet detachment descended on me. It was a reaction trained into me from the time of my recruitment onwards. When an emergency arises, separate all feelings from the circumstances confronting you. React coolly. Be logical.

I could hear how calm my voice was as I asked, "Do we know when?"

"This morning, boss," said Pearson. "Any time now, I think."

"Thank you, Pearson," I responded. "I'll be in touch."

★ ★ ★

It is all too easy to drive too fast or carelessly when dealing with an emergency, and careless driving is dangerous in every sense of the word. I took a deep breath as I left the car park, and then turned on the radio as I always did when driving to work. Public radio was much criticised by the authorities as being biased towards the left, but most people I knew still considered it, privately, to be the best source of news. Once on the motorway I put my car into auto-pilot and considered the situation.

The powers of the police are, or anyhow they were at that time, fortunately, limited. They could not cause Alice to disappear without some involvement from my department, or perhaps MI5 or the military. A police raid could therefore only be for one of two reasons. Either the police believed that they might find something contraband in Alice's flat, either

100

on her computer or in her bookshelves, and I doubted that. For all their radical beliefs, her religious group is actually quite law abiding. Or they might be trying to scare her off. That was not an unusual tactic and I supposed it must be quite effective. A third possibility occurred to me as I turned off the motorway towards the city, with a view of the cathedral ahead, that the police might plant some incriminating evidence in Alice's flat. That would be tricky to deal with, but probably not impossible. Of course, it would only happen if the officers concerned were corrupt, and their superiors were also corrupt, and despite the claims of ethnic minority groups and various protest organisations based in Dublin, Edinburgh or Brussels, it was my experience that most police officers were honest.

There was a police car across the road from the main entrance to the flats. I parked carefully, keyed in the entrance code and climbed the stairs briskly, without actually running. I could hear voices in Alice's flat. I rang the doorbell and waited.

Alice looked flustered. Her face was very red and her forehead looked slightly moist.

"Hi!" I said brightly. "Are you ready?" I strolled in, holding my hat in my hand and jangling my car keys in the other.

Alice looked completely confused, as well she might. I winked at her, hoping she would have the good sense to play along with me. She followed me into her living room.

Two police officers were sitting there, one in the armchair, the other on the settee. Both were looking at me in amazement, even horror. Clearly an ATTF officer – an obviously high ranking ATTF officer – was the last person they had expected to meet.

I pretended to be surprised and worried on seeing the officers. I don't remember now what I said, but I remember putting an arm round Alice as if I thought she might just have been told something devastating. I thought I felt her relax against me a little as I did so, and it felt good.

I must have said something like, "What has happened? Is Amy okay?" or some such query, pretending that I thought the police were there to deliver some bad news.

Both officers were standing by then. One looked embarrassed. Perhaps the other was angry. I made a mental note of the numbers on their shoulder tabs, although I do not think we ever checked on them afterwards. It was just instinct.

The officers were almost stuttering as they made their excuses. They talked about problems in the neighbourhood, and I gave the impression of surprise. By then I knew I had the upper hand. If the police had held anything concrete on Alice they would have told me at once.

One of the officers started muttering about the tent dwellers and about others in the flats being offended by their presence in the park. In turn, I pretended that the ATTF knew all about them (as, indeed, we did) and that the school was sanctioned by some high official body somewhere. I think I said, "There's even a little school over there," which made Alice look sharply at me in surprise, and I implied that it was all done quite deliberately, to prevent protests about the way the homeless were treated.

Quite soon I was able to usher the officers out of Alice's flat. Once they had gone Alice sat down hard on the settee and put her head in her hands, so that I could not see her face. She was not crying. In fact, she was extremely still, her breathing controlled, but a sort of tension rested around her. I turned to the French windows and the Juliet balcony, and let her recover her poise.

After a few minutes, she sighed, and I turned around.

"Thank you, Karl," she said, and stood. I walked over to her. I felt the same old longing to hold her up against me, I wanted to stroke her hair, to let her cry into my shoulder, to kiss her...

Instead I said, "You're welcome!" which sounded foolish. Then I added, "Dinner tonight, I think. I'll pick you up around five if that will suit you?"

Then I turned and left, before I did something that might forever complicate our friendship.

How I wish, now, that I had stayed, and that we had enjoyed at least a few months of complications.

★ ★ ★

Just outside Alice's city there is an ancient church building, once a parish church, I believe, but no longer in regular use by the time I heard about it. It is much beloved by our American cousins who like to have weddings there, and it is used occasionally for concerts in aid of one charity or another, although the old, worm-eaten wooden pews seat only thirty people at the most and the building is not heated, and there are many more convenient sites within the city.

We came to realise that some sort of group was meeting there through one of those fortunate coincidences which help us so much in our work. From Josephine, we knew that a police spy had been successfully placed undercover in the religious group to which Alice belonged, and from that agent we knew that there was talk among a few members of Alice's community about meeting in secret so that they could experience greater freedom than in their scheduled meetings, which were open to anyone. From a completely different source we heard that there had been cars driven to the little chapel and lights seen there, and that there were rumours of strange goings-on. It seemed some people were worried about witchcraft, others about religious extremists. Pearson and I guessed that we would find nothing more than some sort of prayer meeting, and we agreed that I would go along and check it out.

It was a Saturday evening. I dressed casually and borrowed a car from the pool that was more ordinary than mine – older, without the ATTF chip or number plate. We had been told that people seemed to arrive between six and seven in the evening, so I parked in the lane just after seven, when I hoped the meeting, whatever it was, would already be underway. If the group turned out to be suspect they would, no doubt, realise that I might be some sort of law enforcer, and my presence might scare them off. On the other hand, they might think I was a potential convert to whatever organisation they belonged to, and my presence might be welcomed. It was a risk, but instinct told me it was not much of a gamble, all things considered.

The heavy wooden door was not completely closed, but even so it creaked loudly as I entered and several people turned and looked at me as I seated myself in a pew at the back. I did not think anyone looked particularly alarmed, and one of the women at the front, in the row of chairs which faced the sparse congregation, smiled at me in a motherly sort of way.

Another woman, probably only in her early forties, but old-fashioned in her dress and apparently without make-up, stood and also smiled benignly at her audience.

"Friends and visitors," she said, beaming across at the smattering of people distributed in the pews, "it is a pleasure to see you here. Before we begin our worship, there are a few matters we want to make clear. Since you have found your way to this beautiful place, the chances are that you already know that we are here to worship, freely and without restraint. We like to sit in silence, and speak only when prompted by the Spirit. We choose to worship here, as well as in our normal congregations, because we feel that the anger and fear which is rife in our country even affects our worship, and in this place, we trust that we can leave behind, for an hour or so, the frustrations and concerns of everyday life and the sense that so many of us have, of always being watched."

The woman sat and a man stood, a clergyman wearing a distinctive white dog collar over a black shirt.

"Thank you, Friend Madge," he said. "We are here from many different groups, drawn together by two things: our love for God and our love of freedom. It is our hope that you will find peace in your hearts this evening." Then followed some instructions about how the meeting would be conducted. The clergyman sat, and quite suddenly a deep silence descended on the assembled group.

At first, I did what someone with my training would always do. I looked around me and made mental notes about the people in the little chapel. There were twenty-one of us. Sitting at the front, facing the rest of the congregation was the woman referred to as *'Friend Madge'*, the clergyman and three other people. The woman who had smiled a welcome to me was elderly, her hair white and her face softly wrinkled. Next to her was a much younger man in a baggy pullover and jeans, and next to him another woman whose dark clothing and the cross she wore on a cord around her neck, somehow suggested that she was another priest, or maybe a nun. The people in the pews were mostly middle aged, or at least approaching middle age, more women than men, but there was a child of about eight, a pretty girl with her hair in a high ponytail, and two teenage boys. It was the teenagers and the girl who surprised me most. When I was young I could not have sat in silence without giggling, but those three were as still as the adults. I could not see the faces of the boys, only the backs of their heads, but the girl was sideways on to me and I could see that her eyes were closed and her face raised. Can it be said that someone is engrossed in silence? Because that was the word that came into my head – the child was engrossed.

Other than the silence nothing seemed to be happening. So far there was certainly no witchcraft, no fundamentalism, and nothing subversive, unless worshipping in silence could be considered a subversive activity? I wondered what the congregation was experiencing, and since there was nothing else to do, I decided to try it for myself. I settled myself a little more comfortably in my pew and closed my eyes.

At first, having shut my eyes, I became much more aware of the sounds. There were lots of trees around the little church, and I could hear the creaking of their branches in the wind. Some distance away there was the sound of traffic, the occasional whine of electric vehicles and the rumble of trucks. I heard an owl hoot, and either the sound was echoed or another owl answered. Within the church there were the gentle noises of people: a stomach rumbled, someone coughed, someone shifted her position slightly. There was a little skitter-scatter noise. Autumn leaves being blown against a window? Mice?

Gradually I became less aware of the sounds. Or maybe it would be more accurate to say that I became more aware of the sounds within myself, in my mind. I had lived on my own for most of my adult life and so I was used to a certain amount of personal honesty. It is harder to hide from oneself if one wakes alone in the middle of the night. Still, my commitment to my organisation, and perhaps the regular training I had received, had helped me to deal with any reservations which might otherwise have arisen about the nature of our work and the tough decisions we sometimes had to make. As I sat in that quiet chapel I became increasingly aware that I was harbouring some confusion, that somehow my life did not seem as straightforward as is usual.

How can I explain what happened that evening? I know now that such moments are notoriously hard to describe, because somehow words are not enough. Yet I was used to putting things into words, and how could I describe the feeling, as the time passed, that I was seeing myself from the outside as well as living through the silence?

It was as if I became aware of confusion within me, either in my heart or my mind, or in some part of me that was both heart and mind, or neither. It was like a fog, swirling around my once-clear understanding of the world. I knew I was not in control of something deep within me, and my lack of control was frightening. As an ATTF officer I had been trained to be in command, directing my life and the circumstances around me, but in the silence, I became aware that I felt grubby, and that the feeling was not new. Had it started when I involved myself with Maria? Were there other things I had done which did not bear reflecting upon? Even by being here, pretending to worship, was I not practising deception? Was my whole life a deception?

When Friend Madge spoke, I was almost surprised to be brought back to the reality of the little church and the people around me. Surprised, but relieved. The wooden pew beneath me was real, the cool air of the chapel and the sounds of the wind and the traffic were real. The confusion within me had been unreal, a temporary disconnection of my mind from the truths I had embraced for so long. I was serving my country. I did what had to be done. I resolved not to sit in silence with these people again if I could help it.

"Friends," said Friend Madge, speaking quietly into the silence. "It is our custom in these meetings to bring to the Light those we know who might be in danger. We do not use their full names. The Spirit knows who we are thinking of, and even here we need to be circumspect. So, let us hold our friends in the Light."

There was more silence and I thought perhaps no one was going to say anything. Then, "Father Whillerby," said the woman who might have been a priest.

"My sister's friend, missing since her office was raided."

"Anton."

"Jo."

"The Prabhu family."

Then to my surprise, "Alice," said someone. My Alice?

Did her community know she was in danger? I supposed they must do, since they knew about the school in the park.

"Our warden."

"Our soldiers in the Caribbean."

"Jim and Verity."

"That group of kids who sleep in the railway subway."

"My mum."

Then there was another silence. So, we were supposed to hold these people in the Light? What Light? How did one do that? I watched the congregation as some bowed their heads and others looked up at a cross on a wooden screen. I did not close my eyes. I did not want to go back to that place of confusion. I was intent on remaining objective.

Even so, foolishly, I was glad of the prayers of the others. I did not know if the Alice who had been named was my Alice, but it seemed to me that if there were a Light, some sort of kindly power, it was good to think of people holding my Alice up to it, for its protection. I pictured her surrounded by some sort of golden aura, and felt somehow comforted and peaceful even while I told myself it was all superstition.

"Harmless mystics," I reported back to Pearson afterwards, and wrote a brief report that is probably in an archive still, somewhere among the routine reports we delivered to the central offices for storage at the end of the year.

"I guessed as much," responded Pearson.

CHAPTER 7

All that happened in October, and it is strange, looking back on it, how normal November and December were. Not uneventful, of course. It was the nature of my work that something was always happening, but in a way life seemed quite settled. I did not see very much of Alice. She had resolved to be at the execution of her penfriend and I totally opposed the idea, although at least Texas was still using lethal injections, which I thought might be less traumatic for Alice than seeing a firing squad at work. The tent encampment in the park had grown and Alice's crowd continued to run their school, opposed by the police but not, as far as I could judge, by the greater part of public opinion. There were a few small protests and several heated articles in the very conservative local paper, but there were also several letters on the letters' page of the same paper applauding the idea of educating the children of feckless parents, so that they stood some sort of chance of living more productive lives. It did not seem as if the public had yet associated the school with Alice's religious group, although of course the police knew all about the links. As far as Pearson and I could tell, the group involved with the school was being impressively cautious in its communications, so I believed that at least some of my warnings to Alice had born fruit.

All across the country that autumn people were exercised by the homeless. The government of the day even recognised the concern which was being expressed by more and more people, although they only admitted to having moved *'too quickly'*, never to having acted harshly or to having denied anyone their human rights. The statistics seemed to support official policy, too. Unemployment had reached such low levels that they matched the percentages just after the Second World War. There was evidence of people taking very poorly paid work, which was applauded, and the number joining the military rather than settling for low wages, was up. There was even an English battalion in the US army, since theirs was so much larger than ours.

My biggest concern that autumn was Meadows. Not long after the raid on Alice's flat in October, Meadows had again asked to see me. This time her request was more of an invitation than a summons, and I delayed for a week, claiming I was busy, so that she would be absolutely sure that I held all the aces in this game. I also sauntered in ten minutes late and wearing my dress uniform, partly to impress her but partly because I had been invited to a passing out parade later in the day.

I took the lead at once. "So," I asked as I sat down, putting my hat on top of a pile of papers on her desk, "how are your spies working out?"

She looked taken aback, which had been my aim. "Spies?" she asked, sounding uncertain.

"We have it on good authority that you have undercover officers in several faith groups. Obviously, you can't be concerned about subversive activity because that has been our remit for years, so you must be looking for criminal activity. What are they doing? Smuggling in drugs? Fiddling the books?"

Meadows had the grace to blush, but, "We have our reasons," she insisted.

"Naturally," I sat back in my chair and crossed my legs. "I'm sure you always have your reasons. So how can I help you today?"

Meadows moved my hat and picked up a piece of paper

that had been on top of the pile. "We're continuing to wonder about Alice Owen," she said, apparently expecting a response from me.

I stifled a yawn. "Good for you," I said. "She has ceased to be a person of interest to us."

I thought I detected a gleam of something in Meadows' eye – not triumph, I thought, but maybe hope.

"Perhaps you wouldn't be so sure of her innocence if you knew what we know," she said.

I yawned again. "I dare say we *do* know what you know," I said.

Now Meadows was looking a little flustered. She put down her piece of paper, then picked it up again.

"Police Commissioner," I said, "please don't tell me you called me in here to tell me that Ms. Owen is planning a trip to the States?"

She actually gulped. "Well..." She seemed to hesitate. Then, "Well, I wasn't sure if... I don't know whether... I formed the impression that Major Wallace doesn't liaise with you, so I thought..."

"He doesn't," I confirmed.

"Then... how...?"

"Police Commissioner," I interrupted, with a great show of patience, "we are the professionals when it comes to this sort of thing. I am sure the police are fine when it comes to crime and keeping order, but really, you have very little idea about how we do our work. Or," I added thoughtfully, "about what we do, beyond what everyone knows."

Meadows folded her piece of paper in half, and then unfolded it. Her hands were shaking with anger. She glared at me. "I know that you are not answerable to the public, and I am!" she exclaimed. "And I know – believe me, I know – that you are just as capable of protecting your friends as the rest of us!"

"My friends," I said, in a slightly lordly tone, "are anyone who serves this country to the best of his or her ability, who is a good citizen, who lives a productive life and who enables others to do the same. And yes, I hope that I am capable of protecting my friends. It is what I have been trained to do!" I paused, and then added, "But if you are suggesting I favour those I am close to, you couldn't be more mistaken. For example, I would never dream of promoting someone because I liked her, or of paying expenses which could not be justified."

Meadows stood, one fist clenched, her colour high. "How dare you...?" she spluttered.

"How dare I what?" I asked, still seated, and looking as relaxed as a man watching cricket on his DeV. "You seemed to be suggesting there is an element of dishonesty in my conduct. I merely gave you a few examples of the sorts of things an officer might do if he – or she – were dishonest, and which I don't do."

Meadows sat again, wrong-footed and furious.

"Oh, you think you're very clever!" she hissed. Then she sat forward. "Karl Wyss, you know and I know that you are protecting subversives. I don't know what your game is, I don't have any idea what you're up to, but I will find out. Believe me, I'll find out. And when I do..." She sat back in her chair, more in control now. "The ATTF has always thought itself better than everyone else," she continued, "but you're not. And your days are numbered."

I stood in a leisurely fashion and picked up my hat. "My dear Meadows," I said, "all our days are numbered. It's the human condition." I turned to the door, and then looked back. "It was a pleasure talking to you, as always," I said. "Perhaps next time we might have coffee as well?" Then I left.

It was time I went to see Lady Grace.

It was November by the time I made it to Bloomsbury, the days short and dark, but the usual pre-Christmas excitement was beginning to emerge. The media was in convulsions over the presidential election, with claims and counterclaims dominating the airways and our DeVs. I drove up and stayed, for a change, in a rather pleasant boutique hotel close to my old haunts, and enjoyed walking around the streets looking at the colourful lights and the Christmas displays, and doing a little Christmas shopping. I was due to have lunch with Lady Grace, and arrived at her place just after twelve noon.

The same maid, Sherine, I think, let me in and walked ahead of me to Lady Grace's first-floor office. She was seated behind a large oak desk with a portrait of Sir Winston Churchill hanging on the wood panelling behind her. She stood as soon as Sherine announced me, came out from behind her desk and, instead of shaking hands, held my two hands warmly in hers. "Karl," she said. "It's so good to see you!"

We moved across to the window. Lady Grace sat in the upholstered window seat, and I settled in a beautiful armchair against embroidered cushions. "Sherry or whisky?" she asked, then sent her maid off to fetch our drinks. "We'll eat at one," she said. "Let's get the business over first, shall we? If we can?"

Sherine came back in and I took my whisky. "I think you might have guessed," I suggested to Her Ladyship.

"Cheers!" she said. "I think I have," she agreed. "Meadows, I'm sure. And Alice Owen?"

"That's it," I agreed, and told her of my encounter with the police commissioner.

Lady Grace was quiet for a few minutes, apparently contemplating the depths of her sherry glass.

"You handled it well," she said at last, looking up. "It's a good thing you've got your operative in Meadows' office. But, of course…" She frowned a little, then smiled at me. "Sally Meadows was a little closer to the mark than we might like, wasn't she?" She sipped her sherry. "After all, you *are* protecting Alice, aren't you? That police incursion into her flat…"

I opened my mouth to answer her. Had Lady Grace not given me some sort of permission to look after Alice?

"Oh, don't misunderstand me!" she exclaimed. "I see nothing wrong with your actions. Only a fool would think that Alice Owen offered any serious challenge to the smooth running of democracy. But, you know, the police are the police… They see things differently."

"They do," I agreed.

"The problem is, they're parochial," suggested Her Ladyship.

"And power-hungry," I added.

Lady Grace chuckled. "That's easy for us to say," she said. "We're the ones with the power! For the moment… Shall we go and eat?"

As we left her study and walked down the richly carpeted corridor to the smaller of Lady Grace's dining rooms, she said casually over her shoulder, "If I were you, Karl, I'd make sure I knew of a good bolthole, in case Alice Owen needs to get away quickly." She bent to pick up a scrap of fluff from a luxurious rug. "We're living in increasingly uncertain times, you know." Then, to my surprise, she added, "You've met Will and Mia in Reggie's area, haven't you? Why don't you pay them another visit?"

We talked about the American election and the Royal Family over lunch, the current scandal in the palace and the enduring popularity of the Windsors, and agreed that the Americans loved them, if possible, even more than the English. We did not mention Meadows or Alice again, even on parting.

★ ★ ★

When we entered into the New Alliance we, on our side of the Atlantic, were led to believe that it was only a matter of time before there were open borders between our two countries. First, though, England and Wales needed to fall into line with US immigration policy. The problem was that the Americans were moving ever to the right, and we had a legacy of liberalism which sat uncomfortably with our more powerful cousins. I was not particularly concerned by the continuing suspicion the US authorities displayed towards my nation. As an ATTF officer I was accorded easy access to the States, coming and going through privileged channels, any questioning being purely a formality, and taking place in a friendly and open fashion. That autumn I knew Alice was having to fill in forms and provide various proofs, in order to be granted her visa to be present at Simon's execution, but I suppose I still thought the situation was temporary. It was taking our two nations longer than I had expected to synchronise our procedures, and the situation in the Caribbean complicated matters, but I believed the time would come when the English would travel as freely back and forth to the US as we had once travelled to Europe.

I was, of course, foolish, and my only excuse can be that I was not alone. I only realised that Lady Grace had seen the writing on the wall, on the afternoon that the US presidential election results were declared and we understood that Sarah Stonewall, sweetheart of the extreme right, ultra-conservative Christian and founder of *Women in Support of Male Leadership*, had been elected. Since Sarah Stonewall, who was quickly dubbed by those who opposed her 'the SS', lauded male leadership, it being the place of women to stay in the home and to grace the presence of their menfolk, we knew at once that the elected president would be a figurehead and no more, and that Colonel Stonewall and their two sons would, in fact, take the helm. The SS and her entourage favoured strong policing, severe punishments and further reductions in gun control.

Her watch word was '*disciple*'. There was to be discipline in the home, discipline in the schools, discipline in prisons and discipline on the streets. Police powers would be increased. Within a week of the SS's election Pearson told me of a rumour he had picked up, that the US ambassador to England had suggested that our independent Police Complaints Commission be closed down. The rumour turned out to be a little ahead of reality. It took a further six months before that request was actually made, and immediately acted upon.

Listening to the news as I drove over to Dorset, I realised why Lady Grace had said, over lunch, that the ATTF had the power '*for the moment*', and why she had suggested I needed to think about a bolthole for Alice if she needed to get away. It was only as I pulled up in front of MacCormack's office that I realised what I was doing. I was planning to subvert our legal authorities in order to protect a friend. What was more, I was doing it with my boss's encouragement. So, what was happening to the strong, safe world I had dedicated my life to achieve?

★ ★ ★

Perhaps I was not quite honest when I said earlier that those autumn months were relatively normal. The normality, such as it was, was at a strictly personal level. I spent most of my nights in my flat, and enjoyed both the simplicity and the comfort of my anonymous little home. The evenings grew darker, we had to deal with some animal rights protestors at the docks of one of our port towns, and ended up holding their leader at our facility in North Hampshire which did not officially exist. Pearson seemed to be seeing Josephine, our under-cover agent in Meadows' office, on a very regular basis, and reported that Meadows both knew and approved of the relationship. From her point of view Josephine might pick up information about our activities, and to encourage Meadows in that point of view, Pearson and I agreed that she could let drop a few useless bits of information into Meadows' ear. Meadows was, of course, an ardent supporter of the SS, and Josephine reported that most of the staff who surrounded Meadows looked forward to an increase in their power, to match the increase in powers granted to the US police.

What was not at all normal for me, was making my third trip to East Anglia, to visit Will and Mia. The suggestion, of course, had been Lady Grace's, but I did not act on it at once. It was only after the SS was elected, and when I realised that our police really might be granted more power, that I took seriously the need to find a bolthole for Alice.

At first I thought the problem would be easy enough to solve. The ATTF had a few safe houses scattered through my area. One or two of them were really rather pleasant, in fact, purporting to be holiday lets. Then I realised that of course anyone looking for Alice would guess I might hide her in such a place. I needed somewhere people would not associate with me. Lady Grace had seemed to think Will and Mia might help, and as I had no other ideas, I decided an early trip to deliver Christmas presents might be in order, and booked a few days' leave for early December.

★ ★ ★

It was fun shopping for the twins. I hardly knew my own nieces, Walter's daughters, and usually just sent them money at Christmas. The big thing being promoted that year was interactive jewellery. Of course, the bracelets, rings, watches and pendants being advertised in sparkling 3D did not do anything that a good little personal DeV could not do, but they were lovely little devices, very charmingly made, and I bought Harry a lapel badge in the shape of an electric guitar, and Charlie a thumb ring featuring dancing angels.

While I was up in London for an ATTF regional commander's dinner I spent a happy afternoon exploring a couple of the big department stores on Oxford Street. There was a time when people wondered whether we might lose our shops, because so many people were making purchases online, but there is something exciting about seeing wares on display, browsing, picking things up and examining them. I bought Reggie and Rosie a pottery coffee set, handmade in Sedona, northern Arizona, and decorated with Native American symbols. I thought Rosie would love it, although I suspected that Reggie would hardly notice the design. I bought Xavier Booth a first-class bottle of Scottish whiskey, very expensive because of the high tariffs imposed on EU goods. I thought Will and Mia would love the etching I had found in a shop in a side street of Alice's city, depicting the flooded crypt of the cathedral. I spent a happy evening wrapping parcels, and realised it was years since I had prepared for Christmas with so much enjoyment.

The weather forecasters were warning of a heavy winter. My parents used to tell me of a time when it was not unusual for there to be at least a little snow every winter, and when my grandparents' village in Switzerland regularly saw white Christmases, but nowadays snow is a big novelty and temperatures below freezing are fairly unusual. The day I drove over to Reggie's territory was frosty, and I thought how beautiful the countryside was, coated in white and glistening in the low winter sun.

I had arranged to meet Reggie for a late lunch at the same hotel where I had first made his acquaintance, back when Alice was still working and I was still half-hoping that she might moderate her beliefs so that we could marry. Now I was just trying to keep her safe.

Reggie was in uniform, looking much smarter than usual. "Meeting at Mildenhall," he explained. "Discussions about relations with the local community, military policing off base, and then an early Christmas dinner. I wasn't able to make Thanksgiving."

"Should be fun," I commented. "Talking of Christmas…" I produced the wrapped box containing the coffee set. "Not to be opened until Christmas Day."

"Goodness!" Reggie looked genuinely pleased, then a little concerned. "I thought this meeting might be business," he said. "I haven't brought you a gift."

"Oh, no problem." The last thing I wanted was to make such a genial man feel uncomfortable. "I'm not here on business, actually," I added. "Or at least, not official business. I'm on a little mission of my own. I'm on leave."

"Very nice too." Reggie asked no questions. We settled at our table in the corner of that elegant dining room, and scrutinised the menu.

"I ought to have a salad," said Reggie, "given we'll have a full turkey dinner this evening, but the steaks here are very good…" He put the menu down and smiled contentedly. "So how are things in your neck of the woods?"

After that we talked about animal rights activists and eventually, inevitably, about the American elections. "Are things still tricky with your police commissioner?" asked Reggie over coffee. "I remember last time you came…"

"Mm, very difficult," I said.

Reggie looked at me with concern. "Be careful, Karl," he said. "The police are in the ascendency now."

"So it seems," I agreed, but added nothing further.

★ ★ ★

Charlie answered the door to me when I arrived at the vicarage. She was wearing some sort of short, fluffy dress with jeans, very fashionable-looking and rather snug on that cold evening, too. She threw her arms around me as if I were a long-lost favourite uncle, although we had only met on one previous occasion. "Karl!" she said. "You're early."

Harry, her twin brother, came in to the hallway behind her. "Hey, Karl," he said, grinning. "Let me take your bag."

"I'll put the kettle on," said Charlie. "Mum and Dad are out, but they'll be back soon. They've been hospital visiting. We don't need to wait for tea for them – they will have been drinking the stuff all afternoon."

The kids had been watching the big DeV but they turned it off in order to talk to me. They were amusing hosts, telling me about the village and about their school, asking questions about my trip but avoiding anything that might be personal or intrusive. I thought how growing up in a vicarage had given them social skills I had taken years to learn. Then Will and Mia arrived, Mia's glasses steaming up as she walked into the warm lounge, and there were hugs all round and talk about slippery roads and about how there were no longer any gritting lorries. I went upstairs and took the various gifts out of my bag, and told everyone not to open them until the proper time.

By then there was a delicious smell issuing from the kitchen, and we drank gin and tonics while the casserole was heated up and potatoes boiled, then talked light-heartedly over dinner about nothing much, until the twins went up to their rooms and we had cleared the table.

Will opened a box of chocolates. *Belgian* chocolates, I noticed. That was interesting, given that Belgian and Swiss chocolate had vanished from our shops more than a decade earlier.

"So, Karl," Will said, biting appreciatively into a truffle, "what has brought you here?"

"Not that you aren't always welcome!" said Mia with her usual enthusiasm. "You don't need a reason!"

"Thank you." The chocolate I had taken had a hard toffee centre and I was struggling to chew it. I waited until I had swallowed the last of it, declined a second, and decided that honesty was probably the best policy.

"I'm not sure if you can help," I started. "Or maybe point me in the direction of someone else who can... I have a friend who might be in a bit of trouble. She might need somewhere to go – somewhere where she can't easily be found."

I saw Will and Mia glance at each other, a look so quick that I, used as I am to deciphering unspoken messages, was not quite sure what had been exchanged.

Will sounded cautious. "We do, of course, know of a number of places where people who are in difficulty can get help," he said. "It goes with the territory. There are retreat houses, a Healing Centre run by the Franciscans, and counselling centres in several towns locally. It depends on the sort of trouble your friend might be in."

I felt silly. Obviously, if Will and Mia did know of a safe hiding place, they were hardly likely to tell me about it. I was, after all, an ATTF officer whom they had only met on two previous occasions. I trusted them instinctively, but I could not know if they felt the same about me. What was more, I realised, if I told them anything further I would be taking great risks. Were my instincts reliable? Did I want them to know anything about Alice? And if they were to be trusted – and I thought they probably were – what was I doing giving them information it was dangerous for them to know? They were the parents of two teenage kids, they really did not need to be exposed to the sort of trouble I could bring down on their heads. I thought about Maria, who was still writing me enthusiastic and affectionate letters. My life was grubby enough without implicating Will and Mia in the mire. I decided that I would push it no further. It was not fair to them.

Instead I tried to neutralise my enquiry by making it sound

totally innocent. "If my friend's need is primarily spiritual," I said, "would the Franciscan place be suitable?"

"It could be," said Will. "I'll give you a leaflet."

An hour later, after light conversation and after watching the news, Mia followed me upstairs. "I'll just check that the twins gave you a towel," she said, following me into the guest bedroom. Then she took some keys out of the pocket of her hoodie. "By the way," she said, very casually, "you're welcome here anytime, but if ever you want to get away entirely by yourself, I own a little cottage in Wales. It's very basic, and very remote, but we never use it in the winter and you're welcome to stay there if ever you want to." She handed me the large, old fashioned keys, hanging from a ring with a handwritten brown cardboard label attached, on which was written an address.

"Oh, thank you Mia," I said as casually as I could. "That's a kind thought. I might just take you up on it." I put the keys in the inside pocket of my case, wished Mia goodnight, waved to Will who was on the landing, and closed the door. I resolved to drive back via the cottage to check it out. I was pretty sure I had just been handed the keys to my bolthole for Alice.

CHAPTER 8

Pearson and Josephine invited me to their Christmas party when I returned from Wales a couple of days later. Pearson handed me a proper invitation, on a card produced rather expertly on a high-class DeV, looking a little sheepish as he handed it over. "I've told Josie lots about you," he said. "She'd love you to come."

The party was to be in Josephine's flat, although when I arrived I realised that Pearson was obviously living there too, at least for part of the time. His slippers were beside the bed when, as instructed, I took my overcoat in to lay it, with the furs and winter jackets of other guests, on the bed. I felt pleased for Pearson, but also a little jealous. They made a good couple, both working for the same organisation, sharing the same belief systems, free to take their relationship as far as it naturally went. With a pang, I thought of Alice, and longed for her to be there, with a longing that seemed to touch every nerve in my body. Of course, it was not possible. Meadows, as Josephine's official boss, would be at the party too, along with others from the police commissioner's office. And anyhow...

I took a proffered glass of punch and admired the Christmas decorations, chatting with Josephine about a job she had once had during an undergraduate holiday, harvesting Christmas trees in the Borders. Meadows arrived a few minutes later, by which time the living room was already fairly crowded. She was with a small group of smartly groomed middle-aged women, her acolytes I assumed, and they all fluttered and beamed at Josephine as she greeted them, and said what an attractive apartment she had.

I was talking to one of the neighbours when Meadows came over to me. He was, if I remember rightly, a school inspector, and lived in one of the penthouse apartments reserved for high-ranking government employees. His conversation was tedious and he stood just a little too close to me while he spoke, so that I found myself shuffling unobtrusively backwards to create a more comfortable space between us. I would not say that Meadows rescued me, but the boring neighbour moved away as soon as she appeared at my side.

"Karl," she gushed in her society voice, "how lovely to see you!" She looked around the room, as if searching someone out. Then, with assumed surprise, she asked, "Are you on your own?"

"Hardly," I said. "The room seems fairly full to me."

Meadows laughed a high-pitched, artificial laugh. "Ah, my dear Commander!" she exclaimed. "I thought you might have a young – one might almost say a *very* young – companion over for the festive season. From Texas, perhaps?" She giggled a synthetic giggle and looked at me sideways.

Despite the control I had practised for decades I could feel myself blushing. How on the earth could Meadows know about Maria? And *what* did Meadows know about Maria? Or think she knew? Almost at once I guessed the answer. The US police already had greatly enhanced powers as a result of the recent election. No doubt they would liaise with their English counterparts. I remembered Lady Grace saying that we, the ATTF, had all the power *'for the moment'*. The moment, I grasped, was over.

I recovered well, though. Thank goodness for professional training. "My dear Commissioner," I said, "I thought our faithful police knew everything! You are falling down on your job! My nieces decided to go skiing instead of visiting their ageing uncle. I will be spending Christmas alone. And my nieces live in Buckinghamshire, not in Texas! You really must get your facts straight!"

I enjoyed making Meadows feel flustered. For a moment confusion was written all over her face. I jumped in before she could recover. "And what about you?" I asked. "Will you be spending Christmas with anyone special?" I looked pointedly across at Meadows' groupies, standing around the buffet. "With friends, perhaps?" I asked.

Now it was her turn to turn red, and to choke on the punch she was holding in a slightly trembling hand. "I..." she stumbled. "Of course, I will keep open house over the holidays, for all those who work with me." Then, sounding pompous, she added, "It is just good citizenship!"

"Quite," I agreed. "And no doubt they appreciate *everything* you do for them!"

Then I saw that Pearson was, for the moment, not speaking to anyone. "Talking of those who work with us..." I said, and moved over to join him.

"You seem to have upset our police commissioner," commented Pearson with some glee.

"And she has upset me," I said.

★ ★ ★

At one time the US president's inauguration did not happen until two months after his or her election, and the previous president remained at the helm until that day, but as their politics became more and more extreme the situation changed in practice, if not in theory. In practice, as soon as the newly elected president started to publish the executive orders planned for the new administration, those who wanted the support of the White House made sure that they started to be put into effect. An earlier president had successfully reduced the power of the legislature so that it had become possible for the president, in practice, to rule by decree.

On our side of the Atlantic elected representatives were falling over themselves, that winter, to stay in the good books of the SS. This was no easy feat. We have had several powerful women prime ministers who genuinely held the reins of government themselves, and whose husbands took very much a back-seat role. Sarah Stonewall made it abundantly clear that she wanted to be purely a figurehead, *'a role model for married women the world over,'* she declared, *'like your own dear Queen Elizabeth, may she rest in peace',* and her stance stretched our political classes almost further than they could go. There was much talk about the culture of the United States being different from our own, of the need to 're-empower' men, of allowing women to be women, but even so a number of female politicians and several high-profile left-wing men resigned when our prime minister publicly congratulated the US on *'recognising that along with equality, we need to respect and encourage difference'.* There were demonstrations on the streets in most of the large cities, but in reality, the way had been paved by the Christian right in both our countries.

Lady Grace phoned me the day after Boxing Day. "Karl," she said, "do you have any time free in the next week or so?" I thought her voice sounded strained. In fact, I had spent a quiet Christmas in my little flat, cooking and reading, and had nothing organised until a New Year's party which Amy was hosting, where I hoped I would see Alice.

"I could come up tomorrow," I suggested.

★ ★ ★

Lady Grace opened her own front door to me. "Sherine is

126

on holiday until the 31st," she explained, and led me, not to her dignified drawing room, but to the half-basement kitchen which was a huge, attractive room with French windows leading out to a small, sunken garden. Sunlight streamed in, and Lady Grace poured coffee from a pot on a scrubbed pine table and indicated where the plastic milk container stood. "I live very informally while I'm on my own," she added, and pulled out a chair to sit, with her hands cupped around her coffee mug as if she were cold.

I sat too, and sipped my coffee. It was not the Brazilian, I thought. Something softer. Chilean, perhaps?

"We're living in interesting times," I said, wondering why I was there but guessing that all was not well.

"We do," agreed Lady Grace, and stared out into the garden. There were winter pansies in a hanging basket, and a bird feeder, but for the moment no birds.

We were quiet for a few minutes. I knew Lady Grace wanted to tell me something but I was happy to wait. It was very quiet, there was only the sound of a clock ticking and, a long way away, the sound of an aircraft flying overhead.

She sighed and put down her coffee mug. "I don't need to ask if you're following the news," she stated.

"Of course," I agreed. "It's pretty grim."

"Sarah Stonewall is a very bright cookie," Lady Grace went on. "She knows just what she's doing."

"I can believe that," I said. "She certainly manages her electorate with some skill!"

"Indeed."

We were quiet again. "I'm guessing you understand the game she's playing?" suggested Her Ladyship.

"I think so." I sipped some more coffee. Although mild it had a twist to it. Beans grown on higher land, I wondered? "I'm assuming the SS has more influence over the police than over federal agencies or the CIA," I suggested, "so she's giving the police all the powers they want and undercutting the authority of the agencies she can't control?"

"That's about it," she agreed. "The US constitution was written with checks and balances to prevent the sort of thing that is happening now. The state judiciaries have always been subject to local prejudices and the Supreme Court is in the hands of the right in perpetuity. There's been a long standing mistrust of all federal agencies for as far back as I can remember, and a parochial love of local law enforcement."

"So, the police grow stronger and agents with the training and the wider perspective grow weaker," I said.

"Exactly." Lady Grace sighed again. "Which, to be honest, is no more than I would expect."

"And on this side of the pond...?" I prompted.

"Now there you have it!" Lady Grace put her mug down on the table with a bump. "On this side of the Atlantic we do things differently." She paused and then corrected herself. "On this side of the Atlantic we *did* things differently," she amended. "But it seems that once again we are falling in to line. Sir Gerald – you don't know Sir Gerald but he's a good friend to the ATTF – Sir Gerald tells me that this new administration is already putting pressure on us to conform."

I had seen this coming. "Why are we cooperating?" I asked, although really, I knew the answer.

"Because they influence our media, which influences public opinion. Because we turned our backs on too many of our other friends and now we daren't be anywhere but in the protective shadow of the US. Because there are issues to do with political funding. Because we need trade deals...You know it all, Karl. I don't need to spell it out."

"And because," I added, "there are far too many people over here who never were democrats at heart."

Lady Grace turned and looked at me sharply. "But were *we*, Karl? In all honesty, were our actions in the ATTF really the actions of an agency working in a truly democratic fashion?"

I noticed that she was speaking in the past tense. Was the ATTF over, then? Finished?

I thought about her question. "No, we weren't democrats," I had to agree. "But we weren't acting out of self-interest either. We wanted the best for our country, didn't we?" I thought back to the idealism of my youth, to the excitement I had felt when I had listened to Professor Narin all those years ago, lecturing on the responsibility of the intelligentsia to govern citizens in their best interests, not according to their stated wishes.

Again, we were both quiet. A single brown bird flew down to the bird feeder, seemed to inspect the food on offer and then to fly away in disgust.

"I fear," said Lady Grace, "that on my tombstone the epitaph will read, *'she meant well'*."

She was staring out of the window. I had never thought about Her Ladyship's age. I supposed she was my generation, just coming up to retirement. In the bright sunlight of the December morning I noticed for the first time how lined her forehead was, and that her hand resting on the handle of her mug had brown marks on the skin.

She sighed again, and seemed to come out of her revere. "More coffee, Karl? Did you come up this morning or stay last night at the place by the river?"

"I came up this morning." Then I asked, "So what do you think will happen now?"

Suddenly Lady Grace became business-like. She poured herself more coffee, pushed the pot across to me and sat back, crossing her elegant trouser-covered legs and looking much more like her old self.

"That's why I wanted to see you," she said. "My letter of resignation is on my computer upstairs. Later this morning I will send it to the prime minister and the leader of the opposition." She smiled wryly. "It's a face-saving exercise," she said. "I already know that tomorrow the announcement will be made that Lord Peters is to be the new Secretary of State for Internal Security."

"Lord Peters?" I asked. "*The* Lord Peters?"

"Exactly," confirmed Her Ladyship. "Lord Peters, once chief constable of the London Met, sued by the Alliance for Civil Liberties after that fracas over street demonstrations, popular speaker in favour of the Alt-Right and vocal supporter of Sarah Stonewall's *Women in Support of Male Leadership*, knighted the year we went into the New Alliance... that Lord Peters."

It could hardly be worse, I thought. "So, what do you think will be the future for us?" I asked, meaning the ATTF.

"Oh, we'll still be there," she said. "This government knows how useful we've been, and we are ideally suited to do things the police can't be seen to be doing. But we'll be expected to work with the police commissioners. *They'll* have the upper hand, not us." She was quiet for a moment, looking thoughtful. "I don't suppose the general public will be aware of any changes," she added, "but my concern is for the organisation. For people like you."

"I see," I said, and I did. Meadows, my declared enemy, would be strengthened. I would be weakened. Alice would be doubly vulnerable because of me. I thought quickly about my team in the South. Pearson would be all right because of his relationship with Josephine, whom Meadows believed to be on her side. My other operatives were not, I thought, politically vulnerable.

"What will you do?" I asked Lady Grace.

She smiled a little sadly. "I think..." she paused, then suddenly smiled a big, easy smile. "I'll tell you what I'm going to do!" she said, almost gleefully. "I'm going to do something I've wanted to do for years! I'm going to write a history of cotton

130

manufacturing in and around Manchester. It was to have been my PhD subject if I hadn't married Teddy." Then she looked serious again. "I'll be all right, Karl," she reassured me. "But as for you... Look after yourself. Look after you and yours."

CHAPTER 9

I was back in Hampshire by mid-afternoon, and arrived at Amy's house at around nine in the evening, by which time her party was well underway. Cars were parked all along the lane and the fir tree which grew by the road at the entry to Amy's driveway was covered in tiny green and red lights. Amy's house was old, all thatch and low oak beams, but at some point it had been renovated inside, and the partitions between small rooms taken away, so that there was a long lounge with little alcoves created by oddly placed, ancient wooden supports. I had been in that room once or twice, with Alice, but it looked different with the furniture pushed back and a Christmas tree tastefully decorated at one end. I recognised one or two people although I did not know any of them well. I was wearing uniform. I told Amy I had come straight from work although I suspect that, strictly speaking, my visit to Lady Grace had not been work, and anyhow I had not changed into my uniform until I had got back.

Amy introduced me to a couple who lived just down the lane, retired military, of course. We discussed the situation in the Caribbean. Amy's neighbours had lived there for a while many years earlier, in some sort of military or diplomatic capacity, and they spoke of the islanders with affection and sadness. The village vicar was there with a very pretty young wife, as different in appearance from Mia as chalk from cheese, but when we started talking about the problems of rural living without public transport I realised that the two women might have more in common with each other than their looks suggested. I wondered whether a certain type of woman tended to become the wife of a rural vicar, or whether being a rural vicar's wife made those women more down to earth and practical, as these two vicars' wives seemed to be. Amy was very lively and entertaining. She was involved in some sort of charity in London involving Eastern Europeans and the arts, and it seemed they had just done a review of some sort on the South Bank. It had gone down a storm, and attracted excellent reviews. I heard a few sarcastic comments about the election of Sarah Stonewall, but nobody appeared overly concerned and there seemed to be a general feeling that Americans went to these sorts of extremes but that we never would. Later in the evening a couple of American Air Force officers arrived, one with his English wife, the other alone. They recognised my uniform and shook my hand warmly, wishing me a Happy New Year in some southern drawl which, whatever people say, I find very attractive.

And all evening I was aware of Alice. I had not seen her when I first arrived, because she had been sitting in a low chair with Amy's youngest grandchild on her lap, reading her a story. I really wanted to go and talk to her, but people kept coming up to me, and I did not want to be too obvious. Nor was I sure, after my conversation with Lady Grace that morning, that friendship with me was quite such a positive thing as once it had been. And I was not entirely sure that Alice wanted to talk to me.

I thought she looked beautiful. Alice was not conventionally pretty but she had such a smile, and a sort of liveliness of features that drew people in. She was wearing a deep-red velvet dress with long, embroidered sleeves and a high waist, so that it looked slightly medieval, and little red slippers. She, too, seemed always to be talking to people, and several times I saw her going into the kitchen with empty nibbles plates, or returning with new stacks of party food. I think she had been at Amy's for the whole Christmas period, and I thought that at least she had been safe, away from controversial projects and people who might get her into trouble. Only once did I look up from a conversation and see her looking at me across the room. I smiled and she gave a little smile back, before returning to her circle to listen to some uproarious account of a skiing accident.

I managed to speak to Alice as I left. Not everyone had stayed after midnight, some cited babysitters or worries about the weather, or about driving after twelve when the last remaining street lights were extinguished, and Amy's grandchildren had gone to bed right after the indoor fireworks and 'Auld Lang Syne'. A smaller group remained, sitting on the settee, the arm chairs and various poufs and stools, drinking liqueurs in tiny coloured glasses, and steaming coffee. Alice sat on the raised hearth, the skirt of her red dress wrapped around her legs, and fed pieces of wood onto the crackling fire while Amy entertained us with amusing stories about catastrophes that had occurred in the little pottery which was her hobby and which provided, I think, a steady if not magnificent income. When the vicar rose with a yawn and said that he had to get up early to write his sermon, the group broke up. Amy and Alice stood at the door, handing people coats and wishing them a Happy New Year again, and as I passed Alice I just touched her arm and said, "I'll be thinking of you." I looked at Amy and saw she had been watching us, a small, perplexed frown on her face. Then I drove home to my empty flat and my empty bed.

★ ★ ★

Alice was flying out on the 8th of January. I had hoped that I might take her to the airport, but she went up by coach the day before and stayed at a budget hotel overnight. I was busy at work, but she was on my mind all the while. I wished I could have gone with her. I hated the thought of what she was going to witness. I hated the thought of how vulnerable she was. I hated the thought that I could not protect her.

Nor was I quite sure that I could protect myself. Lady Grace's retirement was announced on the first day of January. One paper ran a profile of her life and work, so I suppose the fact that she was leaving her post had been known before her letter of resignation reached the prime minister on the 31st. The media was full of praise for Lord Peters, who was, it seemed, an inspired choice to fulfil a difficult role. As was, by then, always the case, our media was very keen to know how the American press was reporting this development. Of course, they thoroughly approved. The online newsfeeds coming into England from Ireland and Scotland were the only ones to mention Lord Peters' disdain for civil rights and his rather shady dealings while he was with the Met. The big news, however, had nothing to do with political appointments. The weather forecasters were talking about a series of heavy storms expected in the middle of the month which could bring substantial deposits of snow and a spell of freezing weather, and there was much discussion about the fact that we no longer had the means to keep our roads clear.

Meadows contacted me on the morning of the 7th. Pearson and I were sitting in his office looking out on the High Street, where red '*Sale*' signs decorated most of the ground-floor windows. He was looking well. He was sporting a smart new haircut which made him look younger ("Josie's work" he told me, with a grin) and he looked generally rested, a man at peace with his world. I had given him the full week off between Christmas and the New Year, and he was telling me how he and Josephine had driven over to Cambridgeshire to visit Josephine's mother. "She was a sweetie," he said, "just like Josie. I haven't met her father yet. He lives up in Yorkshire. Josie tells me he's just a rude old man, but we'll see…"

We talked about the political situation. Pearson had heard the news about Lady Grace and was a bit alarmed by the appointment of Lord Peters, but he did not know, and I did not tell him, that in reality Lady Grace had been sacked. "We'll have to go carefully with Meadows," commented Pearson. "She really doesn't like you!"

Just at that moment my phone rang, and it was the woman herself. "Ah, Karl!" she started, in that annoying schoolteacher voice of hers. "Did you have a good Christmas? Back at the grindstone now, I'm sure." Then, before I had time to answer, she said, "If you could, it would be really good to meet up sometime soon." Then, almost simpering, "It looks as if we're going to be working much more closely together from here on in. Have you read Lord Peters' New Year letter?"

No such letter had reached my desk. I felt wrong-footed. "Not yet," I said.

"Try to find the time to read it before we meet," she said, and I recognised a command when I heard it. "Can you make my office by twelve today?"

★ ★ ★

In fact, we had not received Lord Peters' letter, and that in itself was a clear indication of the lay of the land. I phoned Reggie when our own efforts to find the missive had proved fruitless, and discovered that he had been passed the letter by Xavier Booth. Reggie had also not received it, but he and Xavier worked so closely together that it was unthinkable for Xavier to keep the contents to himself. The letter purported to be addressed to all area commanders of the ATTF and to all police commissioners, but somehow only the police commissioners anywhere in the country had received it. It stipulated that *'these two branches of our noble law-enforcement community'* were to work closely together, and that the police, '*with their longer history and greater experience*' might '*in many situations*' find themselves taking the lead. The letter warned that it was time to change the culture of '*some organisations*', and suggested that it was imperative we not stand in the way of progress. Lord Peters' sole aim, the letter said, was to make both the police and the ATTF more efficient, and he trusted that we would all cooperate.

Pearson came with me to the meeting. I needed his back-up.

★ ★ ★

Meadows was in her pseudo-military garb and was wearing heavy make-up. It occurred to me, not for the first time, that while younger women can look gorgeous with their faces thus made up, older women just look silly, and indeed, the adornment ages them rather than making them look more youthful. I had to admit, though, that although Meadows looked a little ridiculous in my opinion, she also looked like a woman who knew her star was in the ascendancy. She was more than usually gracious as she extended her hand across her desk to shake mine, and offered us both seats.

She phoned for coffee, then started briskly as, no doubt, she intended to go on.

"Thank you for coming, gentlemen," she said, and her tone told us, even if the other circumstances of our meeting had not, that it was Meadows who had the upper hand now. "I thought, in the light of the welcome and sensible political developments of today, that it would be useful if we were to put our heads together and agree on the way forward in our area, now that we are to be working so much more closely together."

Pearson gave an indignant cough. I smiled at Meadows. "A wise thought," I said, hoping to mask my true feelings about the situation.

"Perhaps," suggested Meadows, "one place to start might be for you to tell me – in confidence of course – about any current surveillance that is ongoing in this county."

I had no intention of doing any such thing.

"I don't think," I said, producing a printout of Lord Peters' letter from the inside pocket of my jacket and scrutinizing it as if checking my facts, "that Lord Peters has requested us to do any such thing."

Meadows looked displeased. "He requires you to work with us!" she insisted.

"Haven't we always worked together?" I said pleasantly, acting the part I needed to act. "The only secrets we have had from you have come from our different government briefs, and I'm sure you have had no secrets from us!"

Meadows looked a bit taken aback. No doubt it would have been easier for her if we had arrived looking angry or surprised by developments, instead of a little bored. We were supposed to be alarmed by Meadow's new powers, but instead we seemed rather disinterested. Indeed, just at that moment Pearson uncrossed his legs and stretched them out in front of him, sliding a little down in his chair, so that his posture indicated that he was relaxed, perhaps waiting for something more interesting to happen.

"I have always found," I said, deliberately setting out to sound more experienced than Meadows, "that it is best to take things at a gentle pace, not jumping ahead of our political lords and masters." I frowned, as if thinking things through as I spoke. "There will, no doubt, be discussions at levels higher than ours about the exact divisions of labour. Lord Peters' experience is all with the policing side of things. It will take him time to come up to scratch on our more sensitive areas of work." I knew Meadows would hate the suggestion that the ATTF was more sensitive than the police, and indeed, it was a pretty exaggerated claim.

"But…" Meadows was betraying her dismay at our failure to fall into line. This was not the way she had hoped the interview would develop.

"Quite," I said, as if I knew that she was about to make a sound point. "You are right. I am sure we will all benefit from the new developments. It is something to look forward to – when the details have been worked out. After all, none of us wants anything other than the good of our country."

I stood, picking up my hat, and smiled across the desk to Meadows. "Thank you for inviting us over. Perhaps our next meeting should take place in Pearson's office – to cement the new, closer relationship between us?"

Pearson rose too, following my lead. "Let us wait for further directives, shall we?" I said, my hand on the door handle.

Out in the street Pearson spoke his first words in half an hour. "Duplicitous bitch!" he exclaimed.

"Now then," I admonished him, smiling. "Meadows is our honoured colleague, with whom it will be a pleasure to work!" And we both laughed grimly.

★ ★ ★

The ATTF's official DeVs are specially programmed so that our messages cannot be intercepted. After the trouble, way back when the Russians were discovered to be manipulating events in the West through their ability to access confidential emails, our people in Oxford had developed a new security system which did not just encrypt messages, but which actually hid the fact that messages had been sent at all. This was a big step forward, and had effectively created a level of secrecy that was the envy of every governmental agency in the world that did not have it.

Reggie contacted me using this system at the end of the

day we met Meadows. I was in a hotel in Dorset, having had a rather more cordial meeting with MacCormack, the Dorset police commissioner, than the morning meeting with Meadows. He was in an uncomfortable position. Politically he was further from Lord Peters than he had been from Lady Grace, because Lord Peters was so ultra-conservative and poor MacCormack was one of the few remaining neo-socialists in the south of England. He had never approved of the ATTF, but on a personal level there had been a lot of respect shared between MacCormack and me through the years, a mutual acknowledgement that while we might have different ideologies, our concerns for the people in our respective spheres of influence were benign. To my initial surprise, MacCormack was considering retirement. "Better for my pension," he said, "if I go before I'm pushed."

I had eaten sparingly that evening. I have been aware all my working life that if I am feeling threatened or if I am uncertain about how situations are going to develop, I eat less. I assume it is the *'fight'* part of *'fight or flight'*, the part-instinctive, part-indoctrinated reaction of any well-trained front-line officer. It was a mild, dark evening. The hotel I had chosen was on the coast, looking out from a clifftop position towards the dark sea and a distant lighthouse. I was sitting on my balcony, the rest of the bottle of wine I had started at dinner at my feet, and the elegant wine glass in my hand. I was thinking, of course, about Alice, hoping she was all right and wondering if she was thinking about me.

My DeV was in my jacket pocket. It buzzed, and I saw from the VDU code that it was Reggie. I was pleased.

"Evening, brother-in-arms!" greeted Reggie. "How are things in the affluent south today?"

I laughed. "As expected," I said. "Thanks for your help in sending over Lord Peters' letter this morning."

There was a short pause. "It's not good, is it?" Reggie said.

"It's not," I agreed.

Reggie made a sort of coughing sound. "Lady Grace has left the country," he said.

"What!" I was really amazed.

"Gone to Vancouver," he said. "I'm told she has a research post. I don't know what she's researching."

"Probably Manchester cotton mills," I said, remembering our conversation.

Reggie sounded surprised. "Really?" Then he added, "Actually, that's probably a good decision. Very non-political."

"How are things your way?" I asked.

"Ah, well..." Reggie chuckled. "Things my way are probably much healthier than in your area. Xavier is furious about the choice of Lord Peters. But privately. Unlike your MacCormack, he's always kept his political views to himself. So, Xavier is keeping me informed and I am keeping him informed, and we're lying as low as we can until we see how things pan out."

I took another sip of wine. "You're fortunate," I commented.

"Yes." We were both quiet. I could hear waves breaking on the shore a long way away. It was getting colder. A shiver ran through me.

"I think," said Reggie thoughtfully, "that I will survive this. Will you?"

I thought about that. "I think I'll survive, in as much as I don't think I'll disappear," I said. "But whether I keep my job..."

"Karl," said Reggie, and I thought there was a degree of urgency in his voice, "make provision for yourself, won't you? And for those you love? This is no time to be taking risks."

"Thanks, Reggie." What could I say? "Give my love to Rosie."

I finished the bottle of wine, sitting on the balcony getting colder and colder. I needed to follow Reggie's advice and make some personal arrangements. But before then, I needed to make sure Alice was protected. And I wanted to make sure that any trouble I might bring down on my own head did not affect Pearson. There was quite a lot of damage limitation to be done, and I was not quite sure where to start. To be honest, the wine did not help. I dreamed confused dreams in which I was running sometimes away from, and sometimes towards, a huge snowman who was carrying a rope. I woke at six in the morning to find that the balcony door had blown open again and the room was chilled through and through. And so was I.

CHAPTER 10

I was back in my flat early that morning. I had been thinking hard about what needed to be done. I was a hundred percent certain that Meadows could not access my ATTF phone, but equally as convinced that, whether or not her people had been watching me before, they would be now. I emailed Alice, who would, I calculated, be in Houston preparing to head up to Stanley where the Texas death row was located, and told her I was just back from Milton Keynes and was due a few days off. I always talked about my work as *'going to Milton Keynes'*. I did not know whether Alice realised what I meant, or not. It was one of those things it was wiser not to discuss.

Simon was due to be executed on the 12th of January. I was still hoping there might be a delay or even a last-minute decree of clemency, although of course it was very unlikely. I planned to meet Alice when her flight got in. I very much hoped that I would be able to take her home, check her flat, and leave her safe and sound, but I could not be sure of that, nor take anything for granted. Meadows had been out to get Alice even before the change of administration. Now that she had the power, she might arrest Alice on any charge, real or trumped up. At this point, I realised, Alice was at greater risk of disappearing than I was.

I had indeed taken a couple of days off. I was due them, and I needed them to lay my plans. I decided that I needed to take action to make sure that Pearson was not implicated in any actions of mine which might, in due course, be censored.

I needed a decoy, and the perfect solution came to me while I was jogging round the park. Back home, I used my non-work DeV to email Lady Grace at her ATTF address. Of course, I realised that she had gone, that her ATTF connections were severed and would no longer work, but I very much hoped they were still being monitored. I sent several emails. In the first I expressed concern about Pearson. I 'told' Lady Grace that Pearson was romantically involved with Josephine, and expressed great concern that, because of this new relationship, he was now more inclined to be loyal to the police than to the ATTF, if push came to shove. My second email was made to sound like a clumsy cover-up, as if I had used the wrong DeV in error. I said that of course I realised that there could be no conflict of interest between the police and the ATTF, and that I hoped Lady Grace would forgive my earlier, rather ridiculous, concerns. The third email, sent a few hours later, was made to sound like a further, panicked effort to cover my tracks. I expressed great appreciation for the work of Meadows and her team, and said how happy I would be to work with her under the new regime. I hoped that anyone intercepting this 'correspondence' would believe that Pearson was no threat to the new order, and that I was feeling endangered and alone. It was Sunday, and the fact that I had sent these emails from home, on a day off, should, I thought, add to the impression that I was feeling insecure.

Next, I accessed Josephine's reports. She was a good agent, and everything she had discovered was well documented. I was deeply grateful, as I doctored her reports, for the IT skills ATTF officers were expected to have. There were spreadsheets showing expenses paid to all the officers on Meadows' personal staff. The payments to her intimates were, I realised, outrageous. I revisited a list of undercover police officers who had been placed in faith communities, against the regulations which applied at that time. I doctored these reports subtly, so that they now appeared to have come from *Citizen B* in Accounts, and dated a couple so that they appeared to have arrived on my DeV before Josephine had come to Hampshire, so that no suspicion would fall on Josephine, who worked in IT. I stored the doctored documents on several DeVs.

Then I tried to think of ways to protect Alice, but I could not. I could not plant misinformation because her life was too open, too well known. Meadows' people had, of course, been watching Alice for months, maybe even a year. I found myself wondering whether I could get her across the border into Scotland or Ireland where she would be safe, but I realised that I did not have the connections. I would have to be satisfied with hiding her somewhere in this country. I thought the place I had in mind was safe. I hoped so. Then I realised that I was operating on a knife edge, that in order to save Alice I needed to gamble on more than just the hope that the plans I had so far laid would work. I needed to make a bigger plan yet.

That was a hard day. It took all morning and the early part of the afternoon to manipulate the IT. When there were real experts involved in tracing communications I knew I had to hide the history of my mails, and then the history of the history. For a period of several months a few years earlier I had overseen operatives whose work was this sort of thing, but of course things in IT change quickly and I found a couple of new ploys that the IT division must have developed since my time. It was probably three in the afternoon before I was completely satisfied.

I had initially planned an enjoyable day cooking for my freezer, so I tried to relax by visiting the large, established supermarket by the railway station and buying the various ingredients I needed. I enjoy cooking, and it gives me great pleasure to come back to my flat after a day, or several days, away, and to delve around for home-cooked food that can just be thawed and heated up.

I have visited that particular supermarket often. It is close to a roundabout, and like most of its patrons I take the relevant exit, park in the extensive car park, and go straight inside. I do not think I had ever, until that day, taken any notice of the people outside the supermarket. In fact, if you had asked me, I doubt if I would have known that there were usually any people around other than shoppers.

Do I blame Alice, or maybe the influence of Will and Mia, for the events of that afternoon? I was right behind a car with Virginia number plates and a Confederate bumper sticker, when I turned off the roundabout. The speed limit on the supermarket access road is low, five miles per hour, so we were crawling up the incline in convoy. There were children in the rear seat of the car ahead. They were bouncing around, and I was watching, not really thinking about them, but vaguely wondering if they were wearing seatbelts, when suddenly something was thrown out of a passenger window. It was a good throw. The item, whatever it was, went high into the air and then landed in the bushes besides the road. I glanced in the direction in which it had landed and saw a small child standing waist-high in undergrowth, rubbing his head. In that fraction of a second before I flicked my eyes back onto the road, I saw the face of the child crumple and his mouth open in a wail of surprise and perhaps pain.

My heart was thumping hard. I felt a mixture of complete surprise and indignation. I glanced again into the bushes, now to my immediate right, but there was no sign of the child. What had just happened? The children in the Virginian car were still bouncing around as the car was parked. There was a space beside them. Without really planning it I pulled in and climbed out of my car.

The driver of the American car was a woman, obviously the mother of the bouncy children, who were whooping and shouting as they jumped around, waiting for their mother to collect a trolley.

"We got one, we got one!" one child yelled, and they high-fived each other.

"But it was my shot!" claimed the other child.

"No, it was *my* shot!" It was the boy shouting, his tone suddenly angry.

"It was *my* shot. Look, you still have your apple core. That's two-one to me!" exclaimed the pretty little girl.

Just at that point the mother returned with her trolley and the children grabbed her arms, trying to get her attention. "Mom, Troy says…" "Mom, didn't I…?" "Mom, it's not fair!" "Mom, you saw, didn't you? It was my shot…"

With that calm voice of patient mothers arbitrating over quarrels when they cannot know who is right or wrong, the mother replied, "No, honey, I didn't see. Whoever threw it, it was a good shot. But I don't know who threw it. So why don't we score one point each? I'm sure there'll be more chances on the way home." She smiled across at me, a little apologetically. "They're always so lively for the first hour after school is out!" Then she hustled them along towards the shop.

I was stunned. One of her children had just deliberately thrown an apple core at a child, and the mother had made no attempt to reprimand her offspring. Worse, she had suggested they might have another chance later!

I am sure I did not stand there with my mouth open. We are trained to be impassive, and I dare say my training clicked in. I think I might even have smiled at the woman and said, "Yes!" But I was deeply shocked, for all that.

It was January, and a grey day. Already the long winter dusk had started. I looked around. A few people were coming and going from the store, collars up, hunched into their coats or jackets, not looking at other people, rushing from one warm, dry space to another. As inconspicuously as I could I stepped off the asphalted footpath that led to the store, and over a low wooden rail into the bushes that provided greenery and some

147

sort of carbon-capture. I waded through the undergrowth towards the place where I had seen the small child.

The ground was rough, builders' rubble had not been cleared here, and the bushes masked the uneven ground so that from the road, especially in summer, the area surrounding the supermarket would look green and lush. Ivy and bindweed tangled itself around other plants and the walking was not easy until, about ten paces in, I found a narrow path, a little like the sheep tracks one sometimes finds in the Welsh mountains. It was getting rapidly darker now, and I used the torch on my DeV to show me where I was treading.

And it was because of the torch that I found the child. The beam was lighting broken bricks, dead leaves, mud and litter, and then suddenly the stick-thin, dirty leg of a little boy. Quickly the child pulled his leg in under him. He was huddled down in the bushes not quite far enough away from the path to be completely hidden.

I turned the DeV off and squatted down.

"Are you okay?" I asked the child.

He whimpered, but didn't say anything. It was hard to tell but I thought he might be about five or six years old. He was shivering, but whether it was from cold or from fear I could not tell.

"Where's you mummy?" I asked.

The little boy eyed me warily. After a pause while we both looked at each other, he volunteered, "Can't tell you."

My eyes had adjusted to the gloom by then. I could see that the child was wearing shorts and a pullover, the sort of clothing children wear to infant school, but very ragged. He had bare feet. *A beggar's child*, I thought, and was surprised when a feeling of sadness washed over me. Instinctively I thought, *Poor little chap!* when I should have thought, *How feckless of the parents!*

"Are you hurt?" I asked. "They threw an apple core at you."

"Yes!" The child sounded almost gleeful. "I eated it!"

"The apple core?" I asked, not quite believing my ears. "You ate the apple core?"

"Yes!" The child grinned for the first time. "I like apples!"

"Right." What else could I say? "Me too."

I shifted my position. It was uncomfortable squatting like that, and the ground was too dirty to sit down. When I moved, the child raised one arm to protect his face. *He's used to being hit,* I thought.

"Do you have somewhere to go tonight?" I asked.

"Go with my mum," the little boy answered.

"Okay. Good." I was sure there was no point in asking more. This little one was already well trained in not answering questions. I was sure I ought to do something about him. But what? If I handed him over to the police, what would happen to him? Homes for vagrant children were funded by the tax payer, and nobody likes to pay taxes to support other people's children, or so we are told. The homes are reputed to be large and rough, with everything done on the cheap. This child had a mother. At least, I hoped, he was loved.

I was wearing leisure clothes, an expensive waterproof jacket and my favourite jersey-knit jumper. I took off the jacket and passed it to the little boy. "Here," I said, "this should keep you dry until your mummy collects you." I held it out to the child.

He looked at me suspiciously. He did not reach out to take it. "My mummy says I shouldn't take things from strangers," he announced. Then he added, "Strangers steal little children." He curled up more tightly in a ball in the bushes. "Are you a stranger?" he asked.

I stood up. "Your mummy is quite right," I said. "Indeed, you should not take things from strangers. And I am a stranger. Everyone you do not know, and who your mummy does not know, is a stranger." I took the jacket off. "But if a stranger just leaves something lying around, if he gets into his car and drives away, and leaves his jacket on the ground, then you can have it, can't you?"

The little boy seemed to think carefully. Then, "If stuff is just lying around we can have it," he confirmed.

"Good," I said. I placed my jacket on the bushes next to the child and left, walking the little path back towards my car without using the light from my DeV. I climbed into the car, tooted the horn and drove away.

I bought my ingredients from a different shop that afternoon, and late in the evening I took a couple of plastic fridge dishes back to the spot where I had found the child. There was nobody there, just litter, broken bricks and mud. My jacket had gone. I left the food where I had found the boy, and went home to the comfort of my cosy flat.

★ ★ ★

I slept that night, but my sleep was full of dreams. I knew that Alice would be in Stanley by now, and that she would be visiting Simon. My dreams were a tangle of threads. I was making love to Alice, feeling a sense of great relief that she was safe, then suddenly Alice had turned into Maria. A group of barefooted children were standing outside my window wailing with grief. Maria was in my bed next to me, her back to me, her shoulders hunched, and she too was weeping. Alice was knocking at my door, wanting to come in, and I dared not let her in because Maria was in my bed. Simon was being put to death, but by hanging, not by lethal injection. Then Simon turned into Alice. She was hanging there, with her neck broken, and the children were standing with me, watching the last jerks and twitches of her body, and still they were crying.

I woke sometime in the dark, early hours. My face was wet and I realised I must have been crying in my sleep. Outside in the wild patch of trees and brambles behind my flat, cats were mating, wailing their ecstasy into the night air. I put on my dressing gown and wandered into the living room. From my kitchen window, which looks out over the car park for the flats, I watched a taxi pull up and a couple get out. They said something to the taxi driver, laughed, and made their way to one of the larger apartments out of my sight. The taxi drove away and the night was pitch black.

I had not turned on any lights myself. I sat on my comfortable settee with my hands behind my head, thinking. My head felt very clear. I could almost feel the tangle of my dreams unravelling.

I realised that there was truth in those dreams, perhaps more truth than I had really acknowledged to myself before. Yes, I felt guilty about leading Maria on, but only now did I truly appreciate that sooner or later my actions would leave her lying, hunched over in her bed, weeping. And over the course of my career, how many other people had I used and abandoned? I had said to myself that I loved Alice, indeed, I really did love Alice, but I had not been honest with her. Nor had I been honest with myself. I was a dangerous person to be involved with. As I sat there it was crystal clear to me that she was in real danger, and that it was me who had brought that danger to her. Meadows only wanted to pursue Alice because she knew, or at least suspected, that I loved her. The truth was that when I first met Alice and felt that attraction to her, I should have walked away. And if I had not walked away then, I should have walked away later, when Lady Grace had told me to marry Alice or leave her. I had made excuses for my behaviour. I could not marry her, but I could not leave her either.

A new, uncomfortable thought occurred to me. If I had walked away, if I had genuinely broken all ties, instead of playing this *'let us just be friends'* game, then might not Alice have met someone else by now? She could have been settled happily with a man from her community, living a little on the edge of what was considered acceptable, feeding homeless people, signing petitions, working in the charity shop, feeling indignant about the actions of our government, but basically safe.

It was when I realised how many of Alice's problems lay squarely at my door, that I realised I needed to do something much more risky to save her. I had to break off all contact with her, or at least, I had to appear to do so. A plan gradually evolved in my mind, a plan based on the realisation that I had never had any right to be involved with Alice. The plan made me feel sick. I hated myself for what I was thinking of doing. But the more I thought about it, the more I felt sure that this was what I needed to do.

As for myself... Well, that night I finally understood what Will had been saying to me as we had sat in the church. There is a huge difference between doing something out of a commitment to good citizenship, and out of love. The previous evening, when I had left my jacket for that little boy, and later when I had taken the fridge dishes of sweet and sour chicken and rice back to the same spot, I had at last acted out of love. I wondered, as I sat in the dark, whether this was the first time since my recruitment that I had really been motivated by such a genuine human emotion. I hoped that what I was planning to do the next day would also be motivated by love. Yet I was new to this sort of thing, new and inexperienced, and the situation was complicated.

CHAPTER 11

The following morning I phoned Meadows promptly at 9.00 am. She was not yet in her office, but her new secretary was there, a good-looking young man who was, I believe, serving an internship before going on to accelerated police training, and who did not know me. I asked if it were possible to make an appointment to see Police Commissioner Meadows. I did not say who I was because it was important I did nothing that looked like pulling rank. The receptionist paused, I guessed he was scrolling down through Meadows' diary, then he answered, "Commissioner Meadows is free to see citizens at 10.30 am, for half an hour. May I tell her who wants to see her?"

"Karl Wyss," I answered. "Spelt W, Y, S, S. It's a Swiss name."

Briefly I heard my name being typed. "All right, Mr Wyss," said the receptionist. "You will need to bring some sort of identification, and since you are Swiss that will have to include some proof of your right to reside in England. Be on time. The commissioner is a busy person, and you are lucky to get an appointment so soon."

"Thank you," I answered humbly. I showered, put on my uniform, drank some more coffee, and then set off for Meadows' office.

★ ★ ★

The new receptionist had not recognised my name, but of course Meadows did, and my mode of making the appointment must have put her on her metal. She had also warned her handsome receptionist, who stood to attention when I came in, and held out his hand to shake mine.

"Commander Wyss," he said. "It's a pleasure to meet you, sir. I've heard a lot about you."

I shook his hand warmly. "Thank you," I replied.

The young man walked over to the door to Meadows' office, knocked and opened it at once. "Commander Wyss," he announced and ushered me in, closing the door quietly behind me.

Meadows was sitting behind her desk, as usual. A waft of perfume met my nostrils as she stood to shake my hand, and I realised her hair was freshly styled. No doubt that was the reason she had been late to the office that morning. She was wearing a smart trouser and waistcoat suit, and there was a lapel badge on the waistcoat with the new symbol of US and English unity, a small flag of St. George imposed upon the stars and stripes, almost as if we were another state in the Union.

"Do sit down, Commander," she said with mock graciousness, and sat herself.

"Perhaps," I said, "given the new relationship that exists between our two organisations, we might use first names? As you know, my name is Karl."

"Ah, Karl… thank you," said Meadows, but she did not offer to let me use her name. What was it? Cynthia, I thought. "Yes, our relationship has changed quite significantly, hasn't it?"

"It has." I fidgeted a little, knowing that I was giving the impression that I felt awkward. I was hoping that my email messages to Lady Grace had already been intercepted and the content passed on to Meadows. If that were so she would already believe that the political changes at the top of our

154

organisations had wrong-footed me, and that she now had the upper hand. "I realise," I said, then hesitated, making it seem as if it was hard to go on. "I realise," I started again, "that we will need to work more closely than we have done in the past."

"Indeed!" Meadows was almost gloating. "I look forward to working with you," she lied.

"Yes." I paused again, then swallowed. What I was planning was a really difficult thing to do. "So, I've come here to suggest that I agree with you, that we might need to share our intelligence from now on."

Meadows was a proud and rather silly woman, but even she was not conceited enough to believe I would come to heel this easily. "And what would the ATTF gain from such openness?" she queried.

I fidgeted again, crossing and uncrossing my legs, and looking over Meadows' shoulder out of the window. Finally, I said, "Perhaps nothing." Then I looked her directly in the eye and added, "Job security?"

For a moment Meadows' expression remained guarded, then slowly a smile dawned on her face. "Ah, yes, I see. *Your* job security."

It was deeply embarrassing. I coughed. "Well, yes," I agreed. Then I looked up, trying to appear a little more confident. "And the security of all my operatives."

Meadows' smile was even broader now. "Oh, I don't think we need to worry about your operatives," she said. "There is no suggestion of closing down the ATTF, and to be honest there are one or two of your operatives to whom I would happily offer a job tomorrow." She paused, no doubt for effect, and I am sure I looked worried. "But you are right to be concerned about your own job. I have not found you an easy man to work with, and if Lord Peters were to ask me, I would certainly have to tell him the truth."

I looked at my feet. "Quite," I agreed, humbly.

Now Meadows was on a roll. "Karl," she said, "if I am to take seriously your wish to cooperate with the police more closely, I will need some sort of token of your commitment."

I had expected this. Indeed, looking at it from Meadows' point of view it was not unreasonable. I hated the way the tide had turned. "Like what?" I almost stuttered.

Meadows sat back, the victor of a long standing and unspoken war. "I would like you to give me all the intel – *all* the intel, you have on Alice Owen. If you do that, I think I will be prepared to tell Lord Peters that there are no difficulties in us working together. Otherwise…"

I had known she would ask this of me. Meadows was out to humiliate me, to kick me now that I was down. I had made the appointment to see her perfectly aware of the cost, but that did not mean I liked it. "Ms. Owens?" I said, sounding unhappy. "We don't have much on her, but we've done a lot of research into the issues around homelessness…"

"I'm sure you have," agreed Meadows, looking very self-satisfied, "And any details you have will certainly come in useful. We are planning a big crackdown – a *big* crackdown. But – let us put our cards on the table, Karl…" I hated her use of my first name like this. It made me want to reach across the desk and slap her conceited, gloating face. "The thing is Karl, we don't need your help there, or with the religious minorities. But we do need your help with Alice Owen. And," she added gleefully, "intel on Ms Owen would serve as – let us say – a token of your goodwill. A little sacrifice, we might say, to demonstrate which side you are on."

There was a long pause. I could think of lots of cutting replies. In my head, I was calling the woman every foul name I had heard in the mouths of villains over the years. Yet I steeled myself, bit my tongue, and looked down at my polished shoes. Finally, "Right," I said, hearing the reluctance I could not keep out of that one word. "Right, Commissioner, I can do that."

She smirked. "Good," she said. "I will expect you here this time tomorrow. And what I say to Lord Peters depends upon what you bring me."

★ ★ ★

Back at my flat, still officially on leave, I thought carefully about what I needed to do. The truth was that we really did not have very much concrete evidence that would count against Alice in a court of law. She was a member of a left-leaning religious minority, but in theory at least we believed in freedom of religion. She had been writing to a prisoner on death row, but the organisation through which she had originally contacted him was not yet a banned organisation. It was true that our cousins across the Atlantic viewed all such volunteer groups as suspect, but here at home it was generally believed that prisoners with contacts outside the penal system were less likely to be troublesome than those who were completely isolated. In taking on this pen-friendship Alice had done nothing to raise the eyebrows of our sheltered and well-meaning, liberal, middle class. The same could be said about the school in the park. There had been enough correspondence in the local papers to indicate that public opinion was not yet convinced that the 'tough choices' made by government when it came to homelessness were fully supported by the more affluent and better educated public.

None of that, of course, needed to be a problem for Meadows and her cronies, with the new influence Lord Peters had given them. There was no question of Alice appearing in a court of law, with a jury and lawyers to hand prosecuting and defending. If those with the authority deemed Alice to be a threat, she would either meet with a very unfortunate accident, be found to have drugs or weapons in her flat, or perhaps go away on holiday and never return. Extraordinary rendition had been carried out by the United States since 1987, if not before, and despite political cover-ups and at least one British judicial enquiry which never got off the ground, before the New Alliance was made, it had continued ever since.

My job, therefore, was not to try to show, by the intelligence I was to pass over the next day, that Alice was innocent. The truth was, she *was* innocent in the sight of the law of the land. My job was rather different. My only hope was to demonstrate that any good that might be achieved by removing Alice from the scene would be outweighed by the harm done among her family and friends by her disappearance. Martyrdom can be very effective in marshalling enemies. It was much better for people like Amy and the religious friends Alice mixed with, to think that our rule was basically fair and well-intentioned, than that they should view us with suspicion or even hatred.

I had found my interview with Meadows incredibly difficult. The woman made me very angry and I hated even giving the appearance of having to submit to the changing regime which made her, to all intents and purposes, my boss. When I got back to the flat I changed out of my uniform into jogging gear, and ran a couple of laps round the park.

Usually that is enough to clear my head, but when I unlocked the encryption on my DeV ready to start examining the documents I would pass to Meadows the next day, I found that my heart was still beating hard and my fingers on the keyboard were clumsy. I locked the device again, and stared out of the window. How was I to calm myself? I knew that if I did not have a peaceful mind, with all extraneous thoughts eliminated, I would make some sort of error. I needed to be a hundred percent focused, but instead I found that my thoughts were jumping from one subject to another. What was Alice doing now? Had I fooled Meadows? Where was the little boy who was now wearing my jacket? *Was* he wearing my jacket, or would it already have been taken from him by someone bigger and stronger? Where had the child's mother been, while he hid in the bushes? What was life like for people like that? Would Alice survive my present actions? Would she ever forgive me?

I stared out of the window at my glorious patch of wild land. A flash of something caught my eye, and I stood up from the table and walked across to the window. It was only January, but already some sort of fine, white blossom had appeared on a bush at the edge of the wilderness area. I watched carefully, staying still, almost holding my breath. Yes, there it was again, a tiny, brown and red bird with a flash of white on its collar. I was suddenly mesmerised. I had heard on some DeV documentary that hummingbirds had arrived on our islands, perhaps blown over in one of the huge storms that signalled climate change in the 2010s. It was tiny, and it was busy, engrossed in sipping nectar from the blossom. It seemed like a miracle.

And it made me think. Humming birds do not belong in Europe. They are New World birds, adapted to suit the flora of very different continents from ours. This bird or his ancestors had almost certainly not come here by choice. Yet that tiny creature was alive. It was making a life for itself. Perhaps somewhere in my patch of overgrown land it would build a nest. Next year there might be more. There could come a time when humming birds were a common sight on our islands.

The bird moved from blossom to blossom, and I was absorbed. And then, gradually, it was as if a sort of understanding crept over me. I was not exactly thinking, and I was certainly not hearing a voice, but a sort of comprehension opened up to me, like a map without lines or colours, but clear and full of direction. I was like a humming bird, blown off course. I was in new territory, or anyhow I had left the old. There had been a time when I had been a respected ATTF officer, a man with a clear vision of how he wanted his world to look, and of his role in bringing that to pass. Somehow, without deciding it should be so, I had left my predicted course. I had sent false emails. I was keeping secrets from Pearson. I was setting out to manipulate information in order to fool Meadows, and the whole hierarchy to whom I owed my loyalty. I had failed to bring in a vagrant child. More, I had colluded to keep that child out of the hands of officialdom.

Had I been blown off course, like the hummingbird? A quiet thread of something in my heart said that yes, I had, but that I still had a future. I was not even sure I had reached my new territory. I was not like the humming bird, drinking nectar at my leisure, mating, building a nest. Was I, perhaps, still in the storm which would blow me to a new place?

With those thoughts came a calm stillness inside me. The little humming bird could not fight the storm that had brought it here, and I saw that I could not fight the situation I was in. The best tactic was probably to ride the storm, to spread out my wings and to allow the winds, the unpredictable, ferocious winds, to take me to my new home.

And one way to ride the storm was to give Meadows the intelligence she wanted on Alice. My Alice, whom I loved.

I sat back at the table, unlocked the encryption again, called up all of Alice's earlier journal entries from the time when she still wrote online, her letters to Simon, and even her online appointment diary from her teaching days, and started to work. My heart beat steadily, slowly. My concentration was complete. With my wings outstretched I was riding the wind of political intrigue and uncertainty. My head was clear. It was out of my hands now.

I worked solidly for eighteen hours, barely stopping for more coffee or to turn on the lights. I passed it all to Meadows the next day. The sense of having direction had faded, but it had not died. Meadows' gloating and preening no longer bothered me. I felt sure I had done my best, but I did not know where it might all lead. It no longer felt like my responsibility. I was like an outsider, looking in, not involved. I went home and slept a long, peaceful sleep in my comfortable bed, in my safe home.

CHAPTER 12

I had intended to take Tuesday off too, and to drive down to my patch of Wiltshire on Wednesday, to talk to Police Commissioner Fox about the forthcoming regime changes. Fox was, of course, the least of my problems. He had always cooperated with the ATTF and the good relations between us and the police in that county meant that, for as long as Fox remained in post, very little was likely to change. Nevertheless, I had always made it my practice to keep on good terms with the police if I could.

Simon was due to be executed on Wednesday. I thought that Alice was expecting to visit him on Monday and Tuesday, and I caught myself thinking, as I showered, how hard it must be to visit someone who was about to be put to death. What would they talk about? I felt the old, familiar urge to protect Alice. I found myself thinking *I should be there!* and then I remembered. Alice must be nothing to me from now onwards. I was not her friend. Perhaps, unwittingly, I had been her enemy all along.

Yet Alice must not know that. I was playing a complicated game. For the moment, at least, she must see no changes in our friendship.

I dressed in joggers ready to go to the gym, and tried to think what the old Karl would do – the Karl I still believed I was when Alice had headed off to the States. I opened my DeV and my hand hovered over the keys for a while, but I seemed unable to type anything. Then my work DeV started to bleep and I hurriedly messaged *'thinking of you'* to Alice, and pressed *send*.

Pearson was on the line, sounding cheerful. "Morning boss!" he said. "Enjoying your time off?"

He sounded so normal. He knew nothing about the turmoil in my life, about the storm I was riding. Nor should he.

I did not really want to say *yes* or *no* so instead I said, "You just caught me. I'm about to go to the gym."

Pearson chuckled. "You're not, you know!"

"I'm not?"

"You obviously haven't checked your emails in the last five minutes," Pearson chuckled. What did he have to be so happy about?

"Tell me," I asked.

"We're summonsed to London," he told me. "It seems there was a big fuss when ATTF officers didn't receive Lord Peters' first email, so this time he's been a little more careful. We *have* received the summons, but only half a day in advance. We are all to be at a formal dinner at the A & F this evening, for drinks at seven."

"Goodness!" The Alliance and Fraternity was a very plush hotel close to Hyde Park, and was generally frequented by diplomats, royalty and anonymous owners of global conglomerates.

"Yes, and then we are to be in conference all day tomorrow."

While Pearson was talking, I was scrolling through my emails. Sure enough, there it was, not an invitation but, as Pearson had said, a summons.

"He's trying to catch us out," I said. "He doesn't want the ATTF to be well represented."

Pearson chuckled again. "We will be, though," he said. "Your friend in East Anglia has been messaging everyone. There'll be a full contingent."

I laughed then, as well. "Good old Reggie," I said. Then, "This email is addressed to all police commissioners too."

"Yes," Pearson agreed. "And here's an interesting thing, boss. Josie told me at the weekend that she was going up to London with Meadows. She didn't know much about it then, but obviously, the police have had more warning."

"Well…" I was thinking on my feet. "What is Lord Peters up to?" I wondered.

"Divide and conquer?" suggested Pearson. Then, "Boss, can I come too?"

I looked at the email again. The invitation was vague, addressed to area commanders, police commissioners and *'those members of staff deemed useful'*. "Meadows has taken Josie," Pearson reminded me.

I laughed again. I had no illusions about Pearson's desire to be at this meeting, it would certainly be unpleasant for all the ATTF staff, but he definitely wanted to be with Josephine. "Of course, Pearson!" I said, "Be my guest! Or anyhow, be Lord Peters' guest!"

"Thanks boss." So now I knew why he had sounded so cheerful. When you are in love even attending boring or demeaning meetings can take on a rosy hue. "I was planning to drive up. Shall we have lunch on the way? I can pick you up at twelve."

★ ★ ★

It was actually a relief to be in the car with Pearson. Everything seemed suddenly so normal. It was not that I put my subterfuge out of my mind, just that it all seemed unreal. Pearson has a tendency to play American country and western music on his car DeV, and although it is sometimes rather predictable, there is something homely and normal about the songs. We drove up through winter drizzle to the sounds of women singing soulfully about the men who had let them down and to men singing emotionally about protecting the ones they loved.

We checked in at about three in the afternoon. The summons had been so last-minute that I wondered how the hotel would manage the room allocations, but it seemed the Ministry of Internal Security had commandeered the whole place. The lobby was full of uniformed men and a small number of uniformed women. Staff were pushing piles of expensive leather luggage around on beautiful, brass handled luggage trolleys, and public-school voices greeted each other exuberantly. I was given a small suite on the second floor, and Pearson told the receptionist that he would stay with his fiancée. Fiancée, indeed! It was the first I knew of it, but I was glad.

The majority of uniforms were navy, indicating police, and I noticed that Lord Peters, who was holding court in the lounge, was also dressed in navy despite his promotion to the ATTF, the medals he had earned glinting on his jacket. There are, of course, more police commissioners than there are ATTF area commanders, and for the first time I wondered whether that might be a problem for us. While I waited for the lift I looked around. Security was tight. I could see at least eight officers, dressed as hotel staff, and I was sure there were more I had not spotted. I thought, *tonight would be a good time to begin an insurgency,* and then I smiled to myself. Had I really moved so far that such a thought might cross my mind?

"What's the joke?" asked a familiar voice to my right. I turned, and there was Reggie, wearing more medals on his smart dress uniform than I might have imagined, and carrying his own holdall. "It's good to see you, Karl."

We shook hands, then entered the lift and told the man our floors. "Second," I said. "Four," said Reggie. A couple of smartly dressed Lower Ranks came in after us, two young, blonde women carrying navy, police issue DeVs. *Secretaries,* I thought. "Penthouse," said one of the women and the lift attendant touched his hat and pressed another button.

As the doors for my floor were opening Reggie said, "Fancy

a walk in the park when you've settled in?" and we agreed to meet in the lobby in half an hour.

★ ★ ★

The ATTF has always treated its officers well and my suite, though no doubt small compared to the penthouse, was very luxurious. The screen on the DeV in the living room greeted me with *'Welcome, Commander Wyss'* and instructed me to scroll down for details of the conference. The fridge was well stocked with whisky (Scottish whisky!) and a variety of other more or less exotic drinks, along with bottles of water. The thick towels, the bathrobe and the linen cloth covering the coffee tray were all that elegant taupe colour which is the trademark of this chain of hotels, and the same colour was picked up on the bedding, the carpet and the curtains. They were very elegant rooms.

I hung up my clean shirts and unpacked everything else. Normally when I enter a hotel room I search it for bugs as soon as I am unpacked, but I was sure there was no point here. I was certain that all the delegates were under surveillance, but I doubted very much whether I would find all the devices. In fact, I imagined that some little gadgets were cunningly built in to the very fabric of the building. I sent a message to Pearson telling him I would see him in the Bush Suite for drinks at seven. He did not reply, and I guessed he was with Josephine. *Young love!* I thought as I donned my overcoat and checked my wallet for my keycard.

The A & F was between the United States Embassy and Hyde Park, just a stone's throw from Selfridge's. It was a few minutes' walk, along the busy street and crossing a road humming with electric buses and taxis, before we were in the park. We strolled along small roads and footpaths towards a more wooded area, at first hardly speaking at all. Reggie had brought an umbrella, and was swinging it as he walked. I felt my personal DeV buzz in my pocket. I switched it off, then wrapped it in my handkerchief to muffle any sound in case someone was listening in.

There were people around – a couple of joggers and a small group of young Americans on bikes. From one of the north-eastern states, I guessed from their accents. Walking along without speaking was companionable and I could feel myself relaxing.

"We're living in interesting times," commented Reggie.

"Indeed," I agreed. "Is Xavier here?"

"Ah yes!" Reggie smiled. "Our venerable police commissioner is at this moment being debriefed by Lord Peters. And afterwards," he chuckled, "he will tell me all about it!"

"You are lucky," I said. Then I thought a little more and added, "Or maybe you've played your cards well."

"No," Reggie said. "No, I can't take any credit for my good fortune. I'm lucky. Xavier is one in a million."

I paused, then, "What do you think this conference is all about?"

Reggie looked thoughtful, and swung his umbrella around in some dead leaves. It was already dusk, and the park looked gloomy in shades of winter green, brown and grey. The occasional solar lamps were dim. There had not been enough sunlight recently to charge them.

"I think," said Reggie, "that this conference is all about demonstrating how the new regime will work."

"Yes, I thought that," I agreed. "Lord Peters is still wearing his police uniform. Lady Grace would have worn formal ATTF garb for an event like this."

"We miss her," said Reggie, no doubt referring to his wife Rosie and himself. "Rosie would like us to move to Canada too."

"The last bastion of civilisation," I said. I was repeating a comment supposedly made by the Canadian prime minister when England and Wales signed the Alliance deal.

"You know as much as me," said Reggie. "The police have always disliked the fact that we were given such power."

"Not Xavier," I pointed out.

"No, and he's not alone." Reggie swung his umbrella in a circle in the air. "I think," he said, "right from the start, before we left the EU–"

"In the good old days," I butted in, smiling.

"Yes! Formally known as *'these trying times!'* Well, back then some of the first elected police commissioners were in it for power and prestige, and to promote their right-wing agendas, and others were in it to serve the people."

"Just like politicians," I said.

"Yes, and just like us!" We were both quiet, then Reggie added, "You know that the Yorkshire area commander, Folkes or Freerson or whatever his name is…"

"Freeman," I interrupted.

"Yes, that's the chap! Freeman has gone on record as saying that the ATTF is an undemocratic organisation and that he's glad that power is being restored to the proper, elected bodies. It was the headline on the one o'clock news today."

"So, what happens to us?" I asked.

Reggie grunted. "Your guess is as good as mine," he said. "But I can't see them getting rid of us, can you?"

A similar power struggle had occurred in the US some years earlier. A president had been elected, one of the first of a stream of men and women who had connected with the popular, uninformed vote of an increasingly illiberal and poorly educated electorate, who had tapped into a prejudice against all federal institutions, in favour of homegrown state and county bodies. Over a period of just a few years, being a federal employee became as unpopular as being a Native American or a woolly liberal to the conservative right.

168

Nevertheless, the Federal Bureau of Investigations, the FBI, continued to operate and was often our first port of call when we, in the ATTF, found ourselves dealing with situations which extended beyond our borders. The CIA was as active as ever, too. Despite their stated commitment to democracy and local accountability, White House staff were never able to manage without their skilled and secret investigators.

I was thinking about the situation across the Atlantic. "I think we'll become the fall guys," I said. "The ones to be blamed when unpleasant facts come to light."

"Yes, Xavier and I think that, too."

We were walking in a small copse made up mostly of deciduous trees, their branches bare and skeletal-like against the light-polluted night sky. A helicopter flew low overhead, the noise of the rotor blades and the engine loud in the relative peace of the park. It shone a spotlight down onto the park, just to the north of us, and then hovered somewhere over towards Oxford Square, it's beam steady on its target. For a minute or two as it passed, our shadows were clear and long under the trees, and then the darkness seemed quite black until our eyes readjusted.

Reggie said, "The game has changed entirely, you know."

"Yes."

We turned and started to walk back.

"My aims haven't changed," Reggie added quietly, thoughtfully. "I joined the ATTF to make my country more secure. You know, Karl, I really believed in it all."

"Me too," I said, sadly. Then, "Do you think you will go to Canada?"

Reggie was quiet. The helicopter moved away, further north. We could hear the gentle hum of electric vehicles in the distance.

"I think," he said, "that I'll stay as long as I can. While there are things to be done. What about you?"

169

"My life is complicated," I said.

"I guessed as much."

"But maybe I'll do the same," I agreed. "I'll stay as long as there are things to be done, and then I'll retire."

"Well..." We were approaching the brighter lights of the street. "You know, you always have friends in the east," he said. "Rosie and me, and I think Xavier too. Don't forget us."

"Thank you." We stood at a pedestrian crossing, waiting for our light to turn green. Reggie turned to me, looking earnest. "Seriously," he said. "We are all going to need friends. Maybe especially you."

★ ★ ★

In the lobby, there was a lot of noise and laughter. I saw at once that Pearson and Josephine were in the centre of an excited group which included a beaming and slightly flushed Lord Peters and an obviously happy Meadows, looking a little uncomfortable in the formal police commissioner's dress uniform which she so rarely wore. Pearson saw me as soon as we entered, and raised a hand in happy greeting.

I went over to the group. Josephine was holding out her right hand to the two pretty clerical officers we had seen earlier, showing off a shiny, new engagement ring.

I patted Pearson on the shoulder. "Well done!" I said. "You're a lucky man!"

"Ah!" said Lord Peters, spotting me. I was sure we had never met, but he obviously knew who I was. "Commander Wyss! A happy occasion, this! An omen of times to come, I am sure! An ATTF officer engaged to a civil servant working for the police! It could not be better! We must have the press here!" He looked around, saw another commissioner, called out, "Joseph! You always have a camera with you! Come here! We need photographs! Come on then, let's make a group.

170

Commander Wyss, why don't you stand behind the young woman, and... Meadows, you are her commissioner, aren't you? You stand behind this handsome young ATTF officer! Good! Perfect! Now, let's make sure that's in all the papers tomorrow." Then, turning to one of the pretty young police officers, "Kowalski, you can manage the social media side, can't you? I want something upbeat. Now, let's toast the happy couple! Come on, everyone! Drinks in the Bush Suite!"

Reggie, I noticed, had stayed on the edge of the circle. Of course, he knew Josephine, it was he who had recommended her to go undercover in Meadows' department. He came alongside me as we filed into the bar where once, when this hotel had been under different management, a much earlier United States president was supposed to have had a glass of orange juice.

"That's interesting," he commented. "Did you know anything about it?"

I smiled reassuringly at him. "I did," I said. "And from my point of view it could not be better." Then, in case we were overheard by somebody, or by something electronic, I added, "It's always a good thing to have happy and settled staff."

"Absolutely," agreed Reggie, and went off to talk to Xavier and a tall, angular woman I did not know.

★ ★ ★

The next twenty-four hours were tedious. I caught up with Francis Fox, my Wiltshire police commissioner, over a fried breakfast. He ate surprisingly delicately for such a large man, dabbing his mouth with his elegant taupe napkin between mouthfuls, and sipping the excellent coffee like a real connoisseur. We talked about local business, and I asked him how he had enjoyed the speeches after dinner the night before. "A lot of politics!" he grumbled. "Won't affect us at all!

171

Waste of time, this whole thing!" Then he sipped his coffee again. "Nice to have a touch of luxury, though. The wife never makes me a breakfast like this!"

We sat through talks and DeV shows about integrated policing and about the profiling of terrorists. There was a whole session after lunch, when we were at our most sleepy, on the subject of the radicalisation of the feckless. It seemed that recent research at the new American University of the Pennines had shown that those they cheerfully and unselfconsciously called 'the underclass' were more prone to 'subversive activities' than those with housing and work. I thought this was so glaringly obvious that I could not imagine who might make grants to students to discover such things. We broke into groups to discuss the implications for policing. We were instructed to work in 'area groups' so my circle consisted of Pearson and the three police commissioners: Meadows, MacCormack and Fox, with Josephine taking notes on her DeV.

MacCormack, the only one among us with any left-wing credentials, started at once with his suggestion. "What we need to do," he said, "is provide housing and work – and if there is no work, we need to provide benefits. No underclass," he announced, "means no subversive activities! It's that easy!"

"Nonsense!" Meadows was full of indignation. "That's all been tried! Look at Britain at the end of the twentieth century! Ridiculous levels of benefit, and an underclass to rival India!"

Fox was calmer. "I think, dear Police Commissioner Meadows, that you may be a trifle misinformed about our social history. I don't believe our benefit system was quite as generous as you seem to think, and the big fear about subversive activities was mostly to do with religious groups."

Meadows went pink. I do not think she was a particularly well-educated woman, and she could not refute Fox's mild admonition. She probably got her information from right-wing campaign leaflets.

Pearson bravely added to the conversation. I seemed to be one of the few area commanders to have brought anyone with me, but there seemed to be no problem with him attending every session. He sat, of course, with Josephine. "Is there any chance of re-introducing benefits?" he asked.

"Not a chance!" grumbled MacCormack. "Tax payers won't stand for it."

Meadows agreed. "And why should they?" she asked.

"Then," persisted Pearson, "perhaps we need to accept that these people, the people the researchers called *'the underclass'*, exist, and consider how we are going to deal with them?"

"Exactly!" beamed Meadows. "My thoughts entirely." Then, with a sideways glance at me, "In Hampshire we are already very proactive on this matter. Commander Wyss has been very helpful in providing my office with intel, and I am happy to say that by the end of this week we will have taken strong action – *very* strong action, to start clamping down!"

Josephine looked at me sharply, surprise flashing from her eyes. I felt, rather than saw, Pearson stiffen. Of course it was news to him that I had provided information to Meadows. I had kept him out of the loop. He would not know what to make of it. Meadows looked triumphant.

I noticed that Pearson and Josephine stayed away from me over afternoon tea. They were both good people, and they suspected that I had let them down. I did not feel I could go over and speak to them. It would not help. I could not explain. They must never know how much I had doctored the documents I had passed on and how careful I had been to protect as many people as I could. Perhaps one day, in the light of the way things developed, they might guess at what I had really done, but perhaps they would not. Maybe my apparent betrayal would be one of those sadnesses they would never quite understand. And it was not good for them to be seen to be too friendly with me anymore.

I stood alone drinking my Earl Grey. Deep guffaws came from a table by the window, the smart young secretaries were talking to each other and laughing, and Lord Peters was surrounded by an admiring group of police officers. This had been my world for most of my adult life, but it did not seem like my world anymore.

CHAPTER 13

I made an excuse to Pearson and Josephine so that they could drive back to Hampshire together, and instead I went down by train. ATTF officers always travel first class, and I sat in a half-empty carriage listening to a couple of Americans discussing baseball and English girls, whom, it seems, they found feisty. I walked across the park to my flat feeling desperately lonely. It was, I knew, absolutely necessary that everyone, not just Meadows and her cronies, but Pearson and Josephine too, should think that I had capitulated to the new regime, but I felt as if I had betrayed them, even while I believed that I was trying to act in their best interests. Those two days at the elegant *Alliance and Fraternity* seemed to have brought into focus the world that I now inhabited. I had stood, drinking my Earl Grey tea and watching all those smartly uniformed people, and a scene from a film I had watched in my youth had come into my head. It had been about a German businessman who had, by devious means, saved the lives of many Jewish people during World War Two. We had been shown the film at school, and I remember at the time being shocked because the actors were all English speaking, but those playing German officers spoke in accents not unlike those of my Swiss family. Standing in the lobby, though, it was a scene that I think must have come early in the story, a scene in a restaurant with uniformed men eating and drinking, that came suddenly, vividly into my head. Those jack-booted officers were the master race, confident and in control. We were English and we did not wear jack boots, but I suddenly felt as if there the differences between us ended.

I let myself into my flat, turned up the heating, and changed into casual clothes. I poured myself a whisky and stood looking out into the darkness of the late afternoon, seeing only the slight movement of trees and my reflection in the glass. The weather had turned bitterly cold, unusual for Hampshire nowadays, and I started to think about the humming bird I had watched, only a couple of days earlier, sipping nectar from the early blossoming shrubs. Would the little bird survive the storm which every news broadcast was predicting? If it had a mate, would the mate survive? And would I survive the storm that was certainly blowing towards me on the harsh political currents of the day? Would Alice?

I think that that was the moment when, at last, like the humming bird, I found my new home. I knew I could no longer ally myself with the law-enforcement communities of my country. I could no longer believe that what they were doing was good for ordinary people, going about their ordinary lives. I had been committed to creating a stable, healthy country but instead my well-meaning activities, my whole career, had contributed to the establishment of some sort of repressive regime, almost a fascist state.

Of course, I had been moving away from the accepted ideology of the ATTF for months, years maybe. But as I stood looking out into the dark, I became clear about where I had landed. Will had been right, that morning when we were sitting in the church and he had contrasted our different motives for acting. I had been motivated by a vision of good citizenship, Will by the desire to love. And now, I understood at last, I had changed. From this point onwards, I realised, I wanted to be motivated by love too.

I drew the curtains and sat in my favourite armchair, my legs stretched out in front of me, the warmth of my flat seeping into my chilled bones, and I thought about Alice. Simon had been executed yesterday. If everything had gone according to plan, she would have witnessed it. She would have done this, this brave and noble thing, out of love. Where did she get her strength? How could an ordinary woman, a person without all those years of training that I had received, cope with such a situation?

And I knew the answer. She gained her strength from something as alien to me as the life of that little boy who was still, I hoped, wearing my jacket. Alice gained her strength by this thing she did, this thing all her community practised, of sitting in silence, of holding people and situations in the Light.

I don't know why, but it seemed good to me to try it in darkness. I had a candle, red with a pattern of green holly leaves, which I had only partly burned on Christmas Day. I lit it, and placed it on my coffee table, and then I turned off the lights. I sat looking at the little, flickering light in the darkness. I heard the quiet hum of my fridge, the gentle sound of a Bach choral coming from the flat upstairs, and the noise of wind in the trees. Who or what was the Light I was trying to approach? I did not know, but I knew that my life was no longer under my control, if, indeed, it ever had been. If there was a Light, a source of love, then I needed it. And if there was no such thing, it did not matter, because I recognised that I had nothing left to lose.

I remembered the people in that little church, the 'harmless mystics' led by Friend Madge. They closed their eyes, the child with the ponytail had lifted her face as if the Light were a real thing, shining down from somewhere in the roof. I closed my eyes too. Gradually, as I pictured the Light, the disgust I had been feeling with myself started to drain away. Even my concern for Alice seemed softer, less urgent. I was not really thinking, but nor was my mind empty. I felt fully conscious and, at last, at peace.

And then a picture started to form, not a visual image but a series of impressions, a feeling of being gently pushed in one direction, of a window opening, of a path being made clear. A vision came, softly creeping in the silence, of a life that could be spent in the Light. I did not understand it. I did not need to. I felt as if I had been given a gift. Like that little humming bird, I had tasted the first sip of nectar from my new home.

★ ★ ★

I had told Alice I would collect her from Heathrow on Saturday. She was due to fly in overnight, and would be exhausted. The flight alone would see to that, and her experiences in the US would leave her, I believed, wretched and disorientated. Even in my line of work it was unusual to see a person die. The life of real ATTF operatives is not anything like as dramatic as the films on our DeVs might suggest. In the early years of the Alliance I had once seen a terrorist, trying to get across the border into Scotland, shot by an English Homeland Security officer, and it had shocked me to the core, so that I had dreamt about it for months, even though I knew the man had not died. And I was planning to make things worse for Alice, because in the car back to Hampshire I knew that I had to tell her that I would not see her anymore, not at all, and I had to come clean about the records I had kept concerning her movements and thoughts for all those years, and I had to tell her how I had passed those records on to the police. I would not blame her if she never forgave me.

In the meantime, I had to go on as normal. The peace I had felt as I experimented with sitting in the Light did not exactly go away. Rather, it went into the background. It was like the days of survival training on Dartmoor, with Khalid and Sam, when we were in our thirties. We would know ourselves to be fit and strong, able and as well trained as anyone in the official military. Yet, three days in, as the winter rain chilled us to the bone and we were forced to eat our rations cold, we would feel almost defeated, and every step, every decision, would be hard work. On one level, we knew we were good, the cream of our group, and we told each other that incessantly, but on another level we would feel ourselves to be, almost all the while, only one peat bog, one poor compass-reading or one blister away from giving up. Of course, we did not give up, and I needed to remember that, although the type of survival I was involved in now was so very different.

I needed to drive to the north of the county that Friday morning. I had a useful contact in a small Hampshire town, and we had agreed to have breakfast together. Neil was young, barely out of his teens, and not obviously very intelligent, but his insight into the youth culture in his area was thorough and his comments astute. On more than one occasion we had been able to prevent young people from being radicalised through his early warnings, and I had been able to pass information that was of no value to us, to the local police constable, who in turn had sorted out a small but annoying problem with vandalism. Neil hoped to join the ATTF, but I was pretty sure he would not make the grade. Anyhow, under the new regime he would do better to join the regular police. I resolved to push him in that direction.

Then I needed to meet Pearson at his office, which I feared could be a rather uncomfortable occasion. Undoubtedly Pearson and Josephine believed I had made some sort of deal with Meadows that betrayed our highest ideals, and in a way they were right. I did not need to wear uniform for either of these appointments, so dressed in mufti I headed off in my car in the still-dark January morning.

★ ★ ★

179

It was close to eleven by the time I arrived at Pearson's office. The Christmas lights were still up, strung across the precinct and looking cheerful in the glum light of the grey day. I parked nearby, in a restricted zone that really served the police, and entered Pearson's office with as cheerful a *hello* as I could muster.

Pearson was on his personal DeV, smiling as he talked, but when I came into the room his smile faded. "I've got to go, love," he said. "See you at one." Then, "Hi, Boss," he said. "Coffee?"

"Please." I put my jacket on the back of a chair and sat down. Pearson was busying himself with making the coffee, not looking at me, and not saying anything.

How could I start? "Pearson," I said, "I think I have some explaining to do."

Pearson did not say anything, or turn to look at me. He was taking milk out of his fridge, stirring the coffee more than was needed.

"You must have been surprised," I tried again, "when Meadows mentioned that I had passed some intel to her."

At last there was nothing more to be done to the coffee. Pearson passed a mug to me and swivelled in his chair, so that he was looking directly at me. He looked, I thought, perplexed. "Josie says you passed her information about Alice Owens," he said, in a flat voice.

"I did," I agreed.

"Meadows is boasting all round her office that you did it to save your own skin. To keep your job," he said.

"That is certainly what Meadows believes," I said. I really, desperately wanted to tell Pearson what I had really done, and why I had really done it, but this was no time for self-justification. I sipped my coffee and looked out of the window behind Pearson. I realised how much I valued his opinion, how hard I was finding his disillusionment.

"She's a good woman, Alice Owen," said Pearson. "She's no threat to society."

"She undercuts authority," I said. "She thinks she knows better than her elected representatives."

Pearson sat forward, an earnest look on his face. "Boss, don't we all think that, in our heart of hearts? You, Josie, me… We all think we know better than Meadows, better than Lord Peters. And we do, don't we?"

"Perhaps." It was such a struggle for me to refrain from telling Pearson what I was really up to.

Pearson sighed. "Boss," he said, "you've been under a lot of stress. These are difficult times. Lady Grace has gone and… Why don't you take a break? Go somewhere warm and sunny. Take some time to think? Don't give Meadows any more information until you are quite sure…"

I stood up, my coffee barely started. "Thank you, Pearson," I said stiffly. "I think I can manage my own stress levels without your well-meaning platitudes. And I have told Meadows everything I intend to tell her." Then I left, closing the door firmly behind me.

That left only one important relationship to terminate. Alice. And I would see her the next day.

★ ★ ★

On any other day, in happier times, I would probably have stayed talking to Pearson until lunch time, sorting out the world's problems or discussing sport. Then we might have met Josephine and had lunch together. Now I had nobody to have lunch with, and nowhere, really, where I needed to be. I knew I was doing the right thing. Friendship with me was not good for people, even as things stood, and matters could only get worse. Once I had seen Pearson and Josephine settled, and Alice living safely, albeit with her wings a little clipped,

I would indeed need to go away. Or I would if the powers that controlled me allowed it. I drove slowly back to my flat, my spirits as bleak as the weather. I did not really want to be on my own, but who could I visit? I briefly wondered about calling in on Alice's sister-in-law, Amy. But no, I needed to break all contact with that family. So I let myself into my flat, made a sandwich and stared miserably out of the window at the wilderness of shrubs and saplings that looked, that lunch time, just disorderly and tangled. Like my life.

Who would have expected Meadows to be the one who would lift me out of my doldrums? I had finished my lunch, put a load of washing into the machine and was just wondering what to do next, when my work DeV rang.

"Commander Wyss," I answered automatically.

"Ah, Karl, I wondered if you would be available. Or whether perhaps you might have been dealing with something too subtle for us ordinary law enforcers."

"Police Commissioner," I responded. "How good of you to call. How can I help you?"

"Oh no!" gloated Meadows. "Don't you remember? You *have* already helped me. You've helped me a lot, in order that I can help you in return! Had you forgotten already?"

I swallowed the bile in my throat. "So why are you phoning?" I asked.

Meadows sounded gleeful. She was almost giggling, in a way that was particularly annoying in a woman who was well past the giggling age. "I just thought I'd keep you in the loop," she said, "since you have been so helpful. I felt sure that you would want to know. We are going to raid the camp in the park tomorrow, and…" she paused for effect, "Alice Owens will be detained by Homeland Security when she tries to leave Texas. So, thank you, Karl. You have already been of great help to me!" Then she ended the call, and I was left holding a silent DeV, shocked to the core.

I had spent all that time working through Alice's records before I had handed them over. I had been ruthless. I had deleted whole pages of her reflections, and I had added things I know she would never have thought or written. I had changed the names of the friends she had mentioned. I had made her sound deeply loyal to the government of the day, with just minor reservations about the treatment of the homeless. I had put in comments praising various actions of parliament through the years spanned by my records. I had made Alice into a harmless, slightly muddleheaded elderly spinster. So how *could* the Americans detain her?

As for the encampment in the park... I felt less stricken by that. I had warned my contacts, the couple who had been feeding me small snippets of news, that times were changing, and they had left. It was inevitable that sooner or later the camp would be broken up. I hoped that not too many children would be taken into care. I hoped that the police would just tell them all to move on. That was not uncommon. Homeless people seemed to be endlessly moved on, so that they became somebody else's problem.

I became aware that I was standing, still looking at the blank screen of my DeV. It was really only the detention of Alice that had taken me by surprise. But had she been detained? My heart was pounding hard. I realised I needed to calm down, to think carefully, to check my facts. I was still a trained and high-ranking ATTF officer. Panic was not in my repertoire.

I sat down, put the DeV back in a charging cradle, and took several deep breaths. I thought carefully about Meadows' words. She had, I realised, behaved in a typically amateur way, since she had warned me in advance of what she was going to do. She was so sure that events had broken me, so sure that I was more worried about keeping my job, than about my friends and associates. She was judging me, I thought bitterly, by her own standards. Well, I hoped I was better than that. I needed to think clearly. I needed to make some plans.

My eyes fell on the three-quarters burned Christmas candle, the one I had lit on the previous evening, in my attempt to sit in the Light. Of course, that was what I should do now. It was, I suspected, what Alice might do. Even if I was no longer able to be her friend, I could at least follow her good example. I closed my eyes, I pictured a waterfall of light flowing over this whole, awful situation, and at some level beyond words, I think, I asked for help.

It was not at all like the previous evening. Once again, I felt a sort of calmness creep over me, but I was less successful at quietening my mind. Although my body was still and I was aware of my heart beating slowly and regularly, my mind was buzzing this way and that, like a creature trapped in a room, trying to get out. Then I realised. I did not think I could do anything to influence US Homeland Security, but I could certainly access their communications. It was one of the strengths of ATTF training, almost a routine practice for us.

I opened my eyes and got up, taking from the top shelf of my bookcase the small, cheap-looking and rarely used DeV that appeared to be little more than a child's toy, but which was as powerful and as cleverly programmed as any DeV in the country. I started it up, clicked on some buttons for super-encryption, and settled down to negotiate the labyrinth of trails and dead ends which, if I progressed patiently and carefully, would eventually lead me to the Texans and their plans.

It was easier than it should have been. There was such mistrust of federal authorities in the USA, and such conceit among local officials of all kinds, that expertise was often ignored in favour of 'local knowledge'. The Texan police and Homeland Security used only the most basic of security protocols, and by mid-afternoon I had discovered that, indeed, the Americans had no concrete evidence of any sort against

Alice. They had received information from our Hampshire police that Alice was a 'person of interest' and that she might be carrying incriminating documents. They had agreed to detain her *'pending investigations'*. There was something in the tone of their badly encrypted emails that suggested a certain impatience with the English police. I guessed that Meadows might have used a rather abrasive tone with them, and that the Texans would instinctively dislike taking instruction from us, who were very much their junior partners. Perhaps Meadows' sense of self-importance was working in my favour.

My problem, of course, was that I had offered to pick Alice up from Heathrow. Texas is six hours behind us, and Alice would not start the check-in process for her flight home for another thirty hours or so. I assumed, knowing a little about how these things work, that it would only be at the airport that she would discover she could not leave. I wished I could contact her, warn her of what would happen, and that the authorities had no real evidence against her. I could not. It was too dangerous. I just had to hope that when they interrogated her, *if* they interrogated her, she would not admit to any of the sentiments I had so carefully expunged from her records.

The good thing about the afternoon spent at my DeV, was that I had accessed the direct communications between Agent Frisch of the Houston police, and his or her opposite number in their Homeland Security. It seemed to me that the best I could do, for the time being, was to monitor their contact to discover what was happening to Alice.

The temptation, of course, was to remain logged in and to check every few minutes to see whether there were any developments. That would be the amateur approach, the tactic of someone who was panicking. I was certain that the Americans would not know I had hacked their security, but I rather suspected that *we* might. There were people in London who monitored all the traffic on the airways. I was an ATTF officer and no eyebrows would be raised if the techies in the capital saw that I was looking at Texas, but they might start to wonder if I stayed logged in. I closed everything down, put on my running gear and, in the dark of the late January afternoon, I went for my usual run in the park.

CHAPTER 14

Saturday was a difficult day. The temptation to keep logging in to the Texas communications was huge, and to help me to resist it, I drafted my monthly report, the first that would go to Lord Peters instead of Lady Grace. These reports were sent by all regional commanders and, in Lady Grace's time, had included personal as well as professional reflections. I tried to adopt the same tone this time, aware that Lord Peters' staff would have access to all my earlier reports, and I included a sentence which stuck in my throat as I wrote it, saying how pleased I was to be working with Meadows. Then, at midday, I allowed myself to look again at Agent Frisch's emails.

There had been another mass shooting in downtown Houston. This was fairly routine, and although it had generated a certain amount of email traffic, I assumed most communication would have been via DeV phone lines. The shooter had herself been shot, and Agent Frisch emailed someone in the police department press room to say that there would be no need for an enquiry into the actions of the police officer who had brought down the shooter, since, as he said, *'the evidence speaks for itself'*. Then I found a small communication in Frisch's inbox, from a subordinate based in Stanley. It brought me neatly up to date.

Accessed subject's belongings. Passport, visa, status as English national in order. No criminal record. Return ticket booked. No indication that subject intends to stay beyond declared period. No subversive literature in subject's possession: mainstream novels on subject's DeV, some religious literature, inclining towards Christianity. No political literature. Subject keeps a handwritten journal which we have obtained for scrutiny. Recommend 48 hour delay to scrutinise notebook.

It was, I thought, what I would have expected. The one imponderable, the thing that made me feel queasy, was that I had no idea what was in Alice's journal. Had she been critical of the prison authorities or of the justice system? Who had she met and spoken to while she was in Texas? She would be in a state of shock following the execution, and people can make unguarded comments under such circumstances.

I wondered, too, about the manner of her detention. Way back, following the atrocity of the Twin Towers, there had been accounts of innocent British travellers of Muslim origin being detained in shackles as they awaited deportation. On the other hand, Alice was white, and there had been such an outcry on our side of the Atlantic about those earlier incidents that I rather hoped our American cousins would be more circumspect now. I hated to think of Alice spending forty-eight hours in a cell.

Agent Frisch's inbox would actually have made quite an interesting sociological study, I thought. In amongst his work emails were personal communications, and I learnt quite a lot about him. His son had earned a scholarship to a local junior college and would study criminal justice. Frisch was grateful to his superior officer for the reference which had been written and for '*not mentioning the small matter of the marijuana*'. He had drafted an email to Pastor Duncan, saying that he could no longer support the shelter for battered women because he understood the staff enabled the women to access abortions. Frisch received regular newsletters from the John Birch Society, which I knew to be the political wing of the Klu Klux Klan. Each morning, presumably when he arrived in his

188

office, the first thing he did was to send an e-card to his wife: sentimental, loving little messages decorated with flowers and animated bluebirds or puppies and kittens.

As I was about to log out, a new email dropped into Frisch's inbox. It was brief and formal with a *'do not reply'* instruction, and it told me that Alice Owen would be subject to *'routine Hotel detention'*. I knew this meant that she would be treated with a degree of courtesy, and that she would not be put into a cell anywhere. We did the same thing on our side of the ocean, although we were more subtle, and tended to say that flights had been overbooked, rather than that we were suspicious of the detained person.

I was, as far as possible, comforted by what I had read. I logged out and considered my options for the day. The gym, I thought, some cooking, then the novel I had downloaded a couple of days earlier.

★ ★ ★

I came home mid-afternoon feeling relatively content. I had a routine at the gym originally devised for me by a coach used by the SAS, and modified and adapted over the years. I was pleased with my performance. I had always needed to do more upper-body work than anything else, and that Saturday I found myself managing the weights with ease. It was already dusk when I returned to the flat. I checked Frisch's inbox but there was nothing of significance there, and so I checked my own, which really, I should have done first. There was a blunt, unemotional message from Pearson. *'Tent encampment closed down noon today'*, it read, then, *'Alice's friends Sabrina and Imram detained pending deportation'*. A separate message, timed only seconds later, simply asked, *'Satisfied?'*

Pending deportation? I could not understand it. As far as I knew, Alice had never had much to do with Imram, but Sabrina was, of course, one of her friends and had been a founding member of the little group who had run the tent school. Yet I knew, beyond any doubt, that I had removed all references to Sabrina from the records I had passed to Meadows. How could this have happened?

And almost at once I knew the answer. Long before I had passed those doctored documents to the police commissioner, she had been watching Alice. It was she who had sent those two police officers to harass Alice the day I had rescued her, and she would undoubtedly have known who Alice's friends were. In a way, this was comforting. Pearson and Josephine might believe that it was information I had passed to Meadows which had brought about these events, and it was perhaps best to let them go on thinking that for now, but I knew, and sooner or later they would realise, that Meadows was only doing what she had intended to do all along, and that nothing Pearson, Josephine or I could have done would ever have prevented these actions from being taken.

Then I realised something else too. I had thought that by passing a modified version of Alice's activities to Meadows, and by separating myself entirely from her, I had protected Alice from the vindictive actions of the police commissioner. I had not. If Pearson or I, or any others of my trusted colleagues, were planning to act against a citizen, and somehow the threat that citizen posed was reduced, then we would no longer act. We were professionals, we took action against people only when necessary. Meadows was not like that. She was, at heart, a bully. If someone got on the wrong side of her, they would be on the wrong side of her for life. Meadows did not like Alice, although as far as I knew, she had never met her. She did not like anything Alice stood for. To use my English grandmother's expression, they were as different as chalk from cheese.

And this, in turn, meant that Meadows would not just curtail Alice's activities. She would not just warn her, as I had fondly supposed, that further involvement with the homeless could lead to more trouble. Nor would she lose interest in Alice if I went away. Meadows' grudge against Alice, and against all her friends, would be a settled matter now, an irreversible fact. And, assuming the Americans released Alice from her hotel arrest after forty-eight hours, this was what Alice would be coming home to.

★ ★ ★

Frisch's inbox was annoyingly empty on Sunday. I supposed that he and his friends would all be at home or at church. Sabbath Day observance was a big thing in Texas, I knew. Any respectable family would be seen at worship, dressed smartly and looking clean and polished. It was an American trait that had not yet caught on in England. Even in the most conservative of our churches people wore jeans and trendy waistcoats to services, and the majority of people still did not attend places of worship at all, although talk about prayer had entered the political arena years earlier, and was considered entirely respectable. My time was hanging heavy on my hands, and, perhaps for the first time since I had left the church choir at around eleven years old, I considered going to church myself. If Alice was at home, she would have gone to her Meeting. Will and Mia would certainly be in their church. Even Alice's sister-in-law, Amy, would be in her local parish church, I thought, although whether she had any particular religious beliefs, I was not so sure. I wondered whether there was a group like Alice's in my town. It seemed probable. I even reached for my DeV, intending to look it up, but then I thought of our ATTF techies in London, and even more about Meadows' less skilful techies, and decided against it.

I tried to have a time of worship myself. I think I was hoping for another encouraging experience like the one on

Thursday evening, and indeed, I did feel a deep sense of peace as I sat in the weak sunshine that came, intermittently, into my living room. To be honest, though, nothing really happened. After a while, I stood up and looked out of the window. The hummingbird was there again, hovering over a rather bedraggled bush, and I saw that the little creature was choosing a blossom, drinking, then moving on. My mind started to wander, and I found myself thinking that you never heard about fat hummingbirds. They drank what they needed. Domesticated animals and humans got fat, I supposed because we were not concerned about survival. Our continuation was assured. Then I understood something new. Maybe, I thought, I was treating the Light the way humans treated food, thinking I could access it (whatever it was) whenever I wanted. Whereas, perhaps, the Light was there for survival not for indulgence. It was not there for pleasure, but to equip me, the way the nectar from flowers gave the hummingbird strength.

And I needed to be equipped. I was in this new, strange territory, in which I had become a rogue ATTF officer. The very rules of my existence had changed. I needed a new sort of wisdom. I needed to see my way forward in a strange land, where all my old attitudes and allegiances could be challenged. Not only that, but as I negotiated this new territory myself I needed to try to protect Alice.

I sat again, and closed my eyes. I thought about the Light and about love, and I felt at peace. I did not receive any profound guidance. In fact, after a while I went to sleep. When I woke, and the sun was obliterated by dark, heaving clouds, the peace was still with me, and I had a sense of energy and purpose, almost of optimism. I listened to an afternoon play on public radio, and made a fruitcake that filled the flat with the smells of home.

CHAPTER 15

I had sent Alice a text when I saw from the Texas communications that she was to be allowed home. I really wanted to say '*I am so glad you are all right. I love you*', but all I actually wrote was '*See you at arrivals. 6.45am*'. I set my alarm for five in the morning but I was awake before it chimed, and I listened to the news on my car DeV as I drove. There were three big items of news. There had been a huge explosion somewhere in the Caribbean, in a small town I had not heard of, on an island I did not know; there was a storm approaching England and Wales that was threatening serious disruption; and a terrorist plot had been unearthed by the police, but prevented before any harm had been done. It had originated among homeless people and the police were taking strong action in order to protect law-abiding citizens. There was nothing about the mass shooting in Houston, and nothing about any disruption to flights, so I hoped Alice's journey would have been straightforward.

My mind felt very clear as I drove. I realised that my original plan, of breaking off all friendship with Alice, was not going to be enough to save her. I also realised that, thanks to Lady Grace and Mia, I had a Plan B. In fact, I realised, Plan B had been there all along.

Alice looked dreadful when she walked in to the place in arrivals where friends, family and taxi drivers waited. She had dark rings under her eyes and her clothes looked rumpled. Of course, she would have travelled economy class, something I had not done for thirty years. She seemed pleased to see me, and I took her case, wheeling it to the short-stay car park while Alice walked one pace behind me.

I needed to warn Alice about what was going on. I needed her to be very careful. I was fairly sure that my car was bug-free, that nobody in the hierarchy would yet realise that I had gone rogue, but I could not risk it. When I had deposited Alice's suitcase in the boot, I steered her towards the wall at the edge of Floor E, where we could look out at nothing in particular but where, I was certain, nobody would have thought it worthwhile installing any surveillance equipment. She looked so weary, and did not ask me why we were peering over the wall at some sort of freight depot. I tried to warn her, "It might be better if we don't talk in the car," I said. "Just for safety's sake." Alice just nodded. I thought, *She's too tired to care.*

Of course, I had no idea what Alice knew. Would members of her community have emailed her about the tent city? Would she know about Sabrina and Imram? Even if her English friends had tried to contact Alice, would the Americans have blocked the mail? I realised, too late, that I should have looked at Alice's inbox, then at least I would have known what she knew. On the way home, I stopped off at a motorway service station, bought Alice a coffee, and tried to tell her that there were difficulties, without going into any detail. Alice looked confused, but also very tired, and I thought that now was not the moment. "Let's get you home," I said, without the explanations I felt I needed to give, and we got back into the car.

★ ★ ★

It was daylight, of course, by the time we reached Alice's flat. I carried her case up and she unlocked the door, sighing as she entered. To my eyes it looked perfectly normal, but I had already guessed that Meadows' minions would have been in while Alice was away. While Alice walked through to the bedroom, I found a block of post-its and wrote, "Has someone been in?" Then, without saying anything, I took my question through.

Alice was looking at her bedside table, a slightly perplexed frown on her weary face. She read my note, went through to the spare bedroom, came back to where I was standing, and nodded. I should have thought of this in advance, but it did not really matter. Of course, the flat would be bugged, and no doubt I could find and disable any surveillance gadgets quickly and easily, but what would be the point? If I did so, it would demonstrate immediately that I knew what Meadows was up to, and that I was not really cooperating with her at all. The myth of my capitulation, unconvincing though it probably was to anyone less conceited than Meadows, needed to stay in place for as long as possible.

I needed to get us both out of the flat, if possible without arousing suspicion. "I forgot to get any milk for you," I said. "I'll pop out and get it now."

Alice was quick off the mark. "I'll come with you," she said. "At least it will keep me awake!"

So I lifted up her case, to prevent the noise of suitcase wheels being picked up by sound monitors, hoped there were no hidden cameras, and we left. We drove over to my flat. I knew where I was going to take Alice, but I needed to do some track-covering first.

★ ★ ★

I left Alice sleeping on my settee, and went through to the bedroom with my ATTF DeV. I thought how much I would miss, when I lost my post, all the clever shortcuts our London techies had installed, although I guessed there would still not be much I could not hack into even without their help. It would just take longer. I checked the CCTV outside Alice's flat and saw us arriving, and then later leaving. I photoshopped the suitcase out of our leaving video, so that it did, indeed, look as if we might just have gone out to the supermarket. After playing around for quite a while, I found that there was only one camera installed in the flat, although there were listening devices in every room. Until the advent of Lord Peters it had been difficult for the police to obtain hidden cameras, since that sort of surveillance was not really part of their brief. It had taken no time at all for the police to obtain those convenient little items. The camera had been installed in the living room, and showed us arriving. Because of the angle, it altogether missed our leaving, so I did not need to doctor anything there.

Then I accessed Alice's DeV, and saw that her friends had kept her pretty up to date with developments. I also found rather clumsy evidence of someone else following her communications. I followed the trail but could not trace Alice's stalker to any organisation I recognised. I guessed that Meadows would have subcontracted her surveillance of Alice, probably because of a lack of resources. I knew that Alice needed to ditch the DeV, or she would certainly be traced to the safe place where I hoped to leave her.

Alice woke mid-afternoon, looking bleary but less white and drawn. I sent her off to have a hot bath, and she came back half an hour later wrapped in my bathrobe, her hair damp around her shoulders, and her face flushed from the heat. We did two loads of washing, so that everything she had was clean, and I added a lovely blue jumper of mine to her case. I checked the suitcase lining but there were no tracker devices there. I had not expected there to be any. The Americans had decided Alice was no threat. With any luck, they had written the whole episode off as some parochial neurosis on the part of an officious English policewoman.

While I was cooking dinner, Alice noted down any DeV

codes, email addresses and phone numbers that she had stored on her device, and which she might need. I had convinced her that we needed to ditch her DeV, although I promised I would provide her with a little disposable DeV 14, the sort that you could just buy in any newsagent and throw away when the battery was used up. Despite attempts to legislate against them, neither Congress nor our parliament had yet succeeded in banning those handy little gadgets. Of course, it was only a matter of time.

I made steak and chips, and plied Alice with good red wine. We talked about neutral subjects, as if the last week had not happened: climate change and the consequent rise in sea levels, whether organic steak (which we were eating) tasted better than the stuff they served in the USA (we both thought it did), and whether I should replace the carpet in my living room with oak floorboards, which had been fashionable for decades, and would look good with my oak doors. I told her about seeing the hummingbird, but for some reason I did not tell her about sitting in the Light. All in good time, I thought. We ate homemade apple crumble and custard, and when Alice started yawning I made up the bed-settee and left her and went through to my bedroom, carrying her DeV.

There are things that can be done to disable DeVs so that nosy outsiders would not realise what has happened. It is not easy, and normally, within the ATTF, we passed those sorts of tasks on to the nerds. However, for a while before I came down to Hampshire I had been closely associated with our electronic communications department, and although DeVs had since become more sophisticated the principles remained the same. It took me a while, and it was after midnight by the time I had achieved what I had hoped for. I checked on Alice, who was sleeping deeply, one hand against her face, the other outside the bedclothes. The temptation to join her was huge, but there were things I needed to do, so I drove over to her flat, planted a handy little widget in her desk drawer so that a casual eavesdropper would think her DeV was still in her flat, and deposited parts of the original DeV in different locations on the way home.

I had been awake since before five on Monday morning and by the time I arrived back at my flat it was nearly two on Tuesday morning. I should have felt tired, but I felt good. For the first time in weeks I felt back in control of my life. And there was more to it than that. I was embracing the fact that I had changed sides. I had always hoped that Alice would leave behind her religious convictions so that we could be together. But I was beginning to share her convictions. Maybe we could be together after all.

CHAPTER 16

One of the many things I loved about Alice was that she did not ask too many questions. Sometimes I thought it was because she did not want to know about my work, but I suspect that early on I must have made it clear that there were boundaries to what I would discuss, and Alice had learnt her lesson well. We rarely discussed religion, either.

She asked no questions when, over breakfast, I told her that I was taking her to a place I knew of where I thought she would be safe. She merely pulled her hood up over her head as we dashed through the bitter-cold rain to the car, then settled herself comfortably in the passenger seat. She looked so much better than when I had picked her up from Heathrow. She said she had slept all night, and that was on top of sleeping for hours during the previous day. She looked much more relaxed too. I realised that Alice trusted me, and it pleased me more than I can say.

It is quite a long drive from Hampshire to Mia's cottage in Wales. I found a classical music station and we listened to some Elgar, and then to an Early Music concert. It was almost dark when we arrived, driving down the narrow lane with grass growing in the middle, and I let us in and turned on the heating. Alice looked stricken, and for a moment I saw the cottage through her eyes: a shabby, cold, rather primitive little place in the middle of nowhere. Leaving her case there, we drove on to a supermarket some distance away and bought enough food for about a week, and several bottles of wine. By the time we got back the cottage was warm, and looked quaint rather than shabby in the light of a pretty little lamp. I cooked a meal while Alice settled herself in, and we ate pork and Chinese vegetables.

I wish now that I had been more open with Alice. I wish I had told her what was going on in my life. But the habit of caution is so deeply ingrained into the way I live, that when she asked, "What is going on, Karl?" I told her I did not know. Of course, that was true, in a way. I did not really know who was planning what, or why, but I knew a lot more than I told Alice, and I could guess even more. Instead of being open with her, I think I tried to explain to her how the whole situation – the tent school, her support of her executed friend – might look to the authorities. I am pretty sure I even said, "You people take the easy option." How could I have said such a thing? What was I thinking about? To this day, that comment is one of my biggest regrets.

I left the next morning and was back in Pearson's office for my regular Wednesday meeting at eleven o'clock. Pearson did not ask about Alice, although I am sure he must have known she was back, and I, of course, said nothing about her. Our conversation was stilted. Pearson was unhappy about the arrests at the encampment in the park and about the deportations, but he was not comfortable about discussing it with me.

We went over the usual details, then I said, "Pearson, I think I might take you up on your suggestion."

"Boss?"

"You said I needed to get away for a bit," I reminded him.

"Oh, yes. Yes, I do think that. This year really hasn't started well, has it?" He sounded a little friendlier than before. I so wished I could tell him what was really going on, but I could not. I should have trusted him, but all I could think was that I must not involve him, with his whole life ahead of him, in my subterfuge.

"So, I thought I'd take a few days off, go and visit some friends," I said. "Do you feel okay about holding the fort here?"

"Oh, sure!" I was not asking anything of him that I had not asked a hundred times before. "How long do you think you'll be away?"

"A week, maybe," I said vaguely.

Back in my car I used my work DeV to contact Reggie in East Anglia. "Any chance I can come over?" I asked.

"Yes, of course," Reggie said. "Rosie will be delighted. When would you like to come?"

"Today, if possible." I clicked off. Now the really tricky part began. If I could achieve what I hoped to achieve in the next week, Alice would be safe. Safe, and possibly in the long run, if Alice wanted it, we could be together. I backed out of my parking place and headed towards the motorway.

★ ★ ★

In theory, it was a gamble taking Reggie and Rosie into my confidence, and sometimes, looking back on that January, I have wondered why I was prepared to be so open with them and so cautious with Pearson and with Alice. I think it must have been because the bonds between ATTF officers were so strong. For years, for decades, in fact, the only people I was able to be truly open with were fellow officers of my rank. The connection was deep, forged through survival exercises on Dartmoor or in the hill country in Spain, through conferences in Scotland or Paris, through briefing sessions in smart London hotels and in anonymous rooms in the City. I think it must be the same for soldiers who have seen active duty. However much you love your nearest and dearest, there is something about sharing together a life nobody else has experienced that creates those tough, iron bonds.

I drove directly to their house. As I arrived Reggie was just getting out of his car. He was dressed formally, in uniform, looking very smart. We went into the house together, and Reggie called out, "Rosie! We're here!"

Rosie came out of the kitchen, a smile on her face. "Hi, Karl!" she greeted me, then, "So how did it go, Reggie?"

"Good, good," he answered her, then to me, "Come on in, Karl. We usually sit in the kitchen in the daytime, and I can smell baking!"

The ground floor of Reggie's house had only three rooms and a cloakroom. The kitchen was huge, with a dining table and a small sofa as well as the usual kitchen furnishings. There was a lot of red: a red shiny splashback behind the work surfaces, red and white patterned blinds gathered in loops at the tops of the windows, a red tea towel, kettle and toaster. The whole place had a cheerful air about it. "Tea?" asked Rosie, switching on the kettle, and putting out mugs. I noticed with pleasure that they were using the Sedona pottery set I had given them for Christmas, and that the bright red desert flowers in the design matched well with everything else in the room.

"I'm guessing," said Reggie, getting straight to the point, "that all is not well in the South?"

"Exactly." I sipped my tea and added a little more milk. "To be honest, Reggie, I've had it!"

Reggie gave a sort of grunt, and looked at Rosie. I saw a flash of understanding passing between them. "Do you want to tell us?" he asked.

"I can go and get on with some sewing," offered Rosie, "if you two want a bit of privacy?"

"No. No, Rosie, stay," I answered. I thought for a moment, then I said, "I'm getting out. I can't do this anymore."

Rosie reached across the table and placed a warm hand on mine. Reggie said, "I knew it would be tough for you."

"It's not just Lord Peters or Meadows," I said. "It's... Well, it's complicated."

"Isn't it always?" Reggie was being sympathetic without asking for details.

"So how can we help?" prompted Rosie.

I swallowed some more tea. The less I told these good friends, the less trouble I would land them in if it all went wrong.

"I want to get someone out of the country," I said. "Into Europe, if possible. And then, if I can, I want to join her."

Neither of them said anything. Reggie tapped a finger on the table as if keeping time to an inaudible tune. Rosie looked into her empty mug. Then Reggie said thoughtfully, "Xavier suspects our local Gypsies of people smuggling."

I vaguely recalled Xavier Booth, the police commissioner, telling me such a thing. "Though the Gypsies don't trust the police, so I doubt if Xavier could help you."

Rosie smiled at Reggie. "The Gypsies trust the clergy," she said. Then, to me, "You'd better call on Will and Mia again."

★ ★ ★

I had not thought about where I might sleep that night, but when Rosie realised the situation she insisted I stay with them. It had been mid-afternoon when I had arrived in Cambridgeshire, and by the time we had drunk our tea it was getting dark outside.

"Never mind," said Rosie, as she let the blinds down and fiddled with some knobs on the cooker. "The evenings have already started drawing out. It will be spring before we know it."

Reggie was still in uniform, but he had taken his highly-polished shoes off and donned some leather slippers. "Better that you stay here," he backed up Rosie's invitation. "I never bring colleagues home, and perhaps we don't want you to be too easily traced? Hotels can be so public!"

I was profoundly grateful. Rosie showed me up to a large room, obviously usually used as some sort of sewing room because there was a sewing machine set up on a lovely, oak table and a dressmaker's dummy with tape measures hanging over one of its shoulders. The bed was a single, and Rosie hurriedly moved some velvet fabric from it, and checked it was made up, under the chintz cover. "I'll fetch you towels," she said. "There's a bathroom down the corridor. It's the family bathroom, but there is no family here, so it'll be all your own!" Then, "We'll eat at seven if that suits you?"

She left me and I walked over to the window. It was dark outside and I could see no lights from other houses. Reggie and Rosie lived on the edge of the village and my room must have been on the field side of the house. I drew the curtains, checked that my personal DeV was off, took out my more secure work device and clicked on Will's number. He answered on the second ring. When he heard that I wanted to talk, he was all for me going over for dinner the following evening. "I have to be in Ely all day," he said, apologising for not being able to see me sooner. I thought it was a bad idea. I did not want his delightful twins to see me, or to know I had been anywhere near their home. Instead we agreed that we would meet in the church at six, when Will had done his diocesan duties. When the call was finished, I spent a few minutes trying to hold the situation in the Light. Then I went downstairs.

★ ★ ★

With an empty day ahead of me, and not wanting to get in Rosie's way, I decided to go out for a drive. Rosie thought it was a bad plan. "There's terrible weather on the way," she said. "A storm coming all the way from America," and she showed me the satellite pictures on the weather channel on her kitchen DeV.

Reggie, about to leave the house wearing jeans and a mustard-coloured jumper, said, "Oh, it won't hit until Monday – Sunday at the earliest, and the west will get it worst. I don't suppose we'll even notice it!"

I drove to the coast, to a little fishing town with a high sea wall protecting it from the tide, and ate fish and chips on the quay, then bought a postcard and a stamp and sent it to Pearson and Josephine. Pearson had wanted me to take some time off, and I hoped the unrealistically sunny scene of fishing boats and sea would convince him that I was following his advice. I calculated the number of miles I had driven in the last few days: from my flat to Heathrow and back via Alice's, then to Wales and back, then Reggie's, and now the east coast. I had driven virtually the full width of the country.

★ ★ ★

The church door creaked mightily as I opened it. The lighting was dim, and at first, I did not see Will. He was kneeling down in a pew, his shoulders a little hunched. He turned around when he heard me, stood up and came towards me, his hand outstretched to shake mine, and a smile on his face.

"So, Karl!" he said. "We meet again!"

I found myself smiling too. "It's good of you to see me," I said.

"No problem, no problem." Will sat down and patted the pew next to him. "What can I do for you?"

"It's tricky," I started.

"Yes," agreed Will. "But a problem shared…"

"I want…" I stopped, then started again. "Will, I really need to get someone out of the country. As soon as possible. Or sooner." I could hear the urgency in my own voice.

"Ah!" said Will.

We both sat in silence. The big church clock boomed a

quarter past the hour. Will said, "Such things do happen. I mean, people do leave the country. Usually, I believe, they head for Scotland, sometimes Ireland. Or France, but that means crossing the Channel, which takes a bit of planning."

"I don't know where to start," I admitted.

Will laughed out loud. "I'm glad to hear it!" he said. "I would hate to think that the ATTF was involved in people smuggling!" Then he looked serious again. "You need to think carefully about this, Karl. When we last spoke here you told me that you were motivated by ideals to do with good citizenship. Do you remember?"

"Yes, of course."

"Mm. Well, a good citizen doesn't smuggle his friends abroad," Will pointed out. He turned in the pew so that he was looking directly at me. "Karl, I don't know you very well. When Reggie first introduced us, I thought what a steady sort of chap you were. This request of yours doesn't seem in keeping with my original impressions. Are you really sure about this? Isn't there another way of dealing with your problem?"

I looked away from him, into the shadows of the stonework. I took a deep breath.

"I'm not motivated by ideology this time, Will," I confessed.

"Ah-ha."

"I think… I hope… that I'm motivated by love." I met his eyes again. "I have been so wrong about so much, Will, but I don't think I'm wrong now. My friend really must get out of the country. She really must. And if I can, I want to follow her."

Will was still and quiet. Then, "Right," he said, "that changes matters." He sat still again, sighed, then warned, "These things can take a little organising. How much time do we have?"

"I think we've got a few days' grace," I said, feeling the relief washing over me.

"Good, good…" Will was silent again. "I think the best thing would be for me to contact you, tomorrow or Saturday. Where are you staying? How quickly can you come over, if I need to see you?"

"I'm at Reggie's," I said, "but I don't want to stay there too long. It isn't fair on them."

Will smiled. "Oh, I wouldn't worry about that," he said. "Rosie will love having you. I'll contact you or Reggie when I've got something for you."

As we stood up, Will patted me on the shoulder. "It's not easy," he said, "living a life motivated by love, but it's the best way to live. Absolutely the best way."

CHAPTER 17

I did not expect to hear from Will on Friday. Reggie had to be in Cambridge, he and Xavier Booth were working on some project together, and I went in with him to look at the bookshops and walk along the backs of the colleges, by the Cam. I had lunch in a pub which was showing the Weather Channel, where a beautiful blonde reporter in a green parka jacket with her hood up, was standing in the snow in New York City, describing the havoc the storm had brought there, and a bearded man with a Northumbrian accent was explaining that, with climate change, we were more prone to getting the full force of storms that started in the States, rather than just the after-effects. For the first time it occurred to me that Alice, in Wales, could be affected by the bad weather that was on the way, but then I comforted myself. We had stocked up with lots of food, and I was sure Alice would be all right, even if she could not leave the cottage at all. In fact, if the roads in the west were closed, it might be all the better.

By Saturday I was aware of the build-up of tension, as I waited to hear from Will. Reggie and Rosie were busy with domestic chores and I spent a few minutes surfing around various ATTF and police sites, to see whether I could get any information about what was going on back home. What I really wanted to do was to talk with Pearson, but it was better that he thought I was by the coast, enjoying the bracing air and probably taking long walks along beaches and getting my equilibrium back. Meadows' site was mostly occupied by some civil disturbance outside the Guild Hall, with protesters complaining about the closure of the Feeding Centre, just when the weather was about to turn so bad and the tent encampment had been closed.

Will finally phoned Reggie at lunchtime, as we sat eating cheese and pickles with Rosie's homemade bread. I did not know why he had not phoned me directly, but it was wise. Electronic links can be deleted if you know what you are doing, but it is better not to create them in the first place. Reggie passed his DeV to me and I went out into the hall to talk to Will.

"I think," said Will cheerfully, "that you have almost become one of my flock!"

I smiled. "Thank you!" I said, feeling pleased.

"And shepherds," Will continued, "are supposed to look after their flocks. We're supposed to lead you beside quiet waters and guide you along the right paths."

I laughed.

"Well, I am ready to give you a bit of guidance," he went on. "But my household, which seems to be full of twins and their friends this weekend, is hardly a place of still waters! So, can we meet in the church again? We've got evensong in the village this Sunday. It'll be over by six, I expect. Can you be there at about six-thirty?

★ ★ ★

I listened to public radio as I drove over, still full of Rosie's excellent roast beef. It seemed that the outlying gusts of the storm had reached the west coast. Houses along quaysides in Wales and parts of Cornwall were being evacuated, and the first snow had fallen in the Hebrides. The emergency services were gearing themselves up for a busy couple of days.

I parked in a sort of drive or unmade-up road by the

church. It looked like a Christmas card, with the lights shining through the stained glass, and a pub just across the lane with more lights. I saw a couple come out of the church and crunch along the gravel path to the last remaining parked car. Then I got out of my car and went inside.

I wandered down the aisle of the empty building. The light in the vestry was on, so I made my way to where Will was disrobing and putting books back onto shelves.

"I almost came to evensong," I said.

Will smiled. "Probably a good thing you didn't," he said. "Villages can be very talkative."

"Yes, that's what I thought."

I sat on the only chair in the room and watched Will gathering some papers together. "You know," he said, "we don't have a sermon in our evening services, just a little homily. To be honest, I find it harder to say what I want to say in ten minutes than in twenty!"

"Do people listen?" I asked. We had gone to a Lutheran church when we visited family in Switzerland in my childhood. I used to find those long talks so boring.

"Oh, I don't suppose so!" said Will, cheerfully. "Well, most of them don't, most of the time." Then he turned and looked directly at me, and smiled. "People can't really hear what you're saying, you know, unless they're ready to hear."

I smiled back. "Yes, that's true."

Will closed a cupboard door firmly and turned a key.

"Do you have to lock up hymn books?" I asked, surprised.

Will chuckled again. "No, communion wine," he explained. "We've agreed to keep the church open, otherwise I wouldn't bother. Come through to the chancel."

We sat in the pews again, this time with Will in the row in front of me, swivelled round so that he could see my face in the gloom of the old-fashioned lighting. "Well," he said, "I think I've found what you need."

"That's a relief," I said. "What do I need to know? What do I need to do?"

"Spoken like a true ATTF officer!" remarked Will. Then he paused. "You probably need to know as little as possible. I know someone – some people – who will take your friend into Europe. It might be better if you don't know the route. Or, indeed, the names of my friends!" He was quiet again, then, "You realise the risks your friend will be taking?" he asked.

"Yes. Yes, I do," I said. "But if she stays… Will, if she stays I really don't know what might happen to her."

"Exactly." Will was still looking thoughtful. "I don't think you can go with her," he added.

"I… No." It had not occurred to me that I could, only that I might join Alice later.

"The risks my friends would be taking would be too great," Will explained. "I'm assuming your friend is not high profile?"

"No, certainly not!" I said. "In fact, it's quite ridiculous that she should have to leave at all."

"But you are high profile," continued Will. "Being caught taking a senior ATTF officer out of the country would earn the ultimate punishment, you know."

We were both quiet. Then, "Let's just get my friend out," I said. "Everything else can wait. As long as she's safe."

"Good," said Will, standing. "The people who are going to help your friend thought at first that they could leave promptly. Tomorrow or Tuesday, even. But I didn't know where she was, or how easy it might be to get her here. And now this storm is threatening to disrupt everything. It would look odd if my friends were seen travelling through really bad weather. So now, we think, maybe at the end of the week. Will that work for you?"

I did not like leaving it so long, but I had no choice. "I can make it work," I said, and hoped I could.

★ ★ ★

It seemed as if Pearson's well-meaning prescription was coming to pass. Since there was nothing that could be done until the worst of the storm was over, I was forced to pass my time walking, reading, and practising holding things in the Light. The walking and the reading came more easily than the praying, if praying was what I was doing. Twice I drove out into the countryside after breakfast, sat in my car somewhere where the view was good, and tried to empty my mind of my busy, frustrated thoughts. I cannot say I was all that successful. I was in the fenland one morning, parked on a lay-by on top of a dyke, looking out over wide, straight ditches filled with slate-grey water, ruffled by the persistent wind. I found myself in gentler countryside a day or so later and the storm had reached us by then. It was snowing steadily but the wind was not as strong as the gales that were causing so much havoc in the west. I thought a lot about Alice, trying to hold her up to the Light, but whenever I thought of her I felt cold and uncomfortable. I supposed it was the influence of the snowy scene in front of me and the rather melodramatic news reporting which Reggie, Rosie and I were watching each evening in their snug kitchen. One morning I went with Reggie on a routine visit to an informant at a service station on the M1. It seemed that the ATTF liked to monitor vehicles going north, although East Anglia is a very long way from the Scottish border. It seemed like a rather unnecessary call, to me. Reggie introduced me to the service station manager, they talked briefly about a couple of white vans which came and went regularly, then we ate eggs and chips in the café before driving home.

Reggie said, with a degree of confidence, as we drove away, "People-smugglers don't use white vans!" Then he glanced sideways at me. "I do these checks for form's sake," he said. "And my informants can use the extra money, so we all benefit. And no harm is done."

It made me think that Reggie was rather sympathetic

towards people-smugglers. Of course, he and Rosie were hoping to go to Canada, so that might well be the case, although of course they would be able to do it legally. I was seriously tempted to take him into my confidence, but in the end I did not.

★ ★ ★

Two things happened on Wednesday evening that alarmed me. The first occurred mid-afternoon, when I decided to check the ATTF and police sites, to see what was going on in my region. I took my regulation ATTF phone and tapped in the usual code, but the DeV remained dead. *Bother!* I thought. *Have I forgotten to charge it?*

I plugged it in and the light turned green at once. The phone was fully charged. *Well*, I thought, *I must have typed in the wrong code*. I tried again. Still it was as dead as ever. I was tempted to use my own personal DeV and to try to access those sites the long way around, but I knew that that was not wise.

I thought for a minute or two, then I went downstairs. Rosie was in the kitchen, doing something on her DeV.

"Hi Rosie," I said. "Is Reggie around?"

"Clearing the snow," she said, nodding towards the front of the house. "Although I'm not sure there's much point. Look at this!" She swivelled the screen round so that I could see the forecast. Even East Anglia, it seemed, was due for more snow and bitter temperatures.

"Oh dear!" I said, and fleetingly I wondered if my DeV reception had just been weakened by the weather. But I knew it was not so.

I grabbed my jacket, put on some shoes, and went out into the snow. At first I could not see Reggie. The drive was clear, mounds of white on either side and glistening tyre tracks on the tarmac where Reggie's car had compacted the snow when he had arrived home earlier. Then a snowball landed hard on my arm, and I turned to see Reggie, grinning, and forming another snowball in his gloved hands.

"Got you!" he said happily, then he saw my expression. He dropped the second snowball and walked over to me. "Something amiss?" he asked.

"I think so," I said. "Probably. Reggie, I can't access my DeV – my work phone."

"That's odd." Reggie looked serious. "Come on, let's try mine."

We went inside, took off our jackets and shoes and went through to Reggie's office. His DeV was on top of a pile of papers. It looked identical to mine, standard ATTF issue. He typed in his code, and I saw the screen come alive at once.

"Mine's okay," he said. "Perhaps there's bad reception in your room? I've never tried to use this DeV up there. Bring it down and try it here."

My device, though, was still dead.

"Huh!" Reggie was thoughtful. "I suppose even the classiest equipment goes wrong sometimes! Use my DeV and put your code in. That should gain you the access you need." He handed the little device over to me.

I typed in my code. Nothing. I tried again. Still nothing. I passed it back to Reggie. "Dead as a dodo," I said.

Reggie's voice remained calm but I could see the concern on his face. "What the hell...?" he said.

"I think," I said slowly, "I rather think, Reggie, that I'm out of the loop."

Reggie looked at me with a worried expression.

"Go and fix us both a drink, will you Karl? I want to see what's going on here." And he pulled out his office chair and sat down, already tapping numbers into his DeV, while I went through to the living room to find the whisky decanter.

CHAPTER 18

It took Reggie almost an hour, and a call to Xavier Booth, before he was able to report back. Rosie and I were sitting in the kitchen watching the large DeV screen which was set into the wall next to the dresser, following the news of the storm. There were trees down, cars off the roads, and schools closed. Judging by the tone of the reporters, it was all very exciting. Reggie came through, still holding his DeV and looking very calm. I recognised at once the expression of an officer dealing with a crisis, disconnected from any emotions. He sat down, looked at me, and then looked at his DeV again, as if something new might suddenly appear on the blank display unit.

"Well, you've really pissed someone off," he said. "Sorry, Rosie."

"Can you tell who?" I asked.

"Not easily. Well, no. But I can tell you that there is a lock on all your ATTF communications, and a *Do not assist* notice if I try to get anywhere close."

"Shit!" I said. "Sorry, Rosie."

Rosie laughed. "Such gentlemen!" she said. "Can you work out what's happened?"

"I really can't," said Reggie. "You know what ATTF communications are like. I tried the police, too. There's a lot of traffic around Meadows' office, but it seems to be mostly to do with some anti-terrorist activity. Not you, Karl. They've already made their arrests."

I felt a sinking feeling. Who had Meadows' crowd arrested? But surely Alice was safely out of the way? Perhaps others from her community had been rounded up? If so, would they give away any information about Alice? Then relief flooded over me. None of Alice's friends knew where I had taken her. And anyhow, the arrested people could be anyone. There were substantial ethnic minority groups in the largest city in my area, by the coast. Was it not more likely that some of them had got on the wrong side of Meadows?

Just then Reggie's DeV gave a little buzz. He clicked on answer, said, "Oh, hi there!" and passed it to me. "Will," he said, "for you."

I took the call where I was. There really seemed no need to pretend anything, when Reggie and Rosie must already realise I was in serious trouble.

"Hello, my wandering sheep!" greeted Will. "Enjoying this weather?" He did not wait for a reply. "Can your friend be here by Thursday evening?" he asked. "Or Friday morning at the latest? The worst of the storm will be over by then and my friends have places to go."

I thought of Alice in Wales, and the state of the roads between East Anglia and the west of the country. "I'm not sure," I said. "But I'll try."

"Good man," said Will. "Don't bring her to the house. The school's closed and the twins are causing mayhem at home. And Mia is running a soup kitchen from the garage! Bring her to the church, will you?"

"I'll do my best," I said, and he clicked off.

"It looks as if I'm off," I said to the enquiring faces at the table.

Rosie said, "In this weather? You're mad!"

Reggie reacted more slowly. Long trip?" he asked.

I nodded. "Yes, I think so," I said. "Long and difficult."

Rosie sighed. "Right, time for food!" she said. "You need to have something warm inside you before you go. And I'll make a flask for you. Have you got a spade in the car? A torch? Some blankets?"

Reggie laughed. "Rosie, my love," he said, "you're talking to someone who's done ATTF survival courses. I think we can trust Karl to take the right precautions!" Then, to me he said, "But of course you can borrow anything you need from us."

★ ★ ★

I was not really very anxious about driving across country in the storm. I wished I had snow tyres, but I did not, and there was nothing that could be done about that. I was, though, quite worried to discover the total block on all my ATTF access. Then, while we were eating rabbit casserole, the second thing really to alarm me happened. Reggie took a call which he seemed to be expecting, and went to his office for privacy. When he came back he looked deadly serious.

Rosie raised her eyebrows but said nothing. Reggie finished his meal, glanced at my empty plate, dabbed his mouth with his table napkin and said, "A word, Karl?" Then he ushered me through to his office.

Once the door was closed he said, "Sorry about that. I don't want Rosie involved...That was Josie on the phone. Josephine. I phoned her earlier and left a message. We go back a long way."

Of course, I had guessed as much. It was Reggie who had sent Josephine down to me, to go undercover in Meadows' office.

My mouth was dry. What had happened to my calm, dispassionate ATTF approach? "And?" I prompted.

"She told me an odd story," said Reggie.

I waited. Reggie was looking at me quizzically. "She and Pearson seem to think that you're working with Meadows. Working *closely* with Meadows."

I sighed. "Well, I'm not!" I said.

Reggie gave me a long, calculating look. "That's what I told Josie," he said, "but there seems to be a fair amount of evidence… Josie tells me that Meadows has been boasting high and low about having you under her thumb, and all these arrests… Josie thinks they're the result of information you gave Meadows. She believes you've done a deal. To keep your job."

Of course, I realised, Josephine would think that. How could she not?

"I haven't," I said, sounding like a sulky teenager.

"I couldn't really imagine it," agreed Reggie. "But what…?"

"I wanted Meadows to think that," I explained. "And I didn't want to involve Pearson and Josephine in my difficulties. They've got their lives ahead of them."

Reggie looked thoughtful. "And all this information Meadows is acting on? It seems a bit like using people for bait."

"Meadows' information didn't come from me." I thought I'd better come clean. "I've got um – a well, friend – and she's in trouble. I passed all my information on her, going back over years, to Meadows. It was to put Meadows off the scent. But I doctored it. I changed a lot. There were no names of real people there, nothing that could incriminate anyone."

"But Meadows thinks it's authentic," ruminated Reggie.

"I certainly hope so!" I said. "It was supposed to show her that my friend was of no interest to her!"

Reggie was quiet, twiddling an elegant fountain pen in his fingers, then tapping it rhythmically on the desk as he thought.

"Meadows is a conceited and unpleasant woman," he said at last, "but she's no fool. She wouldn't be where she is if she wasn't as cunning as the devil."

"That's true." I waited for Reggie to finish.

"Are we talking about Alice Owen?" he asked at last, looking me straight in the face.

I swallowed. "We are," I agreed.

"Then I think that you ought to know," said Reggie, "that Meadows has had a man undercover in her community for weeks. Months, perhaps. And Josephine thinks he's discovered Ms Owen's whereabouts."

I thought it was just a metaphor, but my heart really did miss a beat. "How long has Josephine known this?" I asked.

"Several days. Since Sunday, in fact. She saw no point in telling you, believing, as she did, that you were on Meadows' side now."

"Oh, God!" I could feel myself wincing. I had played my hand so badly.

"Alice hasn't been arrested yet," said Reggie. Then he reached across the desk and touched my shoulder. "Is tonight's journey to find Alice? Are you going to rescue her?"

I looked up. "I hope so," I said.

"And I hope so too," he said, "so let's get you on your way."

CHAPTER 19

Normally I would use the DeV in the car, or turn on one of my personal devices to give me the route I needed, and I was about to do that when Reggie put his hand over mine. "Don't!" he said.

I looked at him aghast. Of course, if I were under suspicion with the ATTF, the last thing I wanted to do was tell them where I was going. I should have thought of that myself.

"Your whereabouts will be known," Reggie said. "And it'll only be a matter of time before they come here. Put in a search for somewhere else."

I thought for a moment, then asked my device for directions to a small town on the Norfolk coast. I used a website to look at various bed-and-breakfasts in that vicinity. While I was doing that, Reggie was rooting around in his office, and he came back with an old route atlas, of the sort people used before they had DeVs in their cars. Together we looked at the roads I would need to take to get to Wales.

"Your best way seems to be via Birmingham and Shrewsbury," he said. "The roads are good, but remember, there are usually ATTF checks around Birmingham."

I looked carefully at the map too. I have a good visual memory and of course I knew the highways of England very well. There was a limit, though, to the amount my memory would store when it came to smaller roads, and I realised I might have to use my instincts for part of the time. Reggie was frowning, then he went back into his office and returned with a compass. "Could be useful," he said. "You never know."

By the time all this was done it was already eight in the evening. Rosie had been in and out of the kitchen while Reggie and I were talking. "Do you really have to go tonight?" she asked. "The wind's got up and it's snowing a blizzard. Wouldn't you be better off waiting until morning?"

It would have been tempting, but I thought of Josephine's report to Reggie, that someone from Meadows' team was on Alice's trail. I knew I did not have a minute to spare.

"I'll go now," I said, pulling on my shoes and wrapping a scarf round my neck.

★ ★ ★

I opened the driver's door of my car, and immediately a flurry of snow landed on my seat.

"Wait a minute!" said Rosie. "Is this your usual car, your ATTF car?"

"It's the only car I have," I said, "If I need to disguise myself I... Oh!"

We were all quiet for a few seconds while I digested the thoughts which must have been crossing all our minds.

Reggie said, "Rosie has her own car. One of the first hybrids. Not glamorous, but it's the car we use when we're... off duty."

"Right." I was thinking hard. Since I obviously could not access a car pool, and since my car carried various useful chips that saved me from having to pay tolls on roads, or parking fees, it was not sensible to drive away in it. If they wanted to, the powers that be could trace me. On the other hand, it was impossible to hire a car, in the Cambridgeshire countryside, on a night like that night, without attracting a great deal of attention to myself.

"You'd better take Rosie's car," suggested Reggie.

I looked at Rosie through the snow-whirling air. She had

screwed up her eyes, but not, I thought, because she was reluctant to lend me her car. It was just the wind. "Yes," she said, "that's the best plan. If we need to, we can say you stole it."

"And your DeVs..." prompted Reggie.

I felt foolish. A trained officer like me should have considered all these things. I was too used to being one of a privileged class. My ATTF DeV was of little practical use to me anyway, now that my access had been cut off, and my ordinary private device would be traceable.

Without saying anything further, Reggie held out his hand. I rooted around in the pocket of my overcoat and handed over my two devices. Reggie peered in the dark as he removed the SIM cards and gave them back to me. I tossed them onto the driveway and ground them into the frozen snow, then handed them back.

Reggie said, "You did a search for the North Norfolk coast, didn't you?"

"Yes."

"Right then, so we'll abandon your car and the phone casings as if you had headed out that way. You can buy yourself some sort of cheap DeV along the way if you need it."

Rosie pressed a button on her device to open the garage door, and smiled as she handed over her car keys. I backed the car out onto the drive, leaving my ATTF vehicle where I had parked it throughout my visit, on the verge.

★ ★ ★

Driving in wintry conditions is entirely different in England, than in Switzerland. Despite climate change and the reduced quantity of snow on the mountains, the Swiss had maintained all their winter services, so that the last time I drove in a snowstorm there, only a few years earlier, the roads had been relatively clear. Here in England and Wales those sorts of local services had long since vanished. The roads out of the village, heading towards the A14 and then, I hoped, the M6, were covered in drifting snow which at first crunched under my tyres, but quickly stopped doing so. It was a bad sign. The tyre treads would be full of impacted and frozen ice, and my wheels would have no grip. There was nothing for it but to drive as slowly as possible and make no sudden moves. I crept past large houses, set back from the lane, their lights shining behind drawn curtains and closed blinds. Here and there people had put Victorian-style lamps at the ends of their drives. There was, of course, no street lighting. The houses looked warm and inviting, and the interior of the car was still cold. I felt lonely.

Once out of the village, conditions grew worse. Quite soon I thought I needed to turn, but I could not. A tree was down and already it was covered in snow. A big drift was building up against the trunk. I slid towards it, unable to use my brakes, and glided to a stop just inches from the tangled branches. Rosie's car was light compared with the vehicles I was used to driving, a lady's car, or a poor person's car. Turning around was difficult, because at first I could not get any traction with my rear wheels, but at last I managed it, and was back on my way, on the only road I could find that was still navigable.

"This is ridiculous," I said to myself. I had probably driven four miles at the most. The windscreen wipers were making heavy weather of clearing the snow, so that I found myself peering out of an ever-smaller gap. The car was a bit warmer, but not comfortably so. Each time I came to an exposed part of the lane I could feel the wind buffeting the vehicle, threatening to push me into the ditch that ran alongside the road.

There was an old-fashioned car radio in the dashboard, but I could not spare a hand to turn it on. For perhaps half an hour I drove like that, the only sounds being the wind, the quiet hum of the engine, and the uncomfortable noise of windscreen wipers struggling to sweep away ice.

I no longer knew exactly where I was, although I felt vaguely confident that I was going in approximately the right direction. A vehicle, or perhaps several vehicles, had driven down the small lanes I was taking, leaving deep track marks. I thought perhaps it was something agricultural, something with wide wheels, and since that vehicle did not turn, and since none of the roads I passed on my left or right showed any signs of use, I just kept following the invisible driver ahead. I knew, of course, that I ran the risk of arriving at a dead-end in a farmyard, but it was a risk I had to take.

I came at last to a slight incline in the road. Just at that point there were hedges, so the lane was a little sheltered. The track marks I was following turned to the left, but one of those small black-on-white signposts one still sees in country areas, pointed straight ahead, and directed me to the A428 to Bedford or Cambridge. I got out of the car and looked at the signpost more carefully. I discovered I was coming from a village called Dry Drayton. I realised I had somehow missed the A14 altogether. How was that possible?

The A428 was good news, though. It would take me, my map told me, towards Northampton, which was in the right direction. While the car was idling, I drank some of the coffee Rosie had given me, and fiddled with the car radio, which was able to tune in to FM, an old wavelength still used in country areas where DeV signals were less reliable, and by people without functioning DeVs at all. I knew no car could be traced if they were using that outdated wavelength, which was one of the reasons new broadcasting licences were not being issued. It was much easier for the authorities if people listened to the radio on their DeVs. Reception was bad, but at last I found a folk and country station, and put my car gently into gear to the sounds of *I will survive*. It seemed appropriate.

★ ★ ★

The lane I was on was hardly more than a farm track, and there were piles of snow at the edge of the main road, blocking my access. It was the first time I used the spade that night. The road was empty, with no vehicles in either direction. Although it was an A road, it had just one lane on either side at this point, and only the very centre of the road was clear, so I drove west, very slowly, astride where the lane markings must have been, if they had been visible.

The going was definitely easier once I was out of the country lanes. There were hedges or trees alongside the right of the road, and then the left, though it was several miles before both sides were protected from the wind. In places the road was almost clear, obviously the wind was sweeping across the hard surface, building snowdrifts on the verges. The land on either side of the road was flat. In fact, it seemed to me that in some places the road was raised a little from the land on the left, which I guessed consisted of those huge fields created by East Anglian farmers and decried by Greens. Here and there the road took wide, sweeping curves, all signalled by road signs which I caught in my headlights. I was going towards Bedford, and making good progress, all things considered. Once or twice I lost my FM signal, but it came back again. There seemed to be no buildings next to the road, and no signs of life at all. The radio played the theme tune to the TV show *Missing You* and I thought of Alice, and hoped that she was curled up under her duvet, warm in the cottage, sealed off from intrusive undercover agents by this wild weather. It was really no night to be out.

Just as the radio station played the chimes of Big Ben, telling me it was midnight, I saw lights ahead of me, the flashing red and blue of an emergency vehicle. I took a deep breath and slowed down even further as I approached the police car. There was a turning to the left but the road ahead was barricaded by temporary barriers with fluorescent strips on them, and one officer was placing cones across the road.

I pulled over to the left, with my wheels in the pristine snow of the verge, and leaned across the passenger seat to wind down my window as the other officer came towards me. I saw, as she waited for me to open the window, that it was a woman, muffled in a huge police-issue overcoat.

"Good evening, Officer," I said in my most polite tone. "Is there a problem?"

"I should say!" said the officer. "The road's blocked up ahead. We don't know what happened. A crash, we think. And now snowdrifts. And the ambulance from Bedford can't get here, even if it wasn't already dealing with other emergencies."

"Can I help?" I asked. I really did not want to be held up. I wanted to get to Alice before Meadows' agent found her, but on the other hand, if someone was injured...

"Oh, thank you, Sir!" The officer seemed surprised at my offer. "But no, I don't think so. We need a four-wheel drive. The best thing you can do," she added, "is go home and stay safe until this storm is over. We don't want you to become another emergency! Have you got far to go?"

I smiled at her. I was playing the role of a genial member of the public. "No, not far at all," I said. "Although I would not have come out to check on my parents if I had realised how bad it is!"

"Well, Sir," she said, "of course you wanted to check on them. I take it they're okay?"

"Fine," I said. "And now I'm going home to my bed! Are you sure I can't do anything?"

"No, no!" the officer insisted, so I indicated left and drove slowly down the only road that was open.

★ ★ ★

226

I found myself on a B road. The police must have come this way, I realised, because I could see their rapidly fading tracks following the centre of the road, as I was doing. A village seemed to be off to the left, but my road went straight on ahead. My compass told me I was driving almost due south now, which was not ideal, but there was nothing I could do about it. The radio was playing a ballad about a child growing up in the ghetto, a song written at a time when protest songs were worth singing, when people thought things could be changed for the better by simply putting moral pressure on governments. I wondered if Alice knew the track, and promised myself that when all this was all over and she was safe, I would play it to her.

I drove steadily but very slowly. It was difficult to see where the road ended and the grass verges started. The hedges were set well back on each side at first, but after a while I came to a place where the bushes and trees stopped and the roaring wind swept across the road, so that the snow was flying horizontally through the bitter air. Rosie's windscreen wipers could not cope, and I had to ease to a halt every five or ten minutes to free them of their load of ice, and once to bend back into shape a damaged wiper, after a particularly fearsome gust had caught it. The one o'clock headlines came on the radio. I had missed the midnight news because I had been talking to the police officer. The news was all about the storm, and the chaos it was causing, and about the fact that we should all stay at home and wait it out. I kept driving. My neck was stiff from concentration, and the car had still not warmed up properly. I began to feel a depression creeping over me. I felt as if I were making no progress at all, like in those dreams when you run and run but go nowhere.

Then I saw a sign besides the road, a sign that jerked me back, out of the nightmare. It was a village sign that rang a bell, the name of a village close to the place where Will and Mia lived. I crept forward. The road I was on was leading in the wrong direction, away from Alice, towards Cambridge again, but I thought that if I kept going... I looked at the map. I was right. The road would take me right through Will's village. By the time I drew up in their drive it was nearly three in the morning. I had driven between two villages that were less than twenty miles apart by any sensible route, a journey which should have taken me half an hour. I had been travelling for seven hours.

★ ★ ★

The vicarage was in darkness. There was a hand-written sign, barely legible, in one of those plastic wallets kids keep their school papers in, pinned to the garage door. *'Breakfast served to all comers',* it announced, *'7.00 – 10.00 am'.* Then there was some writing lost to the damp, a mere smudge of felt-tip pen on moist paper. Of course, Will and Mia would be doing what they could, and no doubt the twins would be helping. The schools would be closed. It was not, I realised, an entirely sensible idea to park in the rectory driveway. In fact, it was crazy. What was I thinking of? Will did not want the twins to see me, and anyhow, what was I planning to do? Ask them to take me in? How would that get me any closer to Alice? I glanced at the small front lawn and saw that someone had built a snowman there. It had been given a wide-brimmed hat, like a cowboy hat, and another five or six centimetres of snow had accumulated on top of that.

I should not bother these good people, I thought. *They are doing enough for me already.* I turned the engine on and backed out into the road. Outside the village I stopped again and drank some of Rosie's soup, from one of the two flasks she had put on the back seat. I scraped as much snow as I could from the roof and the bodywork of the car, and set off again.

As grim nights go, that was one of the grimmest. Without the sheer endurance I had learned in survival training, I am sure I would have given up. I was unfamiliar with Rosie's car, and it did not respond as I expected. On my way to the next village the road took me up a hill, and as I went back down I slithered sideways into a blank, white wall. I climbed out of the car, fearing the worst, but some force was with me that night, because the car had simply lodged itself, bumper first, into a snowdrift, and I was able to dig it out and continue on my way. My feet were wet after that, but for a good twenty minutes I felt comfortably warm because of all the exercise, until the icy wind once again defeated the car's heater and an all-too-familiar chill started to creep through my body once more.

At some point I joined a different B road which took me through a couple of larger market towns and finally on to an A road again, all the time heading towards Bedford which was, at least, better than aiming back towards Cambridge. I saw cars parked at strange angles beside roads, snow heaped on their roofs and bonnets, and I saw lights in windows, but otherwise there were no signs of life. At last I came to a road sign telling me I was on the way to Bedford town centre, and then I came to a roundabout that could have given me access to the A1, except that the same sort of fluorescent-covered barriers and 'Road Closed' signs that had driven me off my previous A road would have prevented me, even if I had wanted to go that way. By then I was desperate to park the car somewhere and to sit in a warm café, if such a thing could be found, and to eat some hot food. I drove wearily past countless red-brick houses, of the sort built in the last century by councils, and now so beloved by a certain sort of American worker. The road turned into a dual carriageway but only one side of it was open, and that only just. I saw a US army personnel carrier heading towards me on the same side of the crash barrier as my little car. We flashed our lights at each other and the passenger in the other vehicle waved cheerfully as we passed, slithering a little on the slippery surface.

It was after seven in the morning, but still very dark. I was crawling along, slipping and sliding on shiny surfaces, sometimes getting better traction where the snow was undisturbed. I continued to follow directions to the centre of the town, and then at last I saw a sign that gave me hope. *'Bedford Hospital'* it said, *'South Wing'*. Then it occurred to me. The one eating place that would still be open in a snow-paralysed town was the hospital café. Nurses and doctors, stranded on duty, needed to eat and drink. I headed that way, thinking no further ahead than a full English breakfast and a cup of builders' tea.

★ ★ ★

The building was ugly, a mixture of different architectural fashions from the post-war era when the National Health Service was being massively expanded, and it now looked rather shoddy because of the continuous cutbacks imposed by successive governments, intent on dismantling a system they called *'socialised medicine'*. There was a car park that required me to pay more, it turned out, than my breakfast was going to cost, and of course I had to pay, like an ordinary member of the public. I no longer had any ATTF privileges.

I had been inside one or two of the old state-funded hospitals in my time, and my expectations were not high, so I was agreeably surprised to find a bright, clean, modern reception area with the usual stationery shop and cashpoint, and a long, shiny desk. A small plaque told me that the Friends of Bedford Hospital had paid for the refurbishment only a couple of years earlier, and I felt absurdly encouraged, in my state of near-exhaustion, to think of a local community still struggling, against the odds, to preserve the old institutions. There were comfortable chairs in bright, primary colours, making the entrance area look more like a hotel reception than a hospital, and several of the chairs were taken up with sleeping people. One or two were in nurses' uniforms, others were wearing ordinary clothes, and a few were wrapped up in blankets, like cloaks.

I followed the signs to the cafeteria. It was much closer to my expectations. There were no windows, and one of the lights was flickering annoyingly. The tables were wooden, old, scarred and stained, and the chairs did not match. It was a typical self-service establishment, with lots of handwritten signs peeling off the walls: 'Customers are respectfully asked to take their dirty dishes to the service points'; 'We cannot take credit cards'; 'Please go to end till for contactless payment'; and, ominously, 'Only food vouchers issued by the Department for Employment can be accepted. We do not accept vouchers issued by food banks'.

The service staff looked like I felt: worn-out, rumpled and in need of a shower or perhaps a stiff drink. I took my tray and pushed it along the metal tray-rest, looking at the food on offer in the steaming containers.

"Breakfast deal," announced the white-haired woman. "Full English and coffee or tea, for fifteen dollars. Or do you have a voucher?"

Goodness, I thought, do I look that bad? Then I considered the night that had just passed, and I thought I probably did.

"I'll pay cash," I said, and smiled at the weary woman.

"Been here all night, love?" she asked. "Fried bread? Beans?"

"No," I said, "I mean, yes to the fried bread and beans – I'll have everything please – but 'no' to being in the hospital all night. It's taken me hours to get here."

She was ladling two portions of beans onto my plate. "It must be someone important, then, to come in this weather." She looked at me kindly. "It must be an emergency," she added, as a statement, not a question.

"Yes," I agreed, "it is." And I thought of Alice in the Welsh cottage. Would she be turning up the fire now? Cooking some breakfast? Peering out of the cottage window at the dark, swirling snow, not knowing how this storm was protecting her?

"Don't fret, love," the woman said, balancing a rather sad-looking fried egg on top of two dark-brown sausages. "The doctors here are good. Saved my Paul, they did, and us with no insurance. You can't ask for more, can you? Tea or coffee?"

The food was, at best, mediocre, but I was desperate for it, and the tea was strong and dark, slightly bitter, but just what I needed. I ate at a corner table, watching tired medics coming in, selecting their food and sitting in the 'Staff Only' area. It was, I thought, all a little squalid. I wondered, briefly, why they were working here when Bedford must now boast lots of good private hospitals.

* * *

I needed that food but inevitably, having eaten so much and not having slept all night, I was suddenly overwhelmed with a desire to sleep. I would never have eaten like that on a survival exercise, and I felt foolish.

I put the contents of my tray in the service corner, as instructed, and left the cafeteria. It was then that I saw the notice pointing to the hospital chapel. Without giving it much thought, I followed the signs.

It was a bright, white-painted room with a high ceiling and elegant lights hanging down. There was a simple table, and chairs pushed back against the walls. Only one person was in the room, a young man with a round, embroidered cap on his head and a colourful mat, performing his prayers.

I sat on the floor just inside the door, not wanting to interrupt him. He had taken off his shoes, and it seemed only polite for me to do the same, since I felt this little room was a mosque until he had finished. Perhaps it was rude to watch him, but it was oddly comforting, the fluidity of his movements, the pauses, the quietly uttered words, the concentration. Then he had finished. He rolled up his mat, and noticed me for the first time.

"Sorry, brother," he said. "I thought I was on me own." I saw that he had tears in his eyes.

"No problem," I said. "I just came in. Are you okay?"

"Yes, man." Then he looked at me again. "It's me mum," he said. "A car skidded into her right outside the house. It weren't his fault, the driver. But she's very poorly. She hasn't recovered consciousness."

"I'm sorry," I said. He was young, perhaps late teens or early twenties.

"You?" he asked.

"A friend," I said. "Her life is at risk too."

"It's all a test," the young man said. "Have faith in Allah – in God." He put his shoes on and left.

★ ★ ★

I was comfortable on the floor. I stretched my legs out and leaned back against the white wall. It was pleasantly warm in the chapel, and outside it was getting light, that stark, grey light of snowy days. I was a long way from Alice, still. I needed energy and quite a lot of luck if I were to reach her that day. I thought of the young man's parting words, that this was all a test. Why would I need to be tested? Tested for what? By whom? But he had also said '*Have faith in God*'. What did that mean? Have faith that God would do what? Protect Alice? Get me to Wales safely?

Then I thought about Will, and about being motivated by love. Suddenly it seemed clear. If there were a God, if the Light were a real, active agent in the world, then all I needed to do was to was to follow the things I was prompted to do by love. I felt prompted – no, impelled – to try to rescue Alice. That was all I needed to know.

I only slept for about twenty minutes, a deep sleep with no dreams, and I woke feeling refreshed, lying on the chapel floor, as if I had been in my own, comfortable bed for hours. I washed my face and combed my hair in the gents, emptied out Rosie's other flask of cooling coffee and filled it up with four cups of rather dubious liquid from a vending machine, and went out to my car. More snow had fallen on it, but not as much as on the previous night. I started the engine, checked my fuel levels, looked at the map, and headed out of the car park, looking for the road to Northampton. There was a chatty news programme on the radio, the host telling stories of good deeds done by neighbours during the storm, and of members of the US military clearing roads and delivering water to people whose pipes had frozen. As I left Bedford it switched to music again, to country songs about falling in love and about broken hearts. '*I waited up all night',* mourned a singer in a rich, dark southern voice, '*but still you did not come.*'

I'm coming, I'm coming, I promised Alice. *I love you.*

CHAPTER 20

Whether it was because that short sleep had done me good, or because it was daylight, I do not know, but the next part of the journey was very much easier. The road to Northampton was another A road, but with a single lane in each direction. It could have been tough going, except that quite soon after I left Bedford I found myself behind a convoy of US military vehicles, which seemed to have come from the base where I had once, years ago, delivered a course on technical surveillance and social media. The effect of the heavy vehicles in front of me was to make the snow deeply rutted, but as long as I wanted to go in the same direction as the military, the driving was easy. Quite soon there were several vehicles behind me too, a police car, a white van and one of those Land Rovers you sometimes see on farms. It was still snowing, and there was a gusty wind, but neither were as severe as they had been earlier, and it was much more pleasant to be in a line of traffic, than out in the wild night on my own.

I stopped off at the Northampton hospital for the same reason I had visited the Bedford one; because I guessed the cafeteria would be open, but also because I was hoping for faster progress after this, and I did not want to stop again, unnecessarily. I was right about the place being open, and I was not alone in my supposition. The modern, clean-looking restaurant was buzzing with people in high-visibility jackets, and I realised that work crews were being organised. I did not linger there, though. The journey from Bedford had taken me an hour and a half, and I downed a quick coffee and was on my way in ten minutes. I was beginning to realise how much ordinary people, without ATTF privileges, had to spend on parking. Then I drove back out of the town to join the M1, hoping that this road, at least, would be open.

I was in luck.

The Americans liked us to call these large motorways *'interstates',* to bring in some sort of uniformity in our road designations, and indeed the M1 north from Northampton is very like an interstate in the USA. Normally there are three lanes and a hard shoulder in each direction, although that morning only one lane was open each way. But it *was* open. It looked for all the world as if a snow plough had been through, and I wondered if it were true, as my FM radio news had reported, that there was not a single working snowplough left in the country. There was a steady line of traffic, which I joined without too much difficulty. Most of the vehicles were predictable: emergency services of all kinds, a few private cars, and then, to my surprise, a public service bus! As we had earlier, we travelled in an orderly convoy. In places the road became hillier, but my tyres gripped the road well enough. On either side of us, on the hard shoulders and up against the crash barriers, there were abandoned cars and quite a lot of trucks, all covered in snow. We passed an area where the road seemed, suddenly, clear, and the car behind me tried at once to overtake. He slithered and slipped sideways into an uncleared lane. I checked in my rear-view mirror. The man, dressed in some sort of fur coat, climbed out of his car and looked back at the slowly moving stream of traffic, a look of bewilderment on his face.

The Watford Gap services were just like any other service station anywhere in the country. I had wondered whether they would be open, but I suppose the same thing had happened there as had happened in the hospitals, staff were unable to go home and they just stayed, working. The lorry park was almost full of parked trucks, many with the cabs misted up, showing that the drivers were using their enforced breaks to catch up with their sleep. I checked my petrol and electric charge. The battery on my hybrid was fine but I bought more gas, using cash again. Rosie's little car was quite efficient, compared with the powerful vehicles I usually drove. The floors of the restaurant and the shop were running with water from people stomping on the floor just inside the doors, to shake off the snow, and the whole place seemed grimy. There was little choice of food. I bought some cereal bars to eat on the way, and left as soon as possible. It was midday, and I had still not travelled halfway.

★ ★ ★

After Watford Gap the journey turned into an endurance test, worse than anything I had been subjected to in training or in the field. I left the M1 to join the M6 to Birmingham. There is a toll road going around well to the north of the city, which I had hoped to take, but it had not been cleared and I was forced to use the other, toll-free road which is much closer to the city, and with which I was less familiar. It was not snowing at all at that point of the journey, although the road was raised, at the level of factory and warehouse roofs, and the wind was buffeting traffic, pushing vehicles towards the mounds of snow in the central reservation. The lane I was using was relatively free of snow, no doubt because of the strong winds, but it was icy, and steering Rosie's light little car was tricky. When I joined the M54 I found myself in difficulty again, the road is anyhow only dual carriageway, not designated an interstate, and only one lane was open. The sky had become very dark again, threatening the next snowfall, and the bare trees on either side of the motorway did little to shelter the traffic. There were few vehicles, and all of us were crawling uncertainly along. At the turning to Bridgnorth it looked as if the road ahead was impassable altogether, and I nearly despaired, thinking I would have to head out cross-country again. I slid to a halt on the hard shoulder, wondering what to do, but just at that moment a police car came the wrong way down the apparently closed road, stopped at the barriers and moved them to one side. I drove slowly to where the two officers were standing, talking, and opened my window.

"Can I get through that way?" I asked.

One of the policemen bent down to speak into my open window. "Well, we've just done it," he said.

The other officer stood behind him, and spoke over his shoulder. "You'd be better off just going home, mate," he said. "There isn't a really safe road in the whole country, if you ask me."

"That's what I'm trying to do," I lied, smiling.

"Caught out, were you?" asked the first officer. "You and hundreds of others. Just didn't believe the forecasters, did we? Me and the wife were the same. Thought they were hyping it up."

"You'll be all right until you get to Telford," the second officer said. "That's where we've come from. But the further north you go, and the further west..."

"Thanks," I said, putting the car into gear and easing forward.

"Good luck!" said the officers, picking up the remaining cones and throwing them into the boot of their car. I thought, *They're going home for their tea,* and I felt suddenly, absurdly envious.

★ ★ ★

238

Once again I found myself travelling in the tracks of a police car. I thought of the song, *Good King Wenceslas* and wished that some heat was in the very tyre marks where the police had driven. I knew my thoughts were becoming a little crazy. I was exhausted, it was getting dark, and I was still miles away from Alice.

Then, as we approached Telford, the road signs actually started to say '*North Wales*', and quite unreasonably, my mood changed again, to one of happy optimism and energy. I was in my second wind.

There is a high point between Telford and Shrewsbury, and to this day I do not think I should have driven that stretch of road. By then it was dark, the snow was falling again in soft, feather-like flakes, and the wind was blowing, first one way and then the other. There was no other traffic, and the marks in the snow of other, earlier vehicles, were rapidly being smoothed over. I was dazed and exhausted. I found myself chanting to myself, from a story book I must have read as a child, *I think I can, I think I can, I know I can, I know I can.* Looking back on it, I think I reached Shrewsbury through sheer determination.

★ ★ ★

I really needed to find a service station or a shop. It was dark, and snowing steadily. My map showed no services on the A5, the road which would take me south of Shrewsbury town itself, so I decided to do my usual trick, and head towards the hospital.

The maps in the road atlas were not totally reliable, the light in Rosie's car was only working intermittently and the torch I had brought did not give off as strong a light as I really needed. I took a turning off to the right, where a road sign indicated '*City Centre*', and found myself driving along

239

a narrow road with houses, a garden centre, and other small businesses on either side. There were no street lights, and I was beginning to think I had made a very silly mistake, when I saw the signs to a well-known supermarket chain. The lights of the petrol station glowed ahead. I turned right again, and saw, to my relief, that the place was open.

I charged the battery for half an hour or so, just to be sure that I was fully prepared for the hillier roads which I knew lay ahead. I filled up with petrol, and realised how empty my wallet was becoming, now that I was avoiding the use of cards, and had destroyed the DeVs which allowed contactless payment. I was all right for the moment, though, and perhaps Alice would have some money. I was getting close. In good weather and in daylight I estimated I was only an hour and a half from the cottage, but once I left the A5 I knew I would be on tiny roads, unclassified, and who knew whether any of them would be passable?

The supermarket advertised that it was open twenty-four seven, but there were very few people in it at nine o'clock on a snowy Thursday evening. There was an elderly woman in the recognisable lime-green uniform of that particular chain of stores, who was stacking shelves in a rather slow and lazy fashion. A large-screen DeV was tuned to the weather station, and the reporter with the Northumbrian accent was showing, with the aid of charts and some wonderful, still photographs, how the storm had crossed the Atlantic, and why a period of very cold weather coming in from the other direction, from Siberia, would prevent a quick thaw from following. We would be saved the floods which were beginning to afflict North America.

I took a basket and wandered up and down the aisles, glad to stretch my legs. I bought chocolate this time, it was energy food and I had been awake for almost thirty six hours, except for that wonderful nap in the hospital chapel. Then I found what I wanted more than anything, a stand selling those cheap little DeV14s, like the one I had given Alice. They came with thirty dollars credit on them, and once it was used up, they could not be topped up. They could be traced, like any other DeV without security coding, but I knew first-hand that the police and the ATTF rarely bothered, because people tended to dispose of them so quickly.

The shelf-stacking woman saw me waiting at the checkout, and smiled as she wandered towards me. "Bad night," she commented, and I could hear the Welsh border sing-song in her voice.

"It is," I agreed. "A good night to stay in and watch TV."

"Lucky you!" she said, as she scanned my few items. "I'm here until midnight."

She turned back to the shelves as I left. I saw that there was a CCTV camera by the door, and another pointing down the central aisle. If anyone was trying to trace me, they would find me, but first they would need to know where to look. Thanks to Reggie and Rosie I had hidden my tracks pretty well, I thought.

I was bone-weary, and the last part of my journey would probably be the hardest, but at the other end lay a warm, snug cottage, and Alice. It was like the last night of survival training. You begin to know, beyond doubt, that you are going to make it.

CHAPTER 21

The little DeV took several minutes to connect to a signal, but once it was properly awake it functioned pretty well. I did not know the postcode of Mia's cottage, but I knew the name of the nearest village and I could remember the route from there. I headed back down the road I had come in on, joined the A5, and circled round to the south of the city. The road was again relatively clear, but I was dreading the point when I would need to turn off. This was the last main road of my journey.

At first the going was good. I easily found the direction I needed. The signs were to mid-Wales now, which added to my feeling that the end was in sight. The road had not been cleared, I thought, but once again there were deep tyre tracks where, I assumed, agricultural machinery had passed. I wondered if this was how the Welsh kept their roads open, now that the local authorities no longer took that responsibility. The way was exposed, but still relatively flat, and my progress was slow but steady. I had turned the radio off at the supermarket, but once we were officially in Wales I turned it on again, and listened to a Welsh language programme, where I recognised the music but had, of course, no idea what the conversation in between was all about. We passed through villages with speed restrictions enforced by cameras, but the chances of breaking any speed limit were zero, and that type of camera only recorded drivers behaving badly. I was concerned about missing my next turn, but the little DeV squeaked helpfully and I found myself driving along a road that was barely two vehicles wide, and hilly. It was pitch dark, and when I was near the brows of hills, or when the ancient lane was not sunken between banks of earth, I could feel the wind tugging at Rosie's little car. *"You're doing well,"* I encouraged it, then felt silly for talking aloud to a machine.

On my right I passed the large, ornate gates of a property I could not see. I thought I recognised it from my previous visit to the cottage, although this was not the route I had taken then. *Nearly there,* I encouraged myself, but then the DeV squeaked again, telling me to turn left into a lane which, I could see at a glance, was impassable.

I drew up, and left the engine running while I tried to make sense of the map. Alice's cottage was on the other side of a line of hills – they are not really mountains in that part of Wales. It should have been possible to turn left where I was now, cross the hills and turn right again. And try as I might, I could not see any other way of getting there.

I climbed out of the car and took a few steps up the lane. The snow had drifted, and in some places it was knee-deep, while in others the walking was easy. I peered up ahead, in to the dark, and I could see nothing. If I were to do the last part of my journey on foot, then according to the map it should have been possible to go cross-country, using a mixture of farm tracks and public footpaths. Wales is an ancient country, with rights of way which must date back to a time before the Romans. I was well trained, though, and survival depends on recognising the possible. I was going to have to walk the long way round, using properly surfaced lanes. I estimated that it would be no more than five miles, a pleasant walk on a summer's day, but one that could kill a man on a night like this.

★ ★ ★

I suppose training and sheer determination take over at such times. I have only intermittent memories of the hours that followed. It was close to midnight by the time I abandoned the car, pulling in just a little further along the lane beyond the impossible turning I was supposed to take, and parking in a gateway so that I would not block the track. I think I locked the car, but I do not know why, it would be easy enough for a concerned farmer or an inquisitive police officer to break into it. I am pretty sure I took the radio with me, although I cannot remember now why I thought that was a good idea. I have a feeling I threw it over a hedge at some point later in the night. I finished the last of Rosie's soup, slopping around coldly in one of the Thermos flasks, and poured away the terrible coffee from the other. I had eaten the cereal bars hours earlier, before Shrewsbury, and the chocolate was rock hard because it was so cold. I ate one bar and tucked the rest into my shirt pocket in the hope that it would thaw. I buttoned my overcoat up to the neck, and set out. I had never been on a survival exercise dressed so inappropriately.

It is hard, now, to untangle my memories. I know that at times I was wading through snow that was almost hip high, and that at other times the lane seemed almost clear. At one point I tried to bypass a snow drift by walking along the top of a stone wall, but I slipped and fell, and landed on a sheep that was sheltering from the storm. I do not know if it was dead or alive. At first, I am sure, the road took me steeply uphill, but I seem to remember dips and other climbs, and I am sure I found some sort of gate between stone walls, where I ate the rest of the chocolate. Clouds were rushing across the sky, sometimes bringing flurries of snow, and sometimes allowing the stars to shine with a brittle brightness in the cold. For a while I could see a light on a hill a long way away. I thought it must be a farmhouse. But I trudged on, and when I looked again it had gone. Had I just imagined it? Had a baby been restless, waking his parents?

I was walking in a daze. I did not feel awake, but it was

not like dreaming either. At times I felt bitterly cold but at other times I was almost unaware of my body. I was driven by my mind, by sheer willpower. I had a deep and growing sense of urgency. Everything else seemed to fade into the background and all I could think about was being with Alice. I would keep her safe. I would protect her. I would not let her fall into the hands of Meadows or her cronies. I would join her, somewhere safe. We would live out our retirement years together... I had to find her. I had to keep going.

There was a place, I suppose an hour or so before dawn, where the lane sloped steeply down to a stream. I think, if I remember rightly, that I was so weary that I sat at the top of the slope and slid down, like a child on a toboggan. I am fairly sure that is a true memory. And then, at the bottom of the slope, I reached the track that would lead to Alice's cottage.

And I knew that something was badly wrong. Very badly wrong.

Apart from that one light, I had seen no signs of life since I abandoned the car. The track leading to Alice's cottage, I clearly recalled, was remote and rarely used. When Mia had given me the keys and I had come this way for the first time, I remember being amused that grass grew down the middle of the lane.

Yet the track in front of me was thoroughly churned up. It looked as if dozens of vehicles, heavy vehicles, had passed that way quite recently.

I was so tired. My mind was functioning slowly. For a few minutes I stood there, not grasping what I was seeing. Then, in a rush of panic that made my heart thump hard, I understood. Many vehicles had passed this way. They had been going towards the cottage. The cottage where I had believed Alice was safe.

★ ★ ★

The paras who trained us must take all the credit for what I did next. Every instinct in my body urged me to run, to race as fast as I could along the track, to reach Alice. Instead I jogged, fifty paces running, fifty walking. And I kept my eyes and ears open.

Then I topped the slope where, for the first time, I could see the cottage. It barely showed up, the roof covered in snow, and the building nestled sideways into the hill. I stood still and listened. Nothing. A wild hope surged through me. Perhaps all those heavy vehicles had not been going to the cottage after all. Maybe, on the news later that day, I would hear of a dramatic rescue, a farmer with a broken leg or a teenager having a lucky escape after a nasty fall, the emergency services going the extra mile to look after our citizens.

I walked slowly down the track, my shoes crunching on the frozen snow. Other than the wind, I could hear nothing. The vehicle tracks seemed to go on, beyond the cottage. I peered in through one of the small windows, but I could see nothing. I turned right along the side of the cottage, and saw that the snow had been badly disturbed there too. I walked round to the back of the cottage.

A window upstairs was broken, and a curtain was flapping in the wind. I tried the back door. It was open. The lock had been broken.

"Alice?" I called, my heart pounding. "Alice, are you okay?"

There was no answer. I walked into the living room. The floor was wet where snow had been trampled in. I climbed the ladder-like stairs. The bed was made and Alice's suitcase was on the floor, open. There was a Dickens book by the bed.

But Alice was not there.

I sat on the floor and wept. "Oh Alice," I heard myself saying. "My Alice!" And the icy wind from the broken window chilled the tears on my face.

CHAPTER 22

To the Clerk of Aylesbury Meeting, from the Rev Will...

Dear Friend,

Please forgive this familiar approach, from one who is not a member of your Society. I am writing concerning a good friend of mine. Karl has something of an unusual history. He is a retired ATTF officer of a fairly high rank, although I think it would be fair to say that he was no longer in good standing with his organisation at the time of his retirement. I have known Karl for a comparatively short time, but have been privileged to be involved a little in his spiritual development. Others have had a stronger influence on him, although the one who has most affected his spiritual journey is, sadly, now deceased.

Karl has just emerged from a very disturbing year, during which he has been led to question everything in which he once believed. He is strongly attracted to the practices and beliefs shared by your faith communities.

It seems to me that Karl needs a period of stability within a congregation such as yours, which I understand is flourishing. I appreciate that, given the nature of Karl's occupation until recently, you may feel that taking him under your wing may be too great a gamble. I am, however, personally convinced that his presence among you will bring you no harm.

I am, of course, willing to discuss this further if you or your Meeting would find it helpful.

In peace,

Will